VARIANT

VARIANT

ROBISON WELLS

SCHOLASTIC INC.

ISBN 978-0-545-49903-3

12 11 10 9 8 7 6 5 4 3 2 1   12 13 14 15 16 17/0

Printed in the U.S.A.   40

First Scholastic printing, September 2012

Typography by Alison Klapthor

To Erin, my best friend

CHAPTER ONE

This isn't one of those scare-you-straight schools, is it?" I asked Ms. Vaughn, as we passed through the heavy chain-link gate. The fence was probably twelve feet tall, topped with a spool of razor wire, like the kind on repo lots and prisons. A security camera, mounted on the end of a pole, was the only sign of people—someone, somewhere, was watching us.

Ms. Vaughn laughed dismissively. "I'm sure you'll be very happy here, Mr. Fisher."

I leaned my head on the window and stared outside. The forest wasn't like any I'd seen. Back in Pennsylvania, parks were green. Lush trees, bushes, and vines sprung up anywhere there was dirt. But these woods were dry and brown, and it looked like a single match could torch the whole place.

"Is there cactus here?" I asked, still gazing out at the trees. As much as I didn't like this version of a forest, I had to admit it was better than what I'd expected. When I'd read on the website that Maxfield was in New Mexico, I'd pictured barren sand dunes, sweltering heat, and poisonous snakes.

"I don't think so," Ms. Vaughn said, not even bothering to look outside. "I believe you'd find cactus more in the southern part of the state."

I didn't reply, and after a moment Ms. Vaughn continued, "You don't seem very excited about this. I assure you that this is a wonderful opportunity. Maxfield is the pinnacle of educational research. . . ."

She kept talking, but I ignored her. She'd been going on like that for close to three hours now, ever since she met me at the Albuquerque airport. She kept using words like *pedagogy* and *epistemology*, and I didn't care much. But I didn't need her to tell me what a great opportunity this was—I knew it. This was a private school, after all. It had to have good teachers. Maybe it even had enough textbooks for all the kids, and a furnace that worked in the winter.

I'd applied for this scholarship on my own. School counselors had tried to talk me into similar programs before, but I'd always resisted. At every school I'd attended—and there had been dozens—I'd try to convince myself that this one was going to be good. This was going to be the school where I'd stay for a while, and maybe play on the football team or run for office or even get a girlfriend. But then I'd transfer a few months later and have to start all over.

Foster care was like that, I guess. I'd racked up thirty-three foster families all around the city since I'd entered the program as a five-year-old. The longest had been a family in Elliott where I'd stayed for four and a half months. The shortest had been seven hours: The same day I showed up, the dad got laid off; they called Social Services and told them they couldn't afford me.

The most recent family was the Coles. Mr. Cole owned a gas station, and I was put to work behind the counter on my first day. At first it was just in the late afternoons, but soon I was there on Saturdays and Sundays, and sometimes even before school. I missed football tryouts; I missed the homecoming dance. I never had a chance to go to any party, not that I'd been invited to one. When I asked to be paid for my work, Mr. Cole told me that I was part of the family, and I shouldn't expect payment for helping out. "We don't expect a reward for helping you," he'd said.

So, I applied for the scholarship. It was part of some outreach thing, for foster kids. I answered some questions about school—I exaggerated a little bit about my grades—and I filled out a questionnaire about my family situation. I got the call the next afternoon.

I didn't even show up at the gas station that night for my shift. I just stayed out late, walking the streets I'd grown up on, standing at the side of the Birmingham Bridge and staring at the city that I'd hopefully never see again. I didn't always hate Pittsburgh, but I never loved it.

Ms. Vaughn slowed, and a moment later a massive brick wall appeared. It was at least as tall as the chain-link fence, but while that had looked relatively new, this wall was old and weathered. The way it spread out in both directions, following the contours of the hills and almost matching the color of the sandy dirt, it seemed like a natural part of the forest.

The gate in the wall wasn't natural, though. It looked like thick, solid steel, and as it swung open, it glided only an inch above the asphalt. I felt like I was entering a bank vault.

But on the other side, the dehydrated forest kept on going.

"How big is this place?"

"Quite large," she said with a proud smile. "I don't know the exact numbers, but it's very extensive. And, you'll be pleased to know, that gives us a lot of room for outdoor activities."

Within a few minutes, the trees began to change. Instead of pines, cottonwoods now lined the sides of the road, and between their wide trunks I caught my first glimpse of Maxfield Academy.

The building was four stories tall and probably a hundred years old, surrounded by a neatly mowed lawn, pruned trees, and planted flowers. It looked like the schools I'd seen on TV, where rich kids go and they all have their own BMWs and Mercedes. All this place was missing was ivy on the stone walls, but that was probably hard to grow in a desert.

I wasn't rich so I wasn't going to be like them. But I'd spent the plane ride making up a good story. I was planning on fitting in here, not being the poor foster kid they all made fun of.

Ms. Vaughn turned the car toward the building and slowed to a stop in front of the massive stone steps that led to the front doors.

She popped the automatic locks, but didn't take off her seat belt.

"You're not coming in?" I asked. Not that I really wanted to talk with her anymore, but I had kind of expected her to introduce me to someone.

"I'm afraid not," she said with another warm smile. "I have many more things to do today. If I go inside, then we'll all get to talking, and I'll never get out of there." She picked up an envelope from the seat and handed it to me. My name, Benson Fisher, was typed on the front in tiny letters. "Give this to whoever does your orientation. It's usually Becky, I believe."

I took the envelope and stepped out of the car. My legs were sore from the long drive and I stretched. It was cold, and I was glad I was wearing my Steelers sweatshirt, even though I knew it was too casual for this school.

"Your bag," she said.

I looked back to see Ms. Vaughn pulling my backpack from the foot well.

"Thanks."

"Have fun," she said. "I think you'll do very well at Maxfield."

I thanked her again and closed the car door. She pulled away immediately, and I watched her go. As usual, I would be going into a new school all by myself.

I breathed in my new surroundings. The air smelled different here—I don't know whether it was the desert air or the dry trees or just that I was far away from the stink of the city, but I liked it. The building in front of me stood majestic and promising. My new life was behind those walls. It almost made me laugh to look at the carved hardwood front doors when I thought back to the public school I'd left. The front doors there had to be repainted every week to cover up the graffiti, and their small windows had been permanently replaced with plywood after having been broken countless times. These were large and gleaming, and—

I noticed for the first time that the upper-story windows were filled with faces. Some were simply staring, but several were pointing or gesturing, even shouting silently behind the glass. I glanced behind me, but wasn't sure what they meant.

I looked back at them and shrugged. In a second-floor window, directly over the front doors, a brown-haired girl stood holding a notebook. On it, covering the whole page, she'd drawn a large *V* and the word *GOOD*. When she saw that I had noticed her, she smiled, pointed at the *V*, and gave a thumbs-up.

A moment later, there was a loud buzz and click, and the front doors opened. A girl appeared, but she was pushed roughly out of the way as two other students—a boy and a girl—emerged, both wearing the uniform I'd seen on the website—a red sweater over a white shirt, and black pants or a skirt. The girl, who looked about my age or a little older, darted down the stairs, sprinting after Ms. Vaughn's car. The guy, tall and built like a linebacker, grabbed my arm.

"Don't listen to Isaiah or Oakland," he said firmly. "We can't get out of here." Before I could even open my mouth he was gone, charging after the girl.

CHAPTER TWO

I watched them run. They raced across the lawn, cutting through the manicured gardens without a pause, and disappeared into the trees. There was no way they were going to catch Ms. Vaughn, if that was their plan. I waited for a few moments, expecting them to reemerge, but they didn't.

I turned and looked back up at the windows. Not everyone was wearing the uniform, but even the more casual clothes looked different from what teenagers had back home. Some seemed old-fashioned—buttoned-up shirts, suspenders, and hats—while others seemed like exaggerated costumes of rappers, all gold chains and bandanas. It was November—maybe they were a little late on Halloween. Maybe they were practicing a play.

I could see that some were still shouting. I raised my hands, gesturing that I couldn't tell what they were saying.

The front door opened again, and a girl came out—the one who'd been shoved. She was grinning and carefree, like nothing had happened. She couldn't have been a day over sixteen.

"You must be Benson Fisher," she said. She stretched

out her hand for me to shake it.

"Yeah," I said, returning the handshake, even though it felt awkward. Teenagers aren't supposed to shake hands. Maybe that was a private school thing, too. Her dad was probably some rich businessman.

"I'm Becky Allred. I do the new-student orientations." She smiled widely, as though nothing was out of the ordinary. Her short brown hair was flawlessly waved and curled—it looked like a hairdo from old black-and-white movies.

I glanced down at the envelope in my hand. "So you're the Becky I'm supposed to give this to?"

"Yep," she said, taking it from me. "Your school records."

I pointed up at the students in the windows, who were still staring down at us. "What's going on up there?"

She waved up at them. "Nothing," she said. "They're just excited to see someone new."

That seemed like an understatement. Some were even pounding on the glass now.

I forced a laugh to mask my confusion. "What's the deal with those guys who ran?" I pointed back toward the forest. Neither of them had come back yet.

Becky's smile never wavered, but her nose and eyes wrinkled. She thought for a moment before responding. "I think they're just running," she finally said. "I couldn't really say why."

She slipped her arm into mine and began to lead me

up the stairs. She smelled good—like some kind of floral perfume.

Her answer wasn't the explanation I wanted. She had to know more about the runners than she was letting on. I hoped it was a practical joke.

"Who are Isaiah and Oakland?" I asked.

She froze for an instant—almost imperceptibly—and then continued walking. "What do you mean?"

Whatever secret Becky was trying to keep, she wasn't keeping it very well. Maybe this was some kind of hazing: Freak out the new guy.

"Isaiah and Oakland," I repeated. "The runner guy said not to listen to them."

Becky stopped and put her hands on her hips, turning toward me. Her smile was glued on her face, and she laughed almost like a real person. "Well, that's about what I would expect from the two of them. Benson, I think you'll find that this school has troublemakers, just like any other school. They're trying to scare you. I mean, what do you expect from two people who are so blatantly breaking the rules?"

I nodded and took another step up the stairs. Her answer made sense. Maybe I'd worry about it if I met anyone named Isaiah or Oakland. What kind of name was Oakland, anyway?

Wait a minute.

"'Breaking the rules'?" I asked, looking back at the forest. "How are they breaking the rules?"

Becky opened her mouth to speak, but no words came out. I watched her stammer for a moment and could feel my stomach dropping. Whatever was going on was stupid. Maybe I was the new kid who didn't have a rich daddy paying my way, but I'd come to Maxfield to get away from the crap I'd put up with all my life in lousy schools. I wasn't going to let a couple of snobby punks play mind games with me just because I didn't have any money. I'd go talk to the principal.

I sighed and trotted the remaining steps up to the wooden door, but it didn't open when I tried the handle. Becky followed, and when she reached me I heard the same buzz and click from earlier. She took the handle and pulled the heavy door open.

"They're—" she began, paused, and then restarted. "No one is supposed to talk to new students before they've had orientation," she said quickly. "It's just one of the rules."

I stood in the doorway and stared at her. She seemed unsure of herself. "That doesn't make any sense. You're not really Becky, are you?"

Her smile popped back onto her face. "No, I'm definitely Becky, and I'm definitely here to help you with orientation. That's my job."

"Your job?"

"We all have jobs here," she said. "We do our part to help out, because we all rely on one another. We're in this school so far away from everyone else—it's like our own little society."

"So I'll have a job?" There was nothing on the website about that, and it felt a little bit like the Coles' gas station.

"Of course," she said. "We all have jobs."

"Can you take me to talk to the principal?" It had felt a little weird before, but I was suddenly hit by the ridiculousness of talking to Becky about any of this. Ms. Vaughn had blathered something about students getting leadership opportunities, but I was sick of having the student body president—or whatever Becky was—give me a pep talk.

"Well," she began, "why don't we go to my office and do the orientation first. I'm sure that will answer some of your questions."

"Let me explain something," I said. "I've just been on a long flight and a long drive. I don't feel well and I want to lie down. I don't want orientation, because I know how a school works. I've been to a thousand schools in my life, and at every single one a counselor or secretary sits me down and tells me that I can join the Honors Society or the Science Club, and I already know that. Can we just go to the principal and do the real stuff?"

"The orientation is the real stuff," Becky said. She again hooked her arm around mine and tried to get me to follow her, but I resisted. I probably had fifty pounds on her, in muscle and height, and I didn't budge.

"I want to see the principal first."

Becky's face burst into a delighted smile, which was as fake as it was big. "You are so decisive. I think that's terrific."

"What?" I couldn't believe how weird she was acting. Nothing in the orientation could be as important as she was making it appear. It was like she was trying to keep me *away* from the principal.

"I'm just saying that we can really use someone like you at this school."

I laughed, though I didn't know why. Maybe because this had to be a joke. "How old are you, Becky?"

"Sixteen, almost seventeen," she said happily. "My birthday's at the end of October."

Her smile was plastered on like a tour guide's. That's what she was: a tour guide, all smiles and scripts.

"No offense," I said, "but can you show me where the real Becky is?"

"What do you mean?" She let her hand slip off the door, and it swung slowly shut.

"I mean that I don't believe a word you've said. This is all some stupid game."

"I'm the real Becky," she said, concern growing in her eyes.

"You're not, and you're not even a good liar. You said

that your birthday is coming up at the end of October. It's already November second."

She opened her mouth but didn't say anything. She took a step back and looked out at the forest. The two runners had just reemerged from the trees, their sweaters glowing a vibrant cherry red in the afternoon sun.

"So," I continued, "enough of the crap." I grabbed the door handle, but it was locked again.

"I am Becky," she said, her arms folded across her chest.

"Why's the door locked?"

"I am Becky," she repeated.

"I don't care," I said. "How do we unlock the door? I want to see the principal."

She turned to look at me, her eyes fierce. "I am Becky Allred. And I'm telling the truth."

"I don't care who you are. I want to see the principal."

Her smile was gone now, replaced by a grim stare. "We don't have one."

What?

"We don't have a principal," she said. "We don't have teachers, and we don't have counselors. That's why I do the orientations."

"There's no—I mean, you don't have . . ."

She tried to put her smile back on, but it was weak and forced. "This school is different from other schools."

"So who teaches the classes?"

"We do," she said. "The students. We get lesson plans."

"I don't believe it," I said. "That doesn't explain your birthday. Why did you lie about that?"

Her grin seemed to be back in full strength. "It's not a lie. I know it seems weird, and it'll be easier to understand when we go through the full orientation. But . . ." She paused, mulling over her words. "We don't have any calendars."

"You're kidding."

"Nope."

"Can't you just look on your computers? Every computer has the date."

"Not ours. But you do get your very own laptop. Did you know that?"

I couldn't believe it—in spite of everything she'd just said, she was still trying to sell me on how great the school was.

"But can't you just email someone? Get on the internet?"

Her nose wrinkled again. "Our computers don't get on the internet."

This was ridiculous. "Well, didn't your family call you on your birthday?"

"No phones, either."

"Let me get this straight. There are no adults in the school. And we can't talk to anyone on the outside."

She bobbed her head in embarrassed agreement.

I pointed at the two runners, who were standing on the lawn now, holding hands and looking back at the forest. I could see little puffs of breath rising from them as they talked.

"He said we can't get out of here," I said. "Is that true, too?"

"Yes."

This could all still be a joke. It had to be a joke.

"I shouldn't have taken the scholarship."

"That depends on how you look at it," she said. Her voice was warm and happy, but detached and distant, like she wasn't really directing her words at me. Another script. "There are some great people in this school. We learn a lot of interesting things, and it can really be a lot of fun."

I bet. I wanted a good school and I got this. Ms. Vaughn had been right about one thing—she'd said this place would be different from what I was used to. I thought she'd meant that we'd actually learn something, and that kids wouldn't get beat up in the parking lot. Instead, she meant that it was a prison.

"What's the point of this place, then? Is it for screwed-up kids?"

Becky laughed. "No, it's just a school. We go to class and we have dances and play sports." She gave me a mischievous grin. "You're not screwed up, are you?"

I pulled away from her, my confusion suddenly erupting into anger. "Why are you calm about this? How long has it been since anyone here has talked to anyone"—I gestured vaguely at the world beyond the forest—"out there?"

Becky glanced quickly at the horizon. The school sat in a low spot in the forest and we couldn't see much more than the rolling, wooded hills and, in the far distance, a faded gray mountain range.

"I've been here for about a year and a half," she said simply. "I don't miss it. Like I said, things are good here."

"Do people graduate?"

"Not yet," Becky said. "But I don't think anyone is old enough." She took my arm again and turned me back toward the door. "How old are you?"

"Almost eighteen," I lied, and then remembered that she had my records. "Well, I'll be eighteen in about nine months. Happy birthday, by the way. You're seventeen, too."

Becky laughed and then stepped to the door. It unlocked again with a buzz, and she pulled it open. "I like you, Benson. You'll do well here."

Chapter Three

The foyer of the school looked like the natural history museum I'd visited back in elementary school. The floor was marble, and dark wood covered the lower half of the stone walls. It was the kind of place that my optimistic twenty-minutes-ago self would have loved and referred to as a beautiful, awe-inspiring palace of education. My current self thought it was an ugly, poorly lit haunted house. And now it was home.

Not for long. Maybe some of the other kids didn't mind being locked in, but I did.

A massive staircase led up to the right, but Becky directed me forward, under a stone archway and down a long corridor. The front doors closed behind us with a soft thud, and despite the tall ceilings, I felt claustrophobic.

"So what were the rules the two runners broke? I mean, for real." I had already decided that I had little intention of obeying the rules here—I wasn't going to stay long enough for it to matter—but I wanted to know what they were. Just the fact that Becky seemed to be in a position of authority worried me. Anyone who had been an unwilling captive for a year and a half and yet seemed as unconcerned as she was didn't deserve a lot of obedience.

Or was she a *willing* captive?

"No one is supposed to talk to the new students. Like I said, it makes more sense if I can explain what the school is like in a prepared presentation."

Right.

"Also, they don't want us to chase after the car. That's against the rules."

"Who are 'they'?"

Becky turned to me and winked. "Ah, that's the real question, isn't it?"

She was starting to drive me crazy. Or maybe *she* was crazy. "And what's the answer?"

The corridor branched, and Becky directed me to the left. I hadn't realized how big the building was from the outside.

She shrugged. "They're the Maxfield Academy. The woman who drove you in and her corporate office."

"You don't know? Don't you want to?"

Becky opened a door and motioned me through. "Of course I want to know, silly. But I *don't* know, so I'm trying to make the most of it."

Inside the small room was a desk surrounded on three sides by tight, cupboard-lined walls. In front of the desk was a small leather sofa. She motioned for me to sit, and then moved to the desk, fiddling with some papers and jotting down a note for herself. The office was immaculately organized. The papers on the desk were in perfect stacks, not a single sheet out of place. There were two pens and a pencil, each one exactly parallel to the others.

Sitting made me anxious. I needed to be out doing something, talking to someone who was as angry about this as I was. I assured myself that there had been others watching through the windows—people who didn't act like Becky. I'd find them.

She picked up a white three-ring binder with my name already on the spine. She walked around the desk and sat next to me on the couch, then crossed her legs and smoothed her skirt.

"Here's the deal, Benson," she said, in a new tone of voice: serious, but still a tour guide, as though she were showing vacationers around the site of a plane crash. "There are some people, like Curtis and Carrie out there, who go running after the car every time it comes. They go stand at the wall and talk about trying to climb over it and get away. They complain about every little thing."

"Like the fact that we're trapped?"

Even Becky's frown was a half smile. "I know that it's hard. But that doesn't change anything. And the sooner you accept it, the sooner you'll be able to enjoy yourself here."

"Accept what? That I can never leave and I can never talk to anyone? What is this place? A prison?"

She shook her head. "It's definitely not a prison, Benson. Does a prison look like this? Do prisoners get great food and a great education? Think of it this way: Even if you had a phone, is there anyone you'd call?"

I thought at first it was rhetorical, but she waited for me to answer.

"I'd call the police."

"That's not what I mean," she said. "If this was a normal school that let you use the phone, is there anyone you'd call?"

Was it that obvious that I was a loner? She knew my name before I'd told her; maybe she'd also seen my answers on the application—the answers that said I didn't have any family.

I decided to lie. "I have lots of friends."

"Do you?" she said, raising an eyebrow. "Friends you'd call to chat with?" She leaned a little closer, watching my face.

Well, I didn't have any at my last school—I'd never met anyone there because I was always at the gas station. And I definitely didn't consider Mr. Cole a friend. There was my caseworker, but she couldn't ever remember my name.

I shook my head. "Not really. But how do you know that?" Almost imperceptibly, Becky's smile wilted. *Oh.*

"Wait. You're the same, aren't you?"

She turned her gaze down, tapping her fingers absently on the binder. "Yes," she said. "All of us are like that."

I couldn't believe it. A whole school full of people like me—no friends, no family. No one who would notice that we were gone.

I pounded my fist into the arm of the couch.

"They take the ones that no one will miss."

Her tour-guide laugh reappeared. "You make it sound so sinister."

I jumped up, rubbing my hands over my face and head. "If it doesn't sound sinister to you, Becky, then you've been here too long." Maxfield wasn't just a prison. It hid what it was doing, seeking out students who had no ties, no homes.

Those had been questions on the scholarship application, though they'd referred to it as a personality profile. *How many close friends do you have? Who do you confide in?* I must have answered just right—*none* and *no one*.

If the school was picking the kids who wouldn't be missed, then were they ever going to let us go? No one was going to come looking for us. Nobody cared.

Becky didn't respond. When I finally turned around, she was still sitting looking as calm as ever. *What was wrong with her? Didn't she get it?*

"We've kinda messed up my official presentation," she said with a smile and a joking sigh, "so let's get right to the details." She held up the binder and motioned for me to come back and sit. I walked to her, but stayed on my feet. "This book is your manual for all things related to Maxfield Academy. It has the rules, a map of the grounds, and a list of services. Everything you'll need."

I stared at her. "I think you're crazy. I think this school has made you insane."

She just smiled. That's all she ever did. She had to be nuts.

"Benson, I'm trying to help."

"Help me or our kidnappers?"

"You," Becky insisted. She handed me the binder and then clasped her hands in her lap. "Now, listen. We need to go over a couple of the bigger rules, and then I'll take you up to your dorm."

Great. I didn't want to go to the dorm; I wanted her to take me back outside. I'd climb the stupid wall and get out of here. I wondered why no one else had done that. It was tall, but there had to be a way. The two that ran after Ms. Vaughn's car—maybe they'd tried. I'd find them and ask.

"Benson?" Becky pointed at the manual.

I opened the binder halfheartedly. The front page had a black-and-white photocopy of the ornate coat of arms that had been on the school's website. The color version had looked so regal, like I was going to some Ivy League school that was going to make everything that was wrong about my life right. This paper just looked like a copy of a copy of a copy.

I sat down again with a sigh, closing the book and looking at Becky. "Are the rules as stupid as everything else?"

She laughed. "They're not stupid at all. Very basic stuff."

I nodded, wondering how someone like Becky would define *basic*. She certainly had a screwed-up version of *normal*.

"There are lots of rules, and you can look them up in your book. But there are four big ones that will get you in a lot of trouble. First of all, no sex." She made a fake grimace. "That's the first thing that all the students think when they hear that there are no adults in the school. But, even though there are no adults, there are these." She crossed the room and pointed to a security camera in the corner. She avoided my eyes, which meant she probably felt as uncomfortable discussing this with me as I felt hearing about it from her.

"Every room, every hallway," Becky continued, still staring up in the corner. "So, they know whether you've been naughty or nice, and if you break big rules—like that one—you will get detention."

"What is detention?"

Becky glanced my way and then returned to her desk. "Detention is bad enough that you don't want to end up there."

"What is that supposed to mean?" I said, putting the binder to the side and leaning forward in my seat. "How about you start giving me some real answers?"

Becky stammered for a moment, her eyes looking everywhere but at me.

"What is detention?" I asked again, speaking slowly.

She exhaled and then looked down. "When people go to detention they don't come back."

"They get sent home?"

"I'm sure they don't."

"What? They get sent to someplace worse?"

Becky broke, her face suddenly contorted in—was it sadness? Fear?

"I don't know," she said firmly, turning away from me. "Nobody knows."

I didn't let up. "Have people been sent to detention before?"

"Can we just say 'it's bad enough that you don't want to end up there' and leave it at that?"

I asked again. "Have people been sent there?"

"Yes."

"And they don't come back?"

"No."

"Perfect." *That fits right in with all the other crap.* For a moment I wondered whether that meant I ought to break the rules immediately—get sent to detention and get out of here. But that couldn't be right, either. Detention couldn't just mean that I'd get sent home. I'd go to the police, and I was sure the school wasn't about to let anyone do that.

I glanced back at Becky. "That's the first rule. What are the other three?"

"No trying to escape," she said, crossing her arms and leaning against the cupboards on the far wall. "No refusing punishments. And no violent fights."

I couldn't help but laugh. "Violent fights? Is there any other kind?"

She grinned. "Yeah, that rule is weird. Most fighting will just get you some minor punishment, but if there's something really bad—like if someone gets seriously injured—then you'd get detention. That's what happens if you break any of the four big rules."

"So how do I know whether my fighting is violent or not?" I didn't plan on getting into a fight—part of the reason I came here was because I didn't want to fight anymore—but I felt like arguing about it.

"You don't," she said. She turned and opened a cupboard full of small boxes. "That's why it's probably best to avoid fighting altogether." She picked three boxes and held them out to me. "Do you want a bracelet, watch, or necklace?"

"What do you mean?"

She handed me the small stack. Each box was about the

size of my fist, with a simple photo on the front and a blue background.

"You can either have a necklace, a watch, or a bracelet. But, let me warn you that these things do not come off. The school doesn't want you to switch yours with someone else's, so once you put it on it's on for good." Becky pointed at her neck. Part of the school uniform was a tie. "I chose the necklace, and I've regretted it for a year and a half. It really chafes under this tight collar."

"What are these for? Why don't they come off?"

"Oh," she said. "Sorry." Becky crossed the room to the door, and as she reached it there was a buzz and a click, just as I'd heard outside on the steps.

"It's the chip," she said, pointing again at her necklace and walking back to the desk. "This will give you access to your dorm and to any places that you've contracted to work. The door can sense your chip, and it unlocks."

I was trapped in a prison, and I had to wear a chip? Were they going to track me?

"What if I refuse?"

She smiled again, turning her head and looking at me out of the side of her eyes. "What if I said please?"

"What?" I blew up at her. "Don't you get how wrong this place is? 'Welcome to Maxfield, here's your tracking device. We watch everything that you do. You can never leave.'"

Becky let me talk, silently listening as I paced the three steps across the room and back. I tried the knob. It had locked again after she'd moved away. I was even a prisoner in this room.

I smacked the heavy wooden door with my palm, and then turned back to glare at her. She stood still.

"Can we sit down?" she said, some of the fakeness disappearing from her voice.

"Will it help me get out of here?"

She raised her eyebrows. "Please?"

I moved to the couch and slumped down against the cushions.

"Let me tell you something, really quick," she said, not quite looking at me and keeping her voice low. She moved from the desk back over to the couch, sitting closer to me now and locking her eyes on mine. "This school has some problems. Your best bet is to follow the rules."

I leaned my head back and stared at the ceiling. "My best bet is to follow the rules."

"I'm serious," she said. "You're right. Things shouldn't happen this way at a school. They shouldn't be happening to us. But they are. And the only options are detention or . . ."

"Or what?"

She sighed. "Will you please just wear the chip?"

I grabbed Becky by the arm and jumped to my feet,

yanking her up off the couch. Too startled to resist, she stumbled after me and I shoved her up against the door, my hands angrily pinning her arms back against the wood. Her eyes were wide with shock.

There was no sound, and as I stared at the still-locked door, my heart felt as though it were being squeezed.

Becky's words were barely audible. "They watch on those cameras," she whispered, her face only inches from mine. "You can only get out with your chip."

I stared back at her, panicked, knowing that there was no way I was getting out of that room on my own. I was trapped. Helpless.

She tried to smile again. "It's okay," she said. "This isn't the first time. And it . . ."

Becky's voice trailed away, but I knew what she meant. I wasn't anything special. I was just another kid—a prisoner or a test subject or who knows what—and I wasn't going to be the last.

I let go of her, and a look of relief washed over Becky's face. She ducked under my still-outstretched arms and moved back to the desk and the boxes I'd dropped on the floor. I turned, stunned and defeated, and watched as she fiddled needlessly with them. She wasn't doing anything—just regaining her composure.

I spoke. "Okay."

"You'll wear it then?" Becky said, her voice lightened

but her back still to me.

"I guess I have no choice."

She turned. Her face beamed, and she held up the boxes. "Which do you want?"

"The watch, I guess."

"That's what most boys choose," she said, quickly returning to her perky old self, though still rattled. Guilt was weighing down on me, but I tried to push those thoughts away. Maybe what I'd done was wrong, but Becky shouldn't be helping the kidnappers, either.

She opened the box and pulled out the plain gray wristwatch, and then took it to her desk. She popped a panel off the back. "You'll be pleased to know that it's waterproof, so you can wear it in the shower."

Yeah. That really makes up for everything. I reluctantly sat back down.

She inserted a small chip that had been lying on the edge of her desk. "So, this will let you in to all the places you need to go—your dorm, your classroom, any place you have the contract for."

"Contract—what's that?"

"Oh yeah. That's not exactly a rule, but here's the ten-second version of how the contracts work: There are a lot of jobs that need to be done around here. There are no adults, which means there are no janitors or gardeners or even teachers. So, every couple of weeks, jobs are posted and we bid to see who does what."

Becky brought the watch to me and put it on my wrist. It snapped snuggly—impossible to slide off.

"We bid with what? Money?"

"Points," she said, sitting down beside me, one leg folded beneath her so she could face me. "We bid how many points we're willing to do the job for, and then they give the contract to the lowest bidder. When you get paid, you can use the points to get clothes or food or whatever. I think that some of the guys in the dorms even bought some video games."

"Does everyone have to have a job?" I had no intention of helping this school.

"Kind of." She smiled, a little more obviously fake than before. She touched my hand again, too, which seemed almost rehearsed. "Things are different than they used to be. Better—way better. For a while, it was every man for himself. But everyone got angry, and no one was satisfied because the good jobs would get down to one point, and you can't come close to buying anything with one point. So, people started getting together and bidding as a group. For example, all of my friends and I bid on the administration jobs. That worked a little better, because I wasn't competing with my friends, but we were still competing with everyone else."

"People want the jobs that bad?" I asked.

"Sure," she said with a laugh. "You can get some fun things. And, as you keep pointing out, we're kinda stuck here, so every little bit of fun helps. Anyway, my group got bigger and then we started making deals with other groups—we won't bid on janitorial jobs if you don't bid on administration jobs. That kind of thing."

"So, like a union." My foster dad two families ago—Mr. Bedke—had been a union organizer, and he was always on the phone trying to get the members to agree on something or other.

"I guess," Becky said. "I don't know much about unions. But in the last year or so we've been pretty formalized. All the jobs are split up between three groups now. We don't bid on each other's stuff, and that means that we all earn a lot of points."

"I'll probably have to join one of those three groups, right?"

"Yep," she said. "Unfortunately, there's a new rule"— she pointed at the security camera—"and I'm not allowed to tell you which group I'm in. But, like I said, my group has the administration contracts. You can ask around. It'd be great if you joined up." She was smiling warmly, and I almost thought she was flirting with me—flirting with me to get me to join her weird union. And after what I'd just done to her. *How did I end up here?*

I leaned back in the sofa, my legs sore from traveling

all day. I tried to think of something I could say or do that would get me out of this school, or at least make things a little more normal, but nothing came to mind.

"Any more rules?" I finally asked.

She shrugged. "Don't be tardy. Wear your uniform during class and meals. No drugs or alcohol, not that you could get them in here. Don't destroy property. You know— common sense stuff. There's a full list in your manual."

Becky stood up. She seemed a little disappointed, but I didn't know why. Was I supposed to try to talk her into spilling the name of her stupid job club?

"Do you want to see your dorm?" she asked.

I sighed. "No, but I guess I don't have a choice."

Becky didn't answer, but her eyes said it all. I was stuck here.

We left her small office, and she made sure the door closed behind her.

"If you need anything," she said, "you can always talk to me." She pointed at a small call button next to her door. "If I'm not here, this will page me. It's part of my contract."

I nodded, but I didn't have any intention of coming back down here. I was going to find normal people. Something told me that any help Becky had to offer was help I didn't want.

We headed upstairs, passing carved wood, huge old paintings, and delicate moldings.

I suddenly realized there were no students in the halls.

"Where is everyone?" I asked.

"They're in the dorms," she said. "It's against the rules to go down and wait for new students to arrive. Curtis and Carrie will get punished for that."

"So they're all locked in their dorms, locked in the building, locked in the wall, locked in the fence."

Becky laughed. "Benson, I get the feeling you're not happy. But, yes, they're all in the dorms. Well, most of them. The group that has the cafeteria jobs will be down there making dinner. You can thank your lucky stars for that."

"Why?"

"When you get into the dorms, everyone is going to ask you to join their group. You don't want to join that one."

I smiled. "I assume that's not yours, then?"

"Ugh, no."

We turned a corner and went up another set of stairs to the fourth floor.

"Here we are," Becky said, stopping at a large wooden door. I heard a buzz. She pointed up at the ceiling, and I saw a round black device. "It sensed your chip. This door will open for all the boys, but not the girls. The buzz means it's unlocked. You'll be in room four twenty-one."

I reached to try the knob, but her hand stopped mine.

"Benson," she said, her voice low. She looked up into my

eyes. "I'm serious. Follow the rules."

Becky paused like she wanted to say more, but then turned on her heel and hurried back the way we'd come.

I opened the door and went inside.

Chapter Four

The hallway was packed with guys—maybe about twenty or so. Most were sitting on the floor, presumably waiting for me, and they popped to their feet as I entered the dorm.

They were all smiles and handshakes, greeting me warmly and reminding me more than a little bit of Becky. In the front of the group was a tall guy, with short, curly hair that had been on the receiving end of a huge amount of gel. He wore glasses with thin black frames and looked to be the tallest of the group. Becky had said no one was old enough to graduate, but he had to be.

"Benson," he said, putting his hand on my shoulder. "It's good to finally meet you."

There was shouting somewhere down the hall, from behind the crowd. The tall guy directed me into a room.

"It's quieter in here," he said. "We can talk."

I followed, more out of curiosity than anything else. Where else was I going to go?

Inside the room was a set of bunk beds, two desks, and

a small sink and mirror. There were no sheets or blankets on the beds—it looked like no one actually lived here. He offered one of the desk chairs to me, and he took the other.

"My name's Isaiah," he said.

The guy who'd run after Ms. Vaughn—Curtis, I think—had said not to listen to Isaiah. I had no reason to trust Curtis, other than the fact that he'd tried to run, and that meant he had his head screwed on at least a little bit straighter than anyone else I'd met. Still, Isaiah seemed harmless.

"Becky told you about the gangs?"

Gangs? I'd never been in a gang—never stayed in one place long enough—but I'd spent my life around them. I thought I'd left them when I flew out of Pittsburgh. Even so, looking at Isaiah, he obviously had a different idea of what gangs were. No one here looked violent or the least bit deviant. They were all clean-shaven, with pin-striped pants and starched shirts. And, from what I could tell, these were their casual clothes—none of them were wearing the uniform.

"She told me a little bit about different groups," I said. "She didn't say they were gangs, though."

"They are gangs," he said. "They're dangerous and irresponsible. You'll find, Benson, that there are a lot of kids who view this school as a free pass to do whatever they want. They love that there are no parents or teachers, and they can behave however they want to."

"Sounds terrible," I said sarcastically.

"It is terrible. Have you ever read *Lord of the Flies*?"

I nodded. Reading was one of the few things I was ever good at in school, probably because I spent so much time by myself.

"Good," Isaiah said, seeming impressed. "Well, here at Maxfield we have a choice of how we want to live. We can either be like the characters in that book—violent and tribal and savage—or we can try to be civilized. I've been here for a long time, Benson, and I can assure you that civilization is the only way to go."

There was sudden yelling from somewhere in the hallway, and Isaiah motioned for one of his friends to close the door.

I looked around at the six guys in the room. They seemed tense, like they were waiting for something—maybe for me to agree to join them. All I really wanted to do was to get back outside and figure out how I could escape this school. Being in foster care was better than being a prisoner. Besides, I only had nine more months until my eighteenth birthday, and then I could be out on my own. No schools, no foster families.

"So," I said, "let me get this straight. You're the nice gang? You follow the rules, just like Becky was talking about. Is she one of you?"

"Yes, Becky is one of us. But we're not a gang. That's my point. We're not like the others. They do nothing but fight and wallow. We recognize that there are problems here—don't think that we love this situation—but we've made a decision. We can be miserable and get ourselves killed, or we can thrive. We have chosen to thrive. We are not a gang. We're the Society."

I laughed, which made Isaiah scowl. "Society? Isn't that just a fancy name for a gang?"

"We don't behave like a gang," he said. "We treat one another with respect. We help one another. We—"

He was interrupted by a crash against the door. Two of his friends jumped to their feet and braced it. I could hear muffled voices coming from the other side.

"Listen," he said to me more urgently. "If you want to be safe, you want to be in the Society. We're the largest group, and no one dares to cause problems with us."

Judging by the pounding on the door, I doubted that was true.

"If you want to be happy, you also want to be with us. We don't get punished like the others, because we hold ourselves to a strict code of conduct. We live right, and we do right."

The door popped open, but the two guys pushed it closed. A third jumped up and held the knob so it couldn't turn.

"Don't you want to escape?" I asked, knowing that our conversation was going to end soon. "Do you always just follow the rules?"

"No good has ever come from breaking them," he said. "No one escapes, and those who try get punished."

All five of Isaiah's Society friends were at the door now, holding it against whoever was on the outside.

"But look at you," I said. "You're obviously older than eighteen. You should be out of high school. How long are you going to stay here and wait?"

"I will stay here as long as it takes. I won't throw myself into danger, knowing it won't help anything. Things here can be good if you stay out of trouble. You just have to follow the rules."

As if on cue, the door burst open about ten inches and the room filled with noise. One of Isaiah's guards kicked at someone in the hall, and another managed to shove the door closed again.

I turned back to Isaiah. "So what is that, if you're following the rules?"

"Havoc is out there," Isaiah said, nodding at the door. "We're protecting you from them."

There was a thunderous crash in the hall, and the door shook. I couldn't believe that all of this was happening just because I had to choose a gang.

"Havoc?"

"That's one of the gangs," he said. He was speaking quickly now. "Just a bunch of punks. When you meet them you'll understand why we had to form the Society."

The door was open a crack now, and the five Society guys couldn't close it.

Isaiah grabbed my shoulder. "We want you, Benson. We're the largest group and we have the most contracts—the good jobs. We do security, medical, administration, teaching—"

"Students do security?"

"We do," he said, his eyes glued on the door. "As directed by the school."

I shook his hand off my shoulder. "So you're helping them keep us in here?"

The door flew open, and the five exhausted Society guards fell back.

A kid stormed through, followed by three of his friends. He was tall and skinny, with brown hair that was too long and hung down almost to his eyes. He still wore the uniform pants, but instead of a shirt he had on an oversize black hoodie draped in gold chains. A tattoo of a hawk's talons encircled his left eye.

"I bet Isaiah told you that you need to play nice, follow the rules. Didn't he?"

I tried to keep calm, but could feel my muscles tense. Even though this new kid was obviously trying to get me to join his gang, he looked ready for a fight. And I didn't have a lot of confidence in Isaiah's guys, either. If five of them couldn't hold the door against these four, I doubted they'd be useful when fists started flying.

"We're Havoc," he said, staring me down. "We take care of our own." He took a step back.

I spoke, keeping my voice as even as I could. I'd dealt with gangs before, and while I didn't want to make him mad, I didn't want to look weak, either. "All the gangs take care of their own."

He raised an eyebrow. "Do they?" He turned quickly to Isaiah and slapped his head, and then shoved him backward onto the floor. Isaiah didn't fight back, but scooted against the wall, out of the way.

It was strange watching it. I'd seen one of the Society guys fighting at the doorway, but none of them moved to defend their leader.

The Havoc kid must have recognized my surprise. "They're putting on a show," he said with a laugh. "They want you to think that they're the peaceful ones, that Isaiah is freaking Gandhi or something. But they fight. You'll see."

He stepped over to Isaiah again and moved like he was going to kick him, but stopped, smiling as Isaiah flinched.

"I'm Oakland," he said, returning to me and puffing out his chest. "I don't know what this little girl told you, but rules around here don't mean a damn thing. There's a camera right there—Isaiah, why don't you go kiss it? Tell it I hit you." He looked back at me. "I can beat the crap out of this moron right here and never get detention."

I paused before responding, trying to choose my words carefully. "So I should join you because you can beat up somebody?" Oakland was taller than I was, but I doubted he was as strong as he was trying to make himself appear. Even with that bulk of his sweatshirt and chains he didn't look very big.

"No," he said, taking a step forward. "You should join Havoc because anyone can beat the crap out of anyone. You need someone watching your back." His lips curled into a snarl that he probably thought was threatening. I wasn't impressed.

There was a crowd at the doorway watching us. Most of them looked like Society kids, I guessed. Havoc was hugely outnumbered, and the Society could have easily stopped them. So Oakland was telling the truth. The Society was putting on a show. But I wondered how much of what Oakland was doing was real, too.

I sized up his three friends, who were now standing a few yards behind him. They were bigger than Oakland, but they looked stupider. Of course, anyone with intelligence wouldn't wear huge gold chains around his neck when he went to a fight.

Oakland's voice was low. "You have a choice, kid," he said. "We point the gun. You choose if you want to be standing in front of it or behind."

I took a breath. "I don't know who you think you are," I said quietly, watching Oakland's eyes, "but I've been pushed around by tougher guys than you—and I've pushed back."

Oakland took another step toward me.

"Back off," I said.

"You're going to join up with Isaiah here," he said, a nasty smile creeping across his face. "You'll be a perfect match—maybe you can share a bunk."

"No. I'm not joining Isaiah. I don't know what else there is, and I don't care. I'm getting out of this place. You girls can stay here and play your—"

Before I could finish the sentence, Oakland shoved me, and I stumbled a few steps to the wall. But as he stepped toward me I launched my fist into his stomach. He staggered back and I leapt at him, grappling him around the waist and throwing him backward onto a desk.

A moment later his goons were on top of me, one trying to pry my arms off Oakland while another jumped on my back. I ignored them and threw another punch, this one glancing off Oakland's cheek. I raised my hand to do it again, but someone got his arm around my neck.

I struggled to fight off the attacker but had to let go of

Oakland to do it. I stood, the other guy's arm tightening around my throat, and I tried to stumble back into the wall to crush him. As soon as I was off Oakland he jumped back at me, his first punches landing in my ribs. I tried to kick him away, but I could hardly breathe.

His fist connected with my face and a moment later I could feel my blood dribbling over my lips and chin. I swung my hand at his chains, caught one, and then yanked. He lurched forward, off balance, and I kicked him in the leg.

But I couldn't keep it up. The arm around my neck was rigid and strong. My lungs were desperate for air but only a trickle was getting through.

I couldn't move—I couldn't get the arm off my neck, and I had run out of strength to stop Oakland. The other two goons were just watching and laughing. Oakland came at me again, but just before his fist connected he fell forward, collapsing into me and then falling to the floor.

Standing behind him was the guy who'd run after Ms. Vaughn's car. Curtis.

"He said he doesn't want to join Havoc or the Society," Curtis said. "That means he's in the V's." He looked at me. "Isn't that right?"

I couldn't speak. I tried to nod, but my neck was immobilized.

"Let him go, Skiver," Curtis snapped. The room was

silent for a moment, and then the arms around my neck released.

I sucked in air and stumbled forward, turning to keep my face to Oakland and Skiver.

"You're with the V's, right?" Curtis said. It was a statement, not a question.

"Sure," I said, and held my hand against my face to stop the nosebleed.

"Then let's get out of here."

He backed out of the room, and I noticed that there were six or seven guys moving with him.

Oakland climbed to his feet. "You're dead, Fisher."

I didn't like getting pushed around. "Bring it on."

Curtis put his hand on my shoulder and led me into the hallway.

"I'm Curtis. And that probably wasn't wise," he said, a smile breaking across his face.

I nodded. I didn't know anything about Curtis, other than that he had tried to run and he warned me about the other two gang leaders. That was good, I guess, but the V's—whatever they were—could be just as bad as the others. Not that it mattered. I just needed to get back outside. I wasn't going to stay long enough for any of this to matter.

Curtis led me through the crowd and down the long corridor. Some of the onlookers we passed looked angry, but others gave me pats on the back and shouts of welcome.

We passed room 421 and kept going.

"I think I'm in there," I called out.

He shook his head. "We're moving you down to the V end."

We passed two hallways that branched off the main one. I stopped at the junction. One side was neat and tidy, with nameplates on each of the doors. The other was vandalized and cluttered. The walls were scrawled with graffiti and the floor was littered with loose papers and dirty clothes. Strings of Christmas tree lights were hung haphazardly along the ceiling, and a dozen bras were draped over them. It looked like a cross between a homeless shelter and a frat house.

"That's Havoc's row," Curtis said. "Stay out of there."

"Right."

He pointed the other direction. "And that's the Society's place. Don't let it fool you, though. They're worse. Anyway, come on."

We passed two more off-shooting hallways—they looked empty—before Curtis led me into a room just two doors down from the end of the main corridor. He stopped at the small sink and tossed me a washcloth. I pressed it against my nose.

A younger kid sat at a desk. Someone closed the door behind us.

"Glad to have you on board," Curtis said, sitting on the

lower bunk. Neither he nor the young kid seemed to have the same weird fashions I'd seen on the others. They were just wearing the uniform, nothing special. "Sorry about Oakland. The Society usually keeps him out of the way. There's no way to stop Isaiah from jumping on all the new students—there are just too many Society guys—but they can usually fend Oakland off for a few hours."

I pulled the rag off my face to see if the bleeding was slowing. It wasn't, so I reapplied the cloth.

"Listen," I said. "Thanks for coming in there, but I don't think I'm going to be sticking around here very long."

"That's why you're perfect for the V's," Curtis answered. He pointed at the other kid in the room. "This is Mason, by the way. Your roommate."

I waved, and then stood and gingerly walked to the sink, my abdomen aching from Oakland's punches. When I checked in the mirror, my face didn't look too bad yet. My shirt was covered in blood, but I didn't see any bruising.

"You're trying to get out?" I asked.

"Some of us are," Curtis said. "We don't know how, but at least we're not just accepting everything."

"What's the V stand for?"

"We're the Variants," he said. "The other two gangs are playing the game. Havoc—that's Oakland's deal—they just want to rule. Get as many points as they can, be in charge, party. The Society thinks that the only way we're getting out of here is to play by the rules, roll over and do whatever Iceman tells us to. The V's are everyone else. If you don't want to be part of that other stuff, we'll take you."

"Iceman?"

Curtis laughed a little. "That's what we call the guy who makes the announcements."

I ran cold water through the towel, rinsing out the blood, and then put the cool cloth back on my face. "So what is this place?"

"Who knows?" Curtis said. "I've been here a year and a half, and none of it makes any sense."

Mason spoke up. "I think they're testing us. We're rats in a maze."

Curtis nodded. "A lot of guys think that. All the cameras always watching us. And every now and then they make us do weird things, like an experiment. Other guys think they're training us for something. And some think maybe it really is a prison."

"You guys do something that would put you in prison?" I'd been in plenty of fights in my life, but I doubted I'd done anything worthy of jail time.

Curtis shrugged. "No one has any ties to home—no friends, no family. With a life like that, not everyone was totally clean before. But I haven't met anyone who did anything terrible. You?"

I shook my head. "No, just a foster kid."

"That's pretty common." He stood up. "I'll take care of changing your room assignment. Mason'll show you around. Don't worry about going down to the cafeteria tonight—we'll find some food for you. For now, don't go anywhere by yourself." Curtis smiled. "You've pissed off Havoc—most new students just ignore Oakland or maybe take a couple hits."

"I thought fighting was against the rules." Then again, very little I'd seen in the dorm seemed to follow the rules.

"The rules are weird," Curtis said with a tired shrug.

"I guess this wasn't 'violent fighting.'"

He smiled. "Exactly. Anyway, I'll be back. Welcome to the V's."

He went out the door and closed it behind him.

"Don't worry, Fish," Mason said. "Just stay close to the rest of us. The gangs have a truce, and they won't start anything big."

I nodded and stood, walking to the small window. I could see a large track behind the school, and miles and miles of forest.

"I'm going to get out of here," I said.

Mason shrugged. "Everyone says that."

Chapter Five

I didn't leave the room that night, and didn't talk to anyone else. Curtis came back with lasagna and bread sticks. It was better than I expected—it tasted more like it came from a restaurant than a cafeteria. Mason sat up reading. I think that he expected me to ask him questions, but I stayed quiet in my bunk.

I went through the manual hoping it would have some answers, but it didn't. It was mostly a retread of what I'd already heard—do this, don't do that. There were no explanations for why any of the rules existed, and they weren't even linked to punishments. I got the impression that the others had just figured out the punishments through experience.

Only twenty-four hours ago I'd been in my old foster home, lying awake, imagining how amazing my new life was going to be. Now I was lying awake, wishing I was back there. This wasn't fair. But since when had life been fair to me?

When dawn came, I was sitting by the window,

searching for any sort of escape route. I didn't see anything promising. Just a couple equipment sheds, a tiny set of bleachers—I had no idea what they'd be for, since we couldn't compete with other schools—and endless pines.

A girl was down on the track, jogging.

"That's Mouse," Mason said, standing behind me. "She's the girl version of Oakland—the two of them run Havoc."

"Mouse?" I asked with a halfhearted laugh. She was a tall, tan brunette, wearing short shorts and a sports bra. She looked nothing at all like her nickname.

"Yeah," Mason said, watching her run. "All of Havoc has stupid names. I guess that's part of their image. Mouse, Oakland, Skiver, Walnut." He left the window to go get dressed.

"And that's supposed to intimidate people?"

"Don't let it fool you. Mouse is vicious."

She followed the oval of the track, jogging fast and steady. I wondered if she was training for an escape. I wished it was me down there—I'd run straight for the woods and get out of this place.

"Can anyone go out on the track?" I asked.

"No. Havoc has the contract for groundskeeping. They can get out there most of the time. The Society's security, so they can go wherever they want. But we can't."

"I ought to join the Society for that," I said, and then

wished I hadn't. I'd just been thinking aloud, but the idea was so good that I wished no one had heard me.

"It won't work," Mason said. "Other people have tried it—joined the Society to get on the security team. But those guys are handpicked by Isaiah, and you'd never make it."

"Why not?"

"You've said no to him. People who say no to Isaiah don't do well in the Society."

"What contracts do we have?"

Mason smirked. "Janitorial and maintenance. Not very flashy, but it pays pretty well."

Mouse bent down to retie her shoe and then stood and continued jogging.

I heard Mason open the closet door behind me. "Hey, Fish," he said. "Your stuff came."

I stood to look. My school uniforms—seven sets of white shirts, red sweaters, and black pants—were all neatly hung. Below them on the floor were shoes and socks, and a bag of school supplies—pads, pencils, and a very small notebook computer, about the size of a paperback.

"Did someone bring them in during the night?"

"No," Mason said, pulling a shirt down from his side. "This is how we get the stuff we buy with points. I'm not sure how it works. At night we lock the closet, and in the morning the new stuff is in there. It's some kind of elevator."

I walked to the closet and inspected the edges, trying to

figure out how it moved. "I was awake all night, I think. I didn't hear it."

Mason shrugged. "You can hear it in other rooms. Ours just isn't as squeaky as some."

I took a shirt from the hanger. I wanted a shower, but didn't really want to deal with a communal bathroom right now.

Mason talked as he dressed. "Some kid, like, a year ago, tried to stay in the closet all night. They must have seen him on the cameras because the closet never moved until he got out. He'd try all kinds of things—waiting until the room was totally dark and sneaking in, or having someone stand in front of the camera while he hid."

I took off my T-shirt and pulled on the uniform. It was heavily starched and stiff.

"They watch us pretty close, huh?"

"Yes, they do," he said. "That's why we do dumb stuff like wear these uniforms. Leaving the dorm without your uniform is against the rules. Not going to class is against the rules. Not shaving is against the rules. Everything is."

I had to get Mason to help me with the tie—I'd never tied one before. He said that was pretty normal for the new guys.

Mason seemed pretty even-tempered. He was a V but didn't have the same drive I did to get out. I had to wonder if he'd joined the Variants simply because he wasn't passionate enough to be Society or Havoc.

We skipped going down to breakfast on Mason's recommendation. He said it might be better if we waited until class to leave the dorms, just to be sure Oakland was already gone. That was fine with me.

Instead, Mason had a box of snack food that he'd bought with points, and he quickly downed a couple of granola bars. He offered me one, but I refused. He'd probably had to go to a lot of trouble to earn the points for the bars, and I didn't want to owe anything to anyone.

At eight o'clock, as guys were trickling back from the cafeteria, there was a loud chime from the hallway.

"You're going to love this," Mason said with a smile as we walked toward the door.

A few of the guys had gathered around a flat-panel TV screen that was mounted on the wall. A man sat behind a desk. He was older—maybe late fifties, I guessed—but his face was lean and muscular. His eyes were cold and dark, and he looked directly into the camera. It felt like he was staring right at me.

I felt a hand on my shoulder and turned to see Curtis. "Meet Iceman."

The man flinched slightly, his eyes flicking from the camera for an instant before looking back at me.

"Students," he said, his voice sharp and dry. "Another disobedient new arrival day. There were several instances of fighting in the boys' dormitory, and you can be assured that punishments will be assigned during class this morning. But more disturbing is the continued actions of Curtis Shaw and Caroline Flynn. While their actions do not constitute a legitimate escape attempt, and they will therefore not receive detention, their repeated disregard for the rules will not be tolerated."

I glanced at Curtis. He still grinned, but the humor was gone from his eyes.

"In class today, you will receive punishments that will . . ." Iceman paused and almost smiled. ". . . *encourage* you to be more obedient in the future."

He stared into the camera for a moment more, and then the screen flickered to blue and the day's schedule appeared.

At five minutes to nine we left the dorm and headed for class. As we walked downstairs I was amazed at how few people we passed. Most of the rooms were empty, and the halls could have fit a lot more students than I saw.

"This place is huge," I said to Mason. "How many kids are here?"

"Not that many. It's mostly empty."

"A hundred? Two hundred?"

"No, not even that many. I think, including you, we're at something like seventy-four."

I nodded, but was surprised. I would have expected a lot more in a school this size. Maybe it was easier to control us if the group was small. Or maybe more were on the way.

The classroom was a little tight for the twenty-five of us in there, but it still looked nicer than any schoolroom I'd ever been in. The floors were wood, polished to a glassy shine. The walls were dark-stained wood, and at the front of the room a wide flat-screen TV was mounted instead of a chalkboard.

Mason took a seat next to the wall, and I sat beside him. It was obvious that the gangs stuck with their own even in class. The Society, recognizable by their immaculate uniforms, hair, and faces, took the front two rows of desks. Havoc was at the back, their uniforms augmented with flashy jewelry and drawn-on tattoos. There weren't any other V's in the room yet, but from what I'd seen we didn't try to dress like one another, the way the other gangs did. I guess that made sense for Variants.

"Are you and I really supposed to be in the same class?" I asked. Mason had to have been at least two years younger than I was.

He laughed, tapping absently on his desk as the other students were wandering in. "There's no freshman, sopho-more, junior stuff here. You just go to class. Oh, and the best part—no grades."

"But there are tests, right? Becky said that."

"Sure," Mason said, raising his hand and waving someone over. "But we never see the scores. We never get a report card."

"Then why does anyone even bother?"

"Points," he said. "Points and punishments. That's what makes the school go round. Speaking of . . . ," Mason said, nodding toward the door.

I looked up to see three girls enter. Becky was in the lead, laughing at something. She scanned the room and when our eyes met she gave me a small wave and smile.

She and her friends sat in the front row, close to the door. I was about to ask Mason about her, but a half dozen more people poured through the door and Mason tapped me on the shoulder and pointed.

"V's," he said.

Two girls took the desks in front of me and Mason. They immediately turned and began to talk.

"Did you really get in a fight with Oakland?" the girl in front of me asked. She had big green eyes and red hair that was almost as bright as her sweater.

I nodded and pointed at my lip, which was still a little swollen. "I'll try not to do it again."

"Why?" she said with a laugh. "I hope you do. I hope I'm there to see it next time. I'm Jane. And that's Lily."

"Hi," I said. "I'm Benson."

Jane's eyes narrowed, but the grin never faded from her

face. "That's a weird name. Who are you named after?"

I shrugged. "No idea."

"Well, Benson, I'm glad you picked the V's. We're not very big, and we need everyone we can get."

"I don't plan to stick around very long," I said, which caused her to laugh again.

"You can't say stuff like that," she said, pretending to be scandalized. "What if the Society hears you?"

Maybe I needed to revise my assessment of the school. Jane seemed happy—truly happy. For some reason, until sitting here in class, I hadn't really contemplated getting to know any girls in this weird prison of a school.

"Where are you from, Jane?"

"Baltimore. Hang on—time for class. Did they tell you about class?"

I shook my head. "Not really."

"They don't teach us reading and writing." She smirked, and then turned back to face forward.

The students quieted down very quickly, much more so than in my schools back home. A girl stood up at the front of the class—she'd been sitting in the desk next to Becky. Her blond hair was pulled into a tight bun and her severe makeup made her skin almost as white as her teeth.

"Welcome to class," she said, a little overly enthusiastic. "We're very pleased to have a new student this morning. Benson, could you stand up and introduce yourself?"

I glanced over at Mason, who smiled and shrugged.

"I'm Benson Fisher," I said. "From Pittsburgh. I'm seventeen. And I think it's absolute bullcrap that you guys are all sitting here, pretending like nothing's wrong."

There were murmurs in the class as I sat back down, followed by a few giggles. Jane turned back and gave me an approving nod. The girl at the front of the class didn't seem fazed at all. Becky faced straight ahead, motionless.

"Welcome, Benson," she said. "I know you'll fit right in." She opened her minicomputer. "My name is Laura, and I'm the teaching assistant in this class. Mason, could you please help Benson out today?"

Mason gave a sarcastic salute.

"Thank you. Before we begin, I just need to announce today's punishments." Laura scanned the classroom, glancing slowly back and forth between her computer screen and the students in the desks. "Ah. Skiver. Fighting. No food today."

Skiver, sitting against the back wall, swore and punched his desk. I looked back at Laura just in time to miss what Skiver did next, but her white face went red, and she stumbled over her next few words.

"It, uh, it looks . . . No one else in here is on the punishment list. Well done. Our lesson today is a little departure from what we've been studying, but you were all doing so well with Materials Science that I guess they've decided we're ready to move on. Today we'll be talking about aesthetics."

Jane and Lily exchanged a look. Lily rolled her eyes.

"Aesthetics," Laura said, reading from her computer, "is the philosophy that deals with the study of beauty. In this course we will be addressing such questions as 'What is art?' and 'What is beauty?'"

Mason leaned over to me and whispered, "It's something new every couple of weeks. Weird junk, like this. At least Materials Science had explosions."

Class seemed to last forever. Laura only spoke for a few minutes, and then she handed out a test that was supposed to gauge our knowledge on the subject. I didn't know a single answer. After the test we watched a video that was nothing but an endless slideshow of statues, vases, and paintings, all with a monotone British guy speaking in the background. A handful of the students seemed to be listening very attentively, but most were just trying to stay awake. Even Laura, who had sat down in the desk next to Becky, seemed bored.

I spent most of the class staring at the back of Jane's head, at her red hair that hung down past her shoulders and touched my desk.

This school wasn't what I wanted or expected, but I had to admit that parts of it were better than back home. I'd sat through a lot of boring classes before, in filthy classrooms that were either blazing hot or freezing cold. I'd watched kids pass drugs around while the teacher's back was turned. And I'd spent many days wishing I could afford to eat at the cafeteria.

I adjusted the notebook on my desk, purposely sliding it so that I could "accidentally" touch Jane's hair with the tips of my fingers.

No. I couldn't get comfortable here. I wouldn't be like the others. Becky had said we were stuck here so we might as well make the most of it. But I wasn't going to be stuck here.

Chapter Six

Stepping out into the hall, I found Jane walking at my side instead of Mason. He and Lily were behind us, chatting.

"That girl, Laura, acts like she's an expert on this stuff," I said, gesturing back to the classroom. "Like she's actually a teacher."

"That's the Society for you," Jane said. "They're the future leaders of America—trapped inside a freak show of a school."

"Has anyone tried to get out of here?" I said, covering my mouth with my hand. "I mean, really tried?"

Jane smiled. "There are microphones as well as the cameras."

I nodded, wondering whether that meant she actually had something to tell me or whether she just didn't want me to get in trouble. I doubted anything I said here could be worse than what I'd said in my introduction in class.

Jane led me to the cafeteria, which was down on the first floor, at the back of the school. I watched the ceilings while we walked and counted at least thirty-two cameras in the four minutes it took to get there. I didn't see the microphones she was talking about, but I didn't doubt her.

The others that we saw in the hall had lost any of the anger I'd seen in them when I arrived. No one was protesting conditions. No one was trying to escape. It looked almost the same as any other school I'd ever been in—some talking, some laughing, some flirting. I wondered how long it took before they'd given up. A month? A year?

The line for lunch was backed all the way out into the hall. Jane and I took our place at the end.

"The food here isn't bad," she said. "Havoc has the contract because food duty offers a ton of points. But part of their points is based on how we rate them. So, they have to make it good."

"How long have you been here?" I said, leaning back against the wall and watching her. Jane had a very light sprinkling of faded freckles on her nose and cheeks.

"Oh, I was one of the first," she said. She folded her arms across her chest.

"How long was that?"

"Two and a half years, I think. I don't keep track anymore."

"How many people were here then?"

She shook her head, her smile disappearing. "Not many. Fifteen. They're all gone now."

The line moved forward a few feet.

"Gone where?"

Her voice hushed, and she absently ran her finger along the wood panels on the wall. "Detention, most of them. No one got out, if that's what you mean. People used to try harder to escape back then."

A girl with black hair and a round face ran up next to Jane, giving me a quick glance before speaking rapidly in hushed tones. "Did you hear about the punishments?"

Before Jane had a chance to reply, the girl continued, "Curtis and Carrie got no food all day and hard labor."

"What?" Jane looked stunned. "They never do that. Not together."

"I know," the girl said. "I don't know what it is, but Dylan took them outside."

Jane shook her head, and the round-faced girl hurried off to spread the story.

"Is that for running after the car?" I asked.

Jane nodded. "The punishments get worse every time. I keep telling Carrie to stop."

I wanted to continue talking, to press her for details, but she'd turned away slightly, not looking at me anymore.

After a few moments we turned the corner and entered the cafeteria. I'd been expecting the usual arrangement— huge pans of sloppy food under sneeze guards, being dished up by bored people with ice-cream scoops. Instead,

65

I found a wall with hundreds of tiny doors. It almost looked like rows of mailboxes in the post office, except that these boxes had small windows and lights.

Jane handed me a tray. "You get one main course, one side, and one drink. It scans the chip in your watch." She was smiling, but looked tired and lost in thought.

I peered in the little windows and saw gorgeous plates of food: enchiladas, fried chicken, lasagna, and half a dozen other things. As others opened the little doors the smells of the kitchen poured out.

I tried to look through the doors to the kitchen behind but couldn't see anything.

Jane opened one and pulled out a salad, heaped with chicken and blue cheese.

"Not bad, huh?" she said. "It tastes as good as it looks."

I finally chose a plate of fettuccine Alfredo. I'd only ever had it as a frozen dinner, but even then it was good. A tiny display above the window lit up as I opened it and the words BENSON FISHER, 1 ENTRÉE scrolled across.

I put the plate on my lunch tray and then followed Jane to the side dishes.

"When I heard that Havoc ran the cafeteria I'd thought they would spit in my food or something."

"They probably would if they could see who was taking it," she said, standing on the tips of her toes to look in a high window.

I opened a door and took a small plate holding two bread sticks. "They don't seem worried about breaking rules."

"A lot of people break rules," she said. "But some of the rules are more serious than others. If you try to escape, you'll get detention. On the other hand, if you don't wear your uniform, your gang will just lose points."

She picked a bowl of fruit and put it on her tray, and then motioned with her head for me to follow her. Around the next corner was a row of vending machines with drinks.

"The gang will lose the points?" I asked.

"Yep," she said. "They do that so that the gangs will keep their members in line. If one of the V guys wasn't shaving, then the rest of us would tell him he has to. Seriously, the school has this all figured out. They make us obey." She popped a crouton in her mouth.

"I saw that shaving rule," I said with a forced laugh. "Do girls have that one, too?"

"Worse than a rule." Jane grinned and gestured to her legs. "We have to wear skirts. Every day."

There wasn't as much selection in the drink machines—just juice and milk. Still, there was no way I was going to complain about my lunch. If it tasted anything like it smelled, it would be the best meal I'd had since two foster families ago.

I chose a bottle of orange juice, but as we turned to leave I noticed a panel of darkened windows on the far wall. The word *discipline* was on a sign above it.

"What are those?"

"More fun," she said. "Sometimes the punishment is like what Curtis and Carrie got—no food at all. Sometimes it's just that you'll only get certain kinds of food. They don't use it much."

"Have you ever been punished?"

Jane laughed. "Everyone gets punished."

I followed her outside. The cafeteria's back wall was floor-to-ceiling windows, and a door was propped open letting in the cool autumn breeze. Jane told me that the V's always ate on the bleachers unless the weather wouldn't let them. I liked to think it was because they were getting a few steps closer to freedom, leaving the confines of the building whenever they could. But it was probably just for the fresh air and to get away from the Society and Havoc. Even so, I loved being outside, and my mind instantly flew back to the wall.

A grappling hook might work. There had to be rope here somewhere.

But first I was going to eat.

I walked next to Jane who, despite her skirt, didn't seem to mind the chilly November air. She'd been here for two and a half years—how old had she been when she came?

Fourteen? Fifteen? I thought of Mason. He was young, too. This was bad enough for me—it must have been a lot worse for the younger ones.

We were the last of the V's to get to the bleachers. The girl from the window was there, her brown hair pulled into short pigtails. She gave me a little wave as she chewed her food.

I counted sixteen V's—eighteen including Curtis and Carrie, who were still off somewhere working. Mason told me that it was the smallest of the gangs; the Society was biggest by far—about double what we were—and Havoc made up the rest. Jane said there were sometimes a few holdouts who refused to join any gang, but they didn't last long. People needed their gangs.

I was the center of attention for a while, answering questions about where I was from and what my life was like before Maxfield, but for the most part the group kept up a normal lunch conversation—how much they hated class, how one girl was excited for winter, how another wondered when we'd get another school dance. No one talked about escape. I tried to bring up the subject once, but it died out fairly quickly.

The whole time we sat there I kept an eye on the trees. There were Society kids out there. One was at the tree line, patrolling on the back of a four-wheeler. I could hear a second one, but couldn't see it.

What would make them act like that? Why wouldn't they just make a break for it?

As I watched them I thought about what they'd need to have to keep the four-wheelers running: gasoline, oil, tools. All of that could help my escape.

After lunch we sat through another class on aesthetics and then had a break. The schedule on the TV screen called it study hall, but Mason told me that no one ever had homework other than reading the textbooks—which we were never tested on anyway—so most people just hung out in the dorms or took a nap.

I explored. Aside from the dorms, the fourth floor had a long common room with heavy wooden tables and leather couches. It smelled like dust and was completely empty.

The third floor was all classrooms—there had to be thirty of them, all almost identical. I tried to do some math in my head. There were seventy-four kids in the school, and my classroom held about twenty-five. So only three or four rooms were being used. Did that mean more kids were on the way? There was plenty of room for them.

Mason had told me that for a while, about a year ago, there were new students every week, sometimes two or three at a time. But then it tapered off. I was the first one in four months—Lily was the last before me.

The second and first floors were more interesting: the

library (which didn't seem to have a single book written in the last hundred years), the cafeteria, the trophy room, a few large multipurpose rooms, a tiny theater, and a dozen small rooms that had no furniture. All of the architecture in these rooms was amazing, with stained wood, painted plaster, and carved stone. But why was there so much space unless they planned for more to come? Or had more been here and left?

Had they all been killed?

I pushed on every door and window, but they were all locked. The sensors didn't make a sound. The V's didn't have a contract that let us outside.

I wanted to check out the basement, too, but the last period of the day was about to start—gym—and I needed to run upstairs to change clothes. As I entered the boys' dorm and headed toward my room, I counted the doors. Sixty-four in the main hall. I didn't know how many others were in the halls that branched off—I wasn't interested in running into either Isaiah or Oakland—but I guessed there were at least that many, if not more. So, 128, and they could fit two guys in each room . . . about 250 guys? And it was probably the same for the girls' dorm?

Were they all going to be filled?

Mason was already dressed when I got to the room. He looked at his watch and grinned. "I almost thought you'd run away."

I took my gym clothes from the closet—a white T-shirt and red shorts. "Maybe I would have if the doors unlocked."

Clouds had rolled in, but it didn't look like they were going to do anything. There was a bit of a breeze, and everyone was cold.

Gym didn't have any set curriculum—it was essentially a free exercise time. Most people were out on the track, jogging or walking. A couple Society kids had a soccer ball. I didn't really want to exercise, but it seemed like the best way to stay warm. The V's didn't have any sports equipment, so we mostly kept to the track. Mason and I started walking together while a group of V girls jogged. After about twenty minutes Lily left them and joined us.

I was making a mental map: the layout of the track, the distance to the tree line, the groundskeeping sheds. I tried to correlate it to what I'd seen from my window—hills in the forest and rocky outcrops that I couldn't see from here. If I was going to run, I had to know this place perfectly.

I watched Havoc. They were clustered in what looked like a sculpture garden—upturned logs carved into faces and shapes, piles of rocks, flowers planted in patterns. Every once in a while Skiver looked in my direction, pointing and saying something to another guy, but they never stood up.

A cool breeze blew past, but it carried forest smells that

brought up vague memories. Had I ever been camping before? I couldn't remember.

"I really should be liking this," I said, more to myself than Mason. "Look at this place. It's nicer than any school I've ever been to. There's no homework."

"No one telling you what to do," he added.

Lily snorted. "Well, no one except whoever is running the school. *Someone* is telling us to walk out in the cold."

"You know what I meant," Mason said. "When we go back to the dorms, we can do whatever we want."

"Except leave the dorms," she said.

I checked my watch. It was past five, and getting colder. "Shouldn't we be heading back in?"

"A bell rings when gym is over," Lily said. "We have to wait for that. The doors don't unlock until it does."

"Why isn't there a schedule?" I asked. "Why don't we just know that gym ends at whatever time, every day?"

Mason spoke. "You know that schedule that was posted on the screens this morning? It changes every day, and there's no pattern to it. Sometimes class starts at nine and sometimes it starts at seven. Sometimes there's no class at all and sometimes we're there till ten at night."

"Why?"

"Why does anything happen here?" Lily answered. "It's all random and stupid."

I had to smile. At least there was someone else who

was as annoyed as I was.

We made a few more loops around the track. The wind was beginning to pick up, and a group was already huddled by the doors, waiting to go inside. Curtis and Carrie appeared around the corner of the school. They sat by the doors. Jane and a few of the other V's left the joggers and ran over to them.

As we walked close to where Havoc was gathered I tried to count them. Even in their gym clothes they looked like thugs. One girl sat on a fat stump, drawing an intricate pen tattoo onto another girl's leg. Oakland was leaning against a long, thin rock that looked like it had been jammed vertically into the ground, and four of his friends sat around him. Unlike the rest of us, a few of the Havoc guys had ignored the rules and worn jackets.

"Are those against the dress code?" I asked, gesturing to hooded sweatshirts.

"Yep," Mason said. "Maybe they'll get dinged for it, but it'll just be points."

"Why are points a big deal?"

"Points are everything," Lily said. I couldn't tell whether she was being sarcastic or not.

Mouse jogged past us and slowed to a stop in the sculpture garden. Despite the cold, she had her T-shirt tied into a knot to show off her stomach, and I'd swear her already-short shorts were rolled at the waist. I know I wasn't the only guy who noticed.

We passed Havoc and again faced the expanse of pine trees. A gust of wind blew past us, carrying tiny leaves and sticks with it, and making me shiver. The only trees nearby with any leaves were the cottonwoods by the road, but those had shed most of their foliage already. Autumn here wasn't pretty.

"So," I said, glancing around to make sure that no one else was nearby. "No one has answered my question. Has there ever been a serious escape attempt?"

Mason didn't immediately say anything, so Lily spoke. "It depends on what you mean by serious. People have tried. From what I've been told, a lot of people used to try."

"And no one has made it?"

"Not that we know of," she said. "Most get caught in the act. Others we just hear about."

"What stops them?" I asked. "Why can't they just get over the wall and go?"

"It's not easy to get over the wall," Mason said simply. "And then you've got to get over that fence. And there are security cameras. And who knows what else."

"I'm going to run one day," Lily said. "Soon."

I looked over at her. She was young and small, but there was something about her eyes that made me believe she might actually be able to. "What are you waiting for?"

She thought for a moment, her jaw set and forehead

wrinkled. "I've never had a good time to do it. Too many Society freaks around all the time."

"What if you went right now?" I asked. "Run into the forest and go?"

"I'm not that fast," she said. She stared at the tree line and the tone of her voice made it sound like she might actually have been considering it. I watched her turn and look for the four-wheeler, which was stopped near the crowd of Society kids at the door. "I don't know. What do you think, Mason? Would the Society chase us over the wall? Would they dare cross it?"

He shrugged. "I wouldn't risk it."

We walked in silence for a while. I wondered what the dangers actually were. I was pretty fast—could they catch me if I ran into the forest? I could run in one direction, hide, and then wait for the others to pass me. It couldn't be that hard, could it? Of course, it shouldn't be hard at all. Every single kid in that school should have agreed with me. If the Society simply refused to enforce the security rules, we'd be fine.

The wind picked up and I had to squint to keep bits of sand and leaves out of my eyes. It stung as it blew against my legs and arms, and I stopped walking so I could turn my back to it.

"I'm going to go check on the doors," I said as the gust faded.

I jogged across the field, leaving Mason and Lily on the track.

It was dumb that they locked us out. I made a mental note to prop one of the doors open the next time we had to come outside. But that would probably be against some stupid rule, too.

I passed the crowd of waiting students and hopped up the front steps.

"It's still locked," someone said. I turned to see Becky, her hands rubbing her arms to stay warm. Her bare legs were speckled with goose bumps, as were mine.

"Hey," I said. "You're admin. Can't you get them open?"

"I wish," she said, her tour-guide personality shining brightly. "I really should be back there jogging."

"Me too."

She took a step toward me, inspecting my face. "I heard about last night. Sorry about the nose."

I shrugged. "Things happen."

Becky leaned forward and whispered, "I shouldn't say this, but Oakland was in the infirmary this morning. I think you might have cracked his rib."

I couldn't help a smile from breaking across my face, and it spread to hers. "Am I going to get in trouble for it?"

She shook her head. "Probably not. The V's might lose a few points, but if it was anything serious it would have been announced this morning. I'd watch out for Oakland, though."

"Okay." I looked back at where Mason and Lily were waiting on the track. "Well, I might be in the infirmary tomorrow if these doors don't open soon."

She nodded and rubbed her crossed arms with her hands. "Me too."

Becky moved back to her friends and I trotted across the grass to the track. Mason and Lily started walking again before I even got to them.

"Is she still trying to recruit you?" Lily asked when I reached them.

"Becky? No, just talking."

"They're all like that, you know," she continued. "Becky, Laura, all the Society girls. Sweet as pie, and fake as Mouse's boobs."

Mason snickered.

"Becky seems nice enough," I said.

Lily pulled her arms inside her T-shirt. "Yeah, Becky's nice. And she'd send you to the gas chamber if the school told her to."

Mason laughed. "That's an exaggeration."

"Says you," Lily said. "And the guys in the Society are worse—arrogant and holier-than-thou. They've turned obedience into a sport."

Just then the bell rang, and we immediately turned and

ran back toward the school. But as we got closer, it was obvious there was a problem. No one was going inside. The doors were still locked.

Lily swore and turned away, looking at the forest.

"They do this, too," Mason said to me, his voice a little more serious than usual. "The school, I mean. Sometimes the doors are locked. Sometimes the power goes out. Sometimes there's no food."

A voice was shouting over the crowd, and I turned to see Isaiah standing on the steps trying to get everyone's attention. "The doors appear to be locked. I'm sure that this is just a malfunction in the mechanism."

The other gangs booed him. The Society was mostly quiet, though it was obvious that they weren't happy, either.

I turned to Mason. "Is it really a malfunction? Maybe the power is out or something, so the doors can't read our chips."

"I doubt it. I swear it's another of their stupid tests."

"Could it be punishment?" I spun, looking for Curtis and Carrie. They were still sitting on the grass, their T-shirts stained with dirt and sweat.

"Maybe," Mason said. "But I bet they're just screwing with our heads."

I gazed out at the western horizon. The sun was dipping behind a distant mountain. "You know how I said that I should be liking this place?"

He gave a short, humorless laugh. "Yeah."

"I do not want to spend the next month or year or who knows how long in some crappy experiment."

He nodded, watching the doors. "There aren't even security cameras outside. If it's an experiment, then what are they watching?"

"There aren't?" *Why hadn't someone mentioned this before?* "Maybe they're hidden?"

"Could be. People out here still act like there are cameras. Of course, the Society will rat us out, cameras or not."

I nodded, not thinking about the doors anymore. "I'll talk to you later, Mason."

Jogging, I headed back to the track where a few of the students were still trying to keep warm. I got onto the track, surveying the edges of the forest, noting areas where the trees were closest.

I did two more laps, finding new energy as I psyched myself up. I watched the mass of students near the door— most of them were huddled together to stay warm, and no one seemed to be looking at me. As I started the third lap, I veered off the track running for the forest.

It was almost instantly warmer there, out of the wind, but I didn't slow down. I sprinted over the rough, rocky ground, bobbing between the trees and around fallen logs. It was getting darker, and I slowed enough to pick a good path. I didn't want to fall and ruin my chance for escape.

My chest was burning as I pushed myself to keep jogging. From the drive in, I guessed that it was about a mile from the school to the wall, and maybe another half mile to the fence. Then again, there was no way of knowing whether it formed a perfect circle around the school. Maybe the wall encompassed other things, too?

I could hear the revving engine of a four-wheeler somewhere behind me. This was it. Trying to escape was one of the big rules. It meant detention.

I was gasping for air by the time I reached the wall. But there was no way to climb it. Twelve feet up, solid brick.

I tried finding a foothold, but it was smooth, the mortar coming out to the edge of the bricks. There were no gaps for my fingers or shoes to grab on to.

The engine was getting close. And I thought I heard a second—or were there three?

I stared, silent and desperate. Fifty yards to my left a fat raccoon sat on the wall, nervously eyeing me in the twilight.

How did you get up there?

Turning my attention to the trees, I looked for one that I could climb—maybe I could get over that way. But someone had planned for that: Between the wall and the nearest trees was a fifteen-foot gap where the vegetation and rocks had been cleared away, leaving only barren dirt. The narrow tire tracks of the four-wheelers were rutted into the earth.

There had to be some way. I climbed up into the closest pine, slowly grappling with the sticky, sap-speckled limbs. It was difficult in the low light, but in a few minutes I got high enough to see over the wall. There was nothing on the other side but more trees.

I could hear the engine below me now—not just the engine but the rough sound of tires crunching over rocks and dry sticks. I didn't waste time looking for it.

I climbed higher, now almost thirty feet in the air. There was no way I could jump. Even if I miraculously made it over the wall, I'd have broken legs or ankles. And there was still a chain-link fence somewhere on the other side.

The engine suddenly quieted, dropping down into a low, rumbling idle.

"Benson!" The voice was harsh and angry. I didn't recognize it.

I slipped, catching myself but feeling the tree sway. It only took me a second before I realized that could help me.

When I shifted my weight back and forth, the pine moved under me. Looking down, I wished that I'd chosen one with a narrower trunk—one that might be more flexible—but it was too late for that. I could already hear another voice on the forest floor below me.

The tree swung a few feet toward the wall, and then back away. With each movement, I threw my weight into the swing, and soon the tree was shaking back and forth, creaking and rocking. I was working too fast to have a good plan—would it bend over the wall and let me jump? What if all the bending made it snap and fall? If it landed against the wall, I could climb it like a ladder—if I managed to hold on. Either way, I was facing a fall.

The voices were shouting now. "Benson, get down here!" "You'll get detention!" "You're breaking the rules!" I ignored them.

The creaking got louder and louder, and each slow swing seemed to strain the strength of the wood. It was too late to give up. I was already in the tree, already trying to jump the wall. If I went back down, I'd get detention, whatever that was. I had to keep going.

As I swung toward the wall I searched for something to break my fall, but the other side of the wall looked like this side—fifteen feet of bare dirt and rocks.

I had to jump. The Society was already below me. I'd already broken the rule.

When the pine swung close to the wall my fingers gripped the branch tighter, as if my own body were unconsciously refusing to take such a suicidal leap.

And I suddenly realized there was something in the forest on the other side. Smoke.

The tree swung back, and I put my weight into it.

It couldn't be fog over there. It was too dry and too

windy. But the dark haze hung over the forest, low in the trees. I couldn't see where it was coming from.

An air horn blared beneath me. They were calling for help.

The tree swung toward the wall, and then back away. I braced myself for the jump. *Next time.*

I could feel the momentum shift under my feet as the tree reached its farthest point, slowed, and began swaying back again. My gaze was glued on the dirt below, the far side of the wall. It looked rocky and hard. I'd have to land just right. Can't lock my knees. Roll with the impact. I might just—

SNAP!

I heard a sharp pop like the sound of a gunshot. The branch below me had broken. I was falling.

I desperately snatched at limbs and branches, but it was too late. I tumbled down through the boughs of the pine, bouncing off branch after branch until I collapsed painfully to the earth. I landed on my knees then fell forward onto my face.

I panted for breath, pain shooting in my legs as I tried to lift myself up.

A foot hit my back, slamming me back down.

"Trying to cross the wall is a detention-worthy offense," a male voice said. I tried to roll over, but he kept his foot in place. I didn't have the energy or breath to fight back.

"Get his hands," a voice ordered—a girl—and I felt someone grab at my wrists. I shook them loose, and then pain burst through my side. A kick to the ribs.

I rolled onto my left. There were three of them, all in their gym clothes. Two boys and a girl. I didn't know the boys, but the girl was Laura, my so-called teacher.

"Hello, Benson," she said, seeing the recognition in my eyes. She held a black stick—maybe it was metal—about two feet long. "No one is allowed to cross the wall. You were told this during new-student orientation."

I couldn't bring myself to say anything. I hurt all over, and it felt like I was breathing through heavy cloth—I couldn't get enough air.

"Now please give your hands to Dylan so that he can bind them," Laura said sternly, as though she were reciting directly from the rulebook. "You will be taken to the school for detention."

Dylan tried to take my hands, but I fought him and after a moment he backed up. I saw him draw something from his belt, but he was obscuring it in his hand. Pepper spray?

"Resisting security," Laura continued, her face red and wild, "is also punishable."

"What is wrong with you people?" I said, fighting for air to speak.

"We follow the rules, Benson," Laura said.

"Don't you want to get out of here?" I gasped. "We—us four—could knock down a tree and be gone."

"That is not true," she said. "Now, Dylan."

Dylan took another step forward, and this time the other boy stepped around behind me. Dylan raised the canister in his hand.

Another voice rang out. "Stop."

Dylan's head shot up.

"He was trying to escape," Laura declared indignantly.

I rolled over again, rocks cutting into my sides. Five others were standing in the woods. Curtis, Mason, Jane, Lily, and Carrie.

"He wasn't trying to escape," Curtis said. "He was going for a jog to try to keep warm." His dirty face was red and tired, and he was panting heavily.

Dylan let out a loud mocking snort, and Laura spoke. "He tried to jump from this tree. He was trying to get over this wall."

Curtis motioned for Mason, who hurried over to me and helped me up. Dylan and the other Society boy seemed unsure of what to do. They wanted to fight—I was sure of that—but they were outnumbered.

"Benson was jogging," Curtis repeated.

"He was going to meet me out here," Jane said. "We'd arranged it. He was in the tree watching for me."

I put my arm around Mason's shoulder and hobbled

slowly back to where the V's stood.

"The fact is," Curtis said, "that's what we're going to say when we appeal his detention. And you know the rulebook, Laura—what's the punishment for making a false accusation for detention?"

"He was trying to escape," Laura said. Her voice was shrill and furious. "Everyone here knows that."

Curtis walked toward Laura and lowered his voice, so quiet I could barely hear him. "And everyone here also knows what detention means. Do you really want that?"

Laura's eyes looked black in the dim light. She was clutching the metal baton tightly with both hands. "If we let him break the rules then everyone here is in danger. Do you want to go back to the way things were before the truce?"

"So you'll kill him to keep the peace?" Curtis asked. He turned and walked back toward the V's. Laura was still fuming, but there was nothing that she could do. There were three of them and six of us. Even with the pepper spray and baton, the odds were on our side.

We hiked in silence for several minutes, picking our way through the uneven forest floor in the quickly dimming light. I hurt all over, but I tried to not let it show.

Curtis moved next to me. Keeping his gaze straight ahead, watching the forest, he whispered, "That's the last time. Don't do something stupid like that again."

I didn't reply.

I knew things now. I knew how Society security guards were armed, and I knew how fast they could respond. The next escape would work.

Chapter Seven

The doors never did unlock that night. We slept outside.

It had been an experiment, just like Mason had said. While I was at the wall, ten sleeping bags had dropped out of the windows of the school. Someone had been in there—must have come up through an elevator, like our clothes did—but no one saw anyone. Just the sleeping bags. Ten of them for more than seventy people.

And, since Curtis had been in the forest with me, the V's didn't end up with any of the bags. In fact, the Society claimed them all, and for whatever reason, Havoc didn't fight them on it. Instead, they tried to cram their whole gang into the two small groundskeeping sheds.

The V's climbed down into one of the deep window wells on the side of the building—deep, broad holes that gave light to the large basement windows. It was fifteen feet wide and maybe eight feet down; we needed help getting in and out. Someone jokingly suggested that we just break the window, but no one looked like they were seriously considering it. I wasn't sure what they were afraid of. Damaging property wasn't one of the Big Four rules, and the punishment couldn't have been worse than sleeping outside all night.

I didn't know where the Society decided to gather. Once we were down in the window well I couldn't see anything. The four-wheeler engines didn't stop running all night, though, and before we all had climbed down I'd seen Isaiah arguing with Curtis about something. I'm sure it was me.

None of the V's said anything about my escape attempt. They all had to know—they saw us come out of the forest, and they saw my bloodied knees and scraped arms and elbows. Maybe escaping was something that all the students tried when they first got here. Even Becky and Isaiah—maybe even Laura. Maybe their devotion to the rules and the Society was something that came from months and years of failing to escape.

I looked down the row at the other V's. Curtis and Carrie were awake, softly talking, though Curtis's eyelids were drooping low. Mason was asleep, his head hanging forward, chin against his chest. Lily was next to him, snoring just loudly enough that I could hear it a few feet away. Jane was beside me, eyes closed. I could feel her body move with each slow breath.

There were hundreds of stars in the rectangle of sky

above us. Thousands maybe. I stared at them. I'd always heard about stars like this. I heard that you could see lots of them once you got out of the city, more than just the few dozen brightest ones that could break through the city lights. It seemed like I'd maybe seen a view like this once or twice, though I couldn't really remember where. Maybe it was just on TV.

As I looked upward I felt a surprising thrill of freedom. I could see so many things in the sky that I never got to see back home—things I'd only heard about. If I got out of that well and got a better look I could probably see the Milky Way. Maybe a planet or two.

"They're beautiful, aren't they?"

Jane's voice was soft, barely a whisper.

"Yeah."

"How are you feeling?"

"Sore. Do you think I'll get detention?"

She took her eyes off the sky for a moment and looked at me. "I don't know. It depends on whether the school believes Laura and Dylan."

I wanted to turn to her, but we were so close together that our noses would probably touch, so I kept my face toward the sky. I also wanted to ask her more questions. How had others gotten over the wall? Did they plan ahead? Take supplies? But I felt guilty. Jane and the others had come into the forest to rescue me. I didn't know if that was a risk—maybe they'd get punished for it. To ask more questions about escape didn't seem the best way to thank her.

"It's cold," she said. She reached out her hands and flexed her fingers open and closed a few times, and then folded her arms again.

"We could start a fire. Would that be against the rules?"

She smiled. "We don't have any matches."

"We don't need them," I said.

Jane raised an eyebrow skeptically. "You were a Boy Scout?"

"No," I said with a little laugh. "But I've seen lots of movies."

"There are movies that teach you how to start fires?"

"Sure. Didn't you ever see *Cast Away*?"

Jane shook her head.

"Never? What about the Discovery Channel—*Man Vs. Wild*, or *Survivorman*? Heck, I think they even had to make fire on *Lost*."

"I don't think I've seen any of those."

"What?"

"I've been in here for two and a half years."

"Those are all older than two and a half years. *Cast Away* is way older."

Jane shrugged and, much to my surprise, rested her head on my shoulder. Her hair smelled good—a little like honey. I thought maybe she wanted me to put my arm around her, but I didn't.

In the window in front of us I could see my dim reflection. I looked just like everyone else. In the low light I couldn't make out any facial features, and I was just another white T-shirt in a row of white T-shirts.

"Why don't we break this window?" I asked quietly. "Get out of the cold. What's the punishment for that?"

Her answer was sleepy and hushed. "You can't break it. People have tried, but it's bulletproof or something. Keeps us inside."

I nodded. The unbreakable glass made it a prison—a prison we now wished we could get back into.

Shortly before she fell asleep, Jane touched my arm. "Don't go anywhere tonight, okay? The Society aren't the only ones who guard the wall."

"There are guards out there?"

"I don't know. There has to be something."

Just before dawn the doors unlocked. In the morning silence we heard the buzz and click even as far away as we were. The Society kids must have spent the night close by; we could hear their groggy shouts of relief, and the sound of the doors opening, before most of us had even stood up. We followed drowsily, a few guys giving the others footholds to climb out of the window well. I was the last out and had to have Curtis and another V pull me up—my side aching with pain as they did so. No one bothered to say much.

Even though everyone had dismissed the lockout as normal, I was expecting something different inside the school. Maybe they forced us out so they could work—paint the walls or install new security cameras or put iron bars on the doors. But nothing was different. This happened all time, they said. Just a stupid test.

Let's give them ten sleeping bags and see how they divide them up.

When we got back to the dorms, I went to the showers and turned the water up as hot as I could stand it. I washed the dirt and rocks out of my knees, and inspected my cuts. Nothing was serious. A deep purple bruise had appeared on my left side, but even that wasn't as big as I'd expected. It felt a lot worse than it looked.

By the time I was finished and back in the room, Mason was getting dressed in camouflage.

"What is that?" I said.

Mason frowned and pointed at the ticker. "No class today. We have paintball."

"You're kidding," I said.

He sighed and pulled on a camo jacket over an olive green T-shirt. The jacket was mostly light colors—tans and browns. "This is our version of high school sports.

Paintball, war games, debate, chess." He paused and grinned. "It's like the nerds meet the military."

I fingered the pair of plain tan sweatpants that hung next to my uniform and then glanced back at Mason.

"Why do you have better clothes than I do?"

"I spent some of my points on it. And you'd better do that, too, when you get some." His serious face broke into a smile. "You're going to get slaughtered out there."

I picked up the gun. It was powered by a canister of compressed air, and a large kidney-shaped hopper on top held the paintballs. "This is crazy."

"I know," Mason said. "Some people think that they're training us. Like, this school is some kind of breeding ground for super soldiers or something."

"You don't?"

"No," he said, sitting down to lace on a pair of boots. "Because they *don't* train us. If the government was in charge of this and wanted us to be learning tactics or something, wouldn't they sit us down and teach us how to do it?"

"I guess so."

"Rats in a cage, Fish. Rats in a cage."

At ten minutes to ten, we left the building, heading out to the woods. It looked ridiculous—more than seventy kids, all in varying degrees of camouflage, trotting out of a school. A few of the outfits were plain, like mine, but some were elaborate. Not only did they have camouflage, but some had fake sticks and leaves attached to their clothes, and a few looked almost like Bigfoot—long hairy grass hanging from almost every inch of their bodies.

"I'm saving up for one of those," Mason said, admiring a Society kid. "It's called a ghillie suit. Snipers use them. If you're wearing that and you crouch down in a patch of grass, you're invisible."

In a way, the walk was exhilarating. I'd never actually played a school sport. And, even though this one was bizarre and fit right in with all the other random crap at Maxfield Academy, it sounded like fun.

I felt a hand on my shoulder and turned to see Curtis.

"Welcome to paintball," he said cheerfully, as though nothing had happened yesterday—to me *or* him. "We're the smallest team, so everybody plays."

"The teams are split up by gang?"

"Yep," he said. "Well, technically we're just supposed to divide up into teams. But a while ago everyone agreed that this is the best way, and we submitted team rosters to the school. They approved it."

I had to laugh. "The school endorses the gangs."

"You should have seen this place before the gangs," he said, shaking his head. "Anyway, we can only use as many players as the smallest gang, so now that you're here each team gets eighteen."

"I've never played before," I said. My grip was tight around the butt of the gun, and my finger rested anxiously on the trigger.

A knot of students had formed about a hundred yards into the woods, and I noticed a bright pink ribbon strung from tree to tree, stretching for a hundred yards in either direction.

"I'm forming a new squad," Curtis said, taking me by the arm and leading me forward to a group of V's. "You, Mason, and Lily." Mason was already following, and Curtis motioned for Lily. She was wearing more camouflage than most of the others, like the ghillie suits we'd seen earlier, but it only covered her upper body, like a poncho. The mask she held in her hand had grass and sticks tied to it, and she'd applied green and black paint to her bare legs. Even though she was probably as old as I was, Lily was short and skinny and looked hilarious in the massive suit, like a kid dressed up for Halloween.

"New squad," Curtis continued when she got there. "Lily's got front. Mason, you're in back, and we'll put Benson in the middle. Lily's the boss." He turned to me. "She's the best. She'll teach you what to do."

He left to organize the rest of the gang, and I wondered for a minute how he got to be in charge. I'd have to ask Mason later.

I turned back to Lily, who was sitting on a rock,

tightening her shoelace. *She* was the best? Maybe it was her hair pulled back into pigtails or her bare legs sticking out from the bulky mass of her ghillie poncho, but she looked more suited for a tea party with her dollies than a paintball game.

"You ever play before?" Lily asked.

"Never."

She pointed to my mask—it had wide, clear plastic covering my eyes and a slotted mouth guard. "Always keep that on. Paintballs hurt, even through your clothes. You could lose an eye or a tooth."

Lily explained how the gun worked, showing me where to load the paint and how to install a new air cylinder.

"Usually the game is something like Capture the Flag," she continued, "but they like to switch things up." She frowned. "Like that crap with the doors last night."

"Right."

"In a minute one of the Society guys will read the game rules, and then we'll head to our positions. We might not even play today—two teams play and one refs."

"They let Havoc ref?"

She rolled her eyes. "Havoc's goons know that we'll be their refs later, so everyone is fair. Usually."

I nodded. There no cameras out here, and I wouldn't have been surprised by anything that Havoc did. Or the Society.

"What did he mean about you being up front and me being in the middle?"

"Those are our positions in the squad. The front person moves up fast and scouts for the other two. Mason's playing back—he should be doing most of the shooting. When you and I are in front of him, we'll be taking most of the fire, and that gives him a little more freedom to move and shoot." Lily's eyes lit up while she talked—the first time I'd seen something approaching happiness from her.

"You're in the middle," she said, "which means you do a little of both. You also cover me. You know how to cover someone?"

I shrugged, smiling at the strangeness of the question. "I guess so. I've seen movies."

"We'll work on it during gym sometime," she said. "I wish we'd known about this change yesterday. We could have been practicing all night."

The bullhorn squawked, and Isaiah called everyone over.

"Sorry I don't have time to explain everything," Lily said as we walked up the slope to where the teams were congregating. "If we end up playing today, stick with me and Mason. Try not to get shot."

"It's just a game, right?" I joked.

"Not exactly." She pointed up front.

I hadn't noticed it before, but all the students were

loosely arranged around a large boulder, which Isaiah was now climbing.

Havoc was on the far side. Even in their paintball gear they were recognizable. Many had new tattoos on their faces, almost like war paint. Mouse was at the front of the group, wearing a black suit that reminded me of the Special Forces I'd seen in movies. The material was thin and form-fitting, and her face was dark and serious—like she was really going to war. Oakland stood beside her, and when he caught me looking he pointed his gun and laughed.

Isaiah held up his minicomputer and gestured for everyone to quiet down. As a hush fell over the forest, he opened it and clicked a few keys. "Search and Rescue," he read. "Havoc is defending and Variants are attacking. The Society is the ref. The winning team will be invited to a party tonight in the trophy room. The losing team will not receive food for two days."

There were groans from the crowd, and players immediately began taunting each other.

"This one's good," Lily whispered to me. "They'll have one of our people, and one of us has to get up there and touch them. And the hostage can't get shot."

"Why would they make us starve? What are we supposed to learn from that?"

"You tell me. They do this a lot."

I looked at Mason but he just rolled his eyes.

Lily's mouth formed back into a bitter smile. "But we don't have to worry about it, because we're going to win."

After a moment's deliberation with the V's, Curtis shouted, "Rosa will be the hostage." One of the older girls nodded, looking a little disappointed but not surprised. She was decked out from head to toe in dark, heavy camouflage that had hundreds of cloth leaves individually stitched onto it. She looked like a cross between a ninja and a swamp monster.

"Rosa's got asthma," Lily whispered to me. "She has the best equipment and gun out of all of us, but she just doesn't last long on the field."

Mason leaned in. "And this frickin' school won't give her any medicine."

Isaiah ushered Rosa up to the front. She handed her expensive gun to another girl.

Isaiah waved his arms to get everyone's attention. "And each team gets a medic," he announced, reading from the minicomputer again. Jane immediately volunteered.

"What does the medic do?" I asked Lily.

"When there's a medic in the game," she said, "if you get hit you just stay where you are and she'll touch you to heal you. But if she gets hit then she's out. And a medic can't heal a head shot. If you're hit in the head, you just leave the field."

Isaiah handed out a white armband with a red cross on

it to Jane and the other medic, and then sent Havoc up into the woods, with Rosa in tow. Several of the Society refs started fanning out into the woods.

Curtis sent our squad to the far left, and we waited outside the ribbon for the refs to blow the whistle. Even though it had been so cold during the night, the midday sun, even under the trees, was warm. Lily, her mask up on top of her head as she waited for the game to start, had sweat dripping down her temples.

I looked out past the ribbon at the forest beyond. Several of the pines and rocks were spotted with paint from old games.

"How big is the field?"

"I once heard twenty or thirty acres," Mason answered. "But I have no idea where that number came from. It's not like we measured it. Just make sure you stay inside the ribbons—those are the boundaries."

"I'm going to run," Lily said, her eyes focused on the uneven terrain. "Stay about fifty feet behind me; when I stop, you stop."

I nodded, but I wasn't thinking about paintball. My mind had gone back to the night before, climbing that tree. Was there a chance I could sneak off the field now? How close did the paintball field get to the wall? How vigilant were the refs? *What if* our *team was reffing?*

No, I thought. There are only as many paintball players

as the smallest team, and since the Society was the biggest, they'd always have players off the field. Even if we were the refs, the Society would be around, maybe patrolling the wall on their four-wheelers.

I glanced back at Lily. I couldn't believe we could buy that stuff with points. It was like they were *trying* to get us to escape.

The whistle sounded and Lily darted under the tape and sprinted forward. I ran after her, but despite her heavy poncho, she was still faster. We ran farther and faster than I thought we would. I had no idea how big twenty acres was, but we ran for a couple minutes before Lily began to slow and watch for Havoc defenses.

The forest was silent except for the crunching under my feet. Lily was walking like soldiers in the movies— crouched low, gun ready. I tried to imitate her.

Somewhere off to the right I heard a girl's voice shout, "Medic!" and then a moment later a boy shouted the same thing. I didn't recognize the voices and turned back to look at Mason to see if he knew who it was. It took me a second to see him, leaning against a tree. He motioned for me to keep my eyes front.

Lily froze, watching something, and she gestured for me to get low. I knelt next to a dry spiky bush, and watched as Lily slowly crouched down. With her legs against the ground, the shaggy ghillie suit obscured her almost completely.

I heard rapid firing from behind me and spun to see Mason spraying paintballs into the woods. I looked for his target, but couldn't see anything. A moment later he stopped.

I lifted up slightly, trying to see the enemy, and my bush erupted in splashes of paint. I fell down on my belly and heard Mason returning fire.

When the shooting stopped, a whistle blew, and a ref jogged over to me and asked me to stand. He inspected my clothes, had me turn around, and then declared, "You're not hit." The balls had exploded on the other side of the bush, and apparently not enough paint got me to count.

I dropped back down and looked forward to Lily. She was on the move again, heading to the right, but motioned for me to stay where I was.

Had I not known her before, I'd have never guessed the professional, commando-like player ahead of me was a short seventeen-year-old girl. Everything about her was different now: the way she moved, the constant level of alertness. Through the smudged paint on her legs I could see well-defined lines of muscle tone. I was glad she was on our team. Hopefully we wouldn't be the ones without food for two days.

I kept low and lost sight of her as she moved over a rise and into a thicket of juniper. Shots suddenly hissed out, and I heard a male voice swear and shout for a medic.

Grinning, I looked at Mason, and he gave me a thumbs-up.

Lily came charging back over the rise and urgently gestured for Mason and me to follow her. I jumped from the bush and ran. My bruise was throbbing, reminding me of the last time I'd been in the forest, but I ignored it.

I almost ran past Lily before I saw her at the last minute, hiding behind a log. I dropped down beside her. Thirty feet ahead was the boy she'd shot—probably the same one who'd shot at me.

"We'll ambush the medic," she said, out of breath. She kept her eyes forward but pointed at a boulder several yards to our left. "You get behind that. When they get here, wait till they get close, and start shooting. Then get down. Mason, get over in that thicket. We want them to think that Benson's alone and doesn't know what he's doing."

"That won't be hard," I joked, but Lily ignored it.

"Go," she whispered.

The injured kid shouted again for a medic. Lily had told me earlier that injured players aren't allowed to say anything else—he wouldn't be able to warn them.

I waited, leaning on the rock high enough that someone would be able to see me. I watched the forest ahead—there was plenty of cover. A tiny stream dribbled down on the far side of the thicket, and tall brush—five feet tall in some places—grew at its bank.

The injured guy rolled and pulled a pinecone out from

under his back. I wondered which of the Havoc kids he was. He looked too short to be Oakland.

I heard the shot—the sharp hiss of compressed air—but I didn't see the shooter before a paintball smacked into my shoulder. A second hit me in the ribs, just above my bruise. I gasped in pain at the sting and then raised my arms in defeat. I was dead.

"Medic!" I shouted, holding my side with my hand. Those paintballs hurt.

I could hear muffled laughter behind the grass, and then two masks pushed through it, identifying their downed player. One of them gestured. Another, crouched low, jogged across the clearing toward me, apparently unaware of Lily and Mason. He cautiously moved around, checking the area, and then gave a signal to the other.

Someone ran straight for the injured guy—the boy with the medic badge. He had just healed the first guy when Lily and Mason opened fire, splattering the guard, the medic, and the newly revived kid. The dead guard swore, and the medic shouted something, yanking off his badge and throwing it to the ground. I noticed now that the last guy—the mask peeking through the grass—stood up, one ball of paint smashed into his goggles. Four kills.

I gave a thumbs-up to Lily and she returned it.

A few moments later, Isaiah's voice echoed over the bullhorn. "The defending team's medic has been killed.

No more Havoc team members can be healed. If you are shot, please leave the field of play."

Lily and Mason formed another ambush around me, taking up new positions to guard against someone doing the same thing we'd done, and we waited for our medic.

Jane appeared a few minutes later, running alone, not moving with a squad as the Havoc team had done. I shouted "medic" as soon as I saw her to help her find me, and she sprinted, moving fast and light. She didn't slow, just lowered her arm enough for her fingertips to drag across my shoulder and then continued into the forest. I stood back up and brushed at the wet paint spots with the back of my hand.

Even though I couldn't see her mouth behind the mask, I could tell from Lily's eyes that she was smiling. "When I told you to act like you didn't know what you were doing, I didn't think you'd take it so literally."

"I'm an overachiever."

"Nice," Lily whispered. "Okay. Same as before. We'll move up and along the ribbon."

Mason and I nodded, and she began running. I gave her fifty feet and then followed, keeping my stance even lower than before.

Lily had described our goal before the game had started. Rosa would likely be held hostage in a group of small defensive forts—nothing fancy, just little wooden structures with peepholes and room to shoot. There were supposed to be five or six of them somewhere at the back of the field.

The slope was getting steeper, and we moved more slowly and deliberately now. Lily would stop at cover—bushes or trees or rocks—and then, when she felt safe, she'd run for the next. Mason and I followed behind.

At a large rock outcropping, she decided to leave the ribbon and head into the interior of the field. We had to be close to the bunkers by now. It wouldn't be long before we ran into trouble.

Lily moved to a cluster of junipers and paused for what seemed like ten minutes, though it couldn't have been nearly that long. Finally, she began to move, creeping up the slope. I watched, giving her some space before I dared to follow. I didn't have any camouflage, and couldn't go slowly like she did. If I left the cover of my rock, I'd be spotted in an instant.

A staccato of shots sounded behind me, and I ducked and spun, turning my gun toward the noise. Someone was shooting at Mason, but I couldn't see him or the shooter.

I peered over the rock toward Lily, but she was nowhere to be seen.

The shooting stopped. Mason hadn't called for a medic, which was a good sign.

My options were limited. Most of the slope was thick

with brush, and anybody could be hiding inside it. I didn't know where Mason was, so I couldn't very well move to help him.

Suddenly there was a flurry of shots, paint splattering all over in the trees and bushes. Mason yelled out "hit!" and stood, paint splattered across his mask.

Jane couldn't heal a head hit. I took a deep breath, watching as he held his gun up and walked toward the ribbon and off the field. I didn't have anyone behind me anymore and someone was hidden in the brush.

Looking back toward the front, I couldn't see Lily at all.

I waited for five minutes, hoping to hear shots as Lily looped back and killed Mason's attacker, but it never happened.

The only sign of life was a Society ref, about forty yards away. I thought about making a break for the wall, but knew I couldn't. The refs all had whistles, and my tan sweats stood out like a white light in this dim forest.

If I couldn't escape, I might as well play the game. I didn't want two days without food.

Clutching my gun, I jumped to my feet and ran to the cluster of junipers where Lily had been. I skidded to a stop behind a gnarled trunk and readied for attack. But there was no sound.

I whispered her name. With her ghillie suit so convincing, she could have been ten feet away from me. No answer.

Crap.

I waited another few minutes, hoping to see some movement or hear a sound, but there was nothing.

I still hadn't fired a shot.

Hoping that I wasn't going to screw up Lily's tactics—I assumed she was still alive since I hadn't heard her call for the medic—I lifted into a crouch and prepared to advance. No one shot at me.

I moved slowly, hunched down, ready to shoot if necessary. My shoes were loud in the rocky dirt, even as I tried to step around dry twigs and brittle grass. I went up the slope where I'd last seen Lily. There were no signs of her— no footprints, no fresh paint marks.

There were more trees here, shorter but denser. I moved from trunk to trunk, watching anxiously. It had been a long time since I'd heard or seen anything, and I began to wonder whether the game was over and I'd missed the bullhorn.

After a few minutes, the first bunker came into view. I dropped to the ground. There was no good cover, so I lay flat on my stomach, my gun aimed at the wooden fort. The front surface was splattered with a dozen different colors of paint, though I didn't know whether that was from this game or a previous one.

Where is Lily?

I moved back to a crouch and headed for the nearest

cover, a large stump. No one fired.

Screw it.

I jumped from the stump and ran toward the bunker, stopping at its base. I took a breath and then leapt up, pointing my gun inside.

It was empty.

I could see through it and out the back door. Behind it was a clearing, and the back of another bunker. I hunched over again, and moved around the side, trying to be quiet and failing miserably.

The clearing was surrounded by five bunkers positioned in a circle, all facing out. Rosa sat cross-legged in the middle, about forty feet away from me, looking bored.

This must be a trap.

I watched the other four bunkers for movement, but didn't see any. Rosa hadn't seen me.

If I remembered the rules right, I only had to touch her. I just had to get to her before I got shot.

If she hadn't seen me, then maybe no one else had either. If I made a run for it, they'd have to take a few seconds to react. Even if this was a trap, I had to have a few seconds.

How fast can I run forty feet?

I set the gun down in the dirt. I wasn't going to need it. Either I got to her and won, or I didn't get to her and I was dead.

I took one last look for Lily. She wasn't anywhere.

I was on my feet before I realized it, running at full speed toward Rosa. I couldn't see her eyes through the glare on her mask, but as I neared, she shielded her body with her arms.

Gunfire erupted from everywhere and I felt the impact of dozens of balls hitting me in the chest, arms, and head. I tried to stop running and tripped into the dirt.

"Nice one, Fisher," said a voice I recognized. "Did you really think we didn't hear you ten minutes ago?"

I rolled over and saw Oakland standing at the door to one of the bunkers, his gun still trained on me. There were people in two other doors, and one in a ghillie suit in the tall grasses at the edge of the clearing. I'd never seen any of them.

Clumsily, I stumbled to my feet, raised my hands over my head, and called out "hit."

Another shot slapped the back of my head, and the wet trickling paint felt like blood. I spun to see Mouse.

"Hit!" I shouted again.

Another ball snapped into my back, just below my shoulder blade, and I turned back to face Oakland. Where was the ref?

"Think you're pretty awesome?" Oakland shouted, and fired five more shots. They would have hit me in the groin if I hadn't moved an instant before. I was glad that he couldn't see my face, because I was having trouble hiding how much it hurt.

An instant later a Society ref appeared in the clearing, blew her whistle, and looked me up and down.

"Looks like overkill," she said, frowning at the mass of paint spots on my body. "Did they shoot you after you called 'hit'?"

I glanced back at Oakland. Maybe I could get him to lay off a bit. "No."

The ref looked suspiciously at the Havoc team, and then back at me. "Head off the field." She blew her whistle to resume play.

There was the loud hiss of a gun behind me—two sharp pops—and then Lily's voice. "We win."

I turned to see her hand on Rosa's arm.

Mouse's mask was dripping with paint, and Oakland had been shot in the neck.

CHAPTER EIGHT

Hey, Benson," Jane shouted, catching up with us and bumping me with her shoulder. The gangs were slowly forming back together as the players trickled out of the forest.

"Thanks for healing me."

"No problem," she said, stepping back and taking a good look at my tan sweats that were now polka-dotted with red and blue paint. She grinned. "I go to all that trouble and look what you do."

I tried not to smile. "I was being heroic."

Jane glanced over at Lily and Mason.

"Don't look at me," Mason said, holding up his hands. "I wasn't there."

Lily, still looking ahead at the forest floor, smiled. "It was definitely something."

Jane laughed and bumped me again. "I told you this place was fun."

"Yeah." I glanced over at Lily. I wondered whether she'd been playing for fun, too. The way she acted on the field, I'd have guessed it was for survival.

Soon, Curtis and Carrie joined us, holding hands, and in a few minutes almost all of the V's were back together, joking and celebrating. Lily explained her actions several times, and the others relayed their stories. We'd probably been walking for ten minutes before I realized that I was actually having fun. I felt like I was with friends, and it felt good.

Jane told me about the party we could expect—it was the most regular of the rewards for winning at paintball. The school sent food in through one of the elevators, and it was always something amazing. Havoc did a pretty good job with the cafeteria food, but the food at the party was more like a five-star restaurant's. They even sent the kinds of food that we never got through the cafeteria: soda, candies, cakes, brownies, and all sorts of snacks. The parties usually lasted long into the night, and the school waived the rules about curfew and uniforms. It sounded great.

We emerged from the forest and stepped onto the grass surrounding the track. My legs were sore as we walked—I could still feel the imprint of each paintball, and I knew it would be worse tomorrow—but I ignored it. I was having too much fun.

"So, Benson," Jane said, talking loud enough for

everyone to hear. "Lily gave her version of the win. How about yours?"

"It was *Saving Private Ryan*," I said. "The massacre on Omaha Beach."

As our eyes met she gave me a mischievous grin, and the crowd fell silent as they looked to me. We were entering the sculpture garden on the edge of the track, and I hopped up on top of the carved stump.

"Did you ever see the end of *Butch Cassidy and the Sundance Kid*?" I asked, turning to face the V's and preparing to tell my embarrassing story.

But I instantly knew from their faces that something was wrong. Their smiles were gone, replaced with blank and somber stares. Jane was holding her breath, and Lily bit her lip. Mason stepped through the crowd and grabbed my arm, pulling me down from the stump.

"What?"

Instead of answering he pointed down at the carvings.

Heather Lyon
Died in the war
Will be missed

On the side, shallower and less well carved, someone had scrawled, *I love you.*

I stared at Mason, too horrified to speak, and then

looked at another of what I had assumed to be sculptures—this one a pile of basketball-size rocks. The top one was flat and someone had painted words on it.

JEFF "L.A." HOLMES
SUMMER '09

Curtis put his hand on my shoulder. "This is the graveyard. I'm sorry. Someone should have told you."

"What do you mean?" I said, now frantically moving from grave to grave. "How are these people dying?"

Mason spoke. "What did I tell you? This place is dangerous."

Curtis nodded, following me as I moved from a log to a small wooden plaque to a large smooth stone. The stone had fresh flowers on it that couldn't have been more than a few days old. I read the name—some other kid, just like me.

"It used to be worse," Curtis said. "Before the truce."

"What was the war?"

"It was as the gangs were forming. Things got pretty bad."

I stared at him and then at the faces of the other V's. There were tears on a few cheeks. Jane had turned away. My chest felt tight and I could feel my hands balling into fists, almost on their own. These people hadn't been killed by the school. They'd been killed by other students. There were a dozen graves, at least.

"Come on," Curtis said. "Let's get back inside."

I refused to go to the infirmary, even though Mason pestered me for the rest of the day. When we'd gotten back to the dorm and I took off my shirt, the one small bruise from my failed escape had multiplied into at least fifteen welts on my chest and back, and eight more on my arms. There were two lumps on the back of my head, under my hair, and someone had hit me in the ankle—that one broke the skin.

After showering, I spent the evening in my room. I didn't want to talk to anyone, and I definitely didn't want to join the party. On the walk back I'd felt like maybe I was fitting in and that seemed like a good thing. Maybe this school, for all the craziness, was better than any other alternative. The food was good, the paintball was fun, and I was making friends—real friends. But the graveyard had changed that. I didn't want friends and I didn't want food. I wanted to get out.

Curtis dropped by as the sun was going down and tried to talk me into going to the party, but I told him I was too sore and too exhausted from sleeping in the window well. It was a lousy excuse—he'd been through worse yesterday and hadn't gotten any more sleep than I had—but I guessed he knew the real reason why I didn't want to go. Still, he played along.

"You can get some ibuprofen down in the infirmary," Curtis said.

"I'd have to deal with some Society moron."

"You'd like the girl who works down there," he said. "Blond, cute."

I was lying flat on my back, but nothing was comfortable. "Laura is blond and cute, too. And she tried to send me to detention."

"That's Laura," Curtis said. "This girl's cool. Anna."

"No thanks." I'd already heard about the infirmary from Mason. In addition to Anna, Dylan worked there. I didn't want to see him again, let alone ask him for help.

Curtis nodded, leaning over to look at a small photo of the Brooklyn Bridge that Mason had hung above his desk. "Your loss. There are a lot of cute girls here."

I sighed, staring at the bunk above me. "I know." I rolled onto my side but found it just as painful as my back. Curtis was still there, like he was waiting for something. "I'll give Maxfield one thing: There's a lot to be said for the uniforms in this place. Girls at my schools never wore skirts."

He laughed. "Anyone in particular?"

I shook my head, and even that sent little bolts of pain up my neck.

"I think Jane likes you," he pestered. "The V's have all the best girls. Jane, Gabby, Rosa, Lily. Carrie, of course, but she's taken."

"I'm getting out of here," I said, closing my eyes. "Not dating."

"Have it your way." I heard his footsteps against the hardwood floor as he left the room.

This was all so stupid, so fake. The people in here only knew about things going on inside the school, and they'd convinced themselves that it was all okay. They dated. They studied. Lily had said that in her spare time she planned new paintball tactics. And now they were downstairs celebrating that they'd won a game. In the last three days I'd gotten kidnapped, been on the losing side of two fights, fallen out of a tree while trying to escape, and been shot repeatedly. And this afternoon, at the graveyard, I'd discovered that my problems were just beginning. It could get a lot worse.

Mason came back from the showers a few minutes later. I was lying down, eyes closed. I felt like crying but didn't want to let the security cameras see.

"Who do you follow?" I asked, needing to talk about something outside the walls of Maxfield Academy. I cracked open one eye. "Sports teams, I mean."

Mason looked puzzled. "Nobody, I guess. Not anymore, of course." He dug through his closet for some casual clothes. "I follow paintball."

I stared at the bunk above me. "What sports did you like? Before you got tossed in here."

"Used to play a little baseball."

"The Giants took the Series last year. Where are you from, anyway?"

He tapped on the photo by his desk. "New York. I tore that out of a textbook a couple months ago. Don't tell on me."

"The Yankees are having a good year. Mets, too. The Knicks won't. They never do."

Mason pulled a sweater on, getting dressed for the party. "I barely remember the teams. It's been too long, I guess."

I rolled onto my side. *I need medicine.*

"I'm not going to be here long enough to forget," I said, more to myself than to him.

I tried to sleep, but it just wasn't coming. I hurt too much to get comfortable, and my brain kept replaying my escape attempt, trying to think of a new solution to getting over the wall. I could make a rope. It wouldn't be hard to use the bedsheets. For the first time ever I could see how that movie cliché got started—it was by far the easiest substitute for rope I could think of. But then what would I do with it? The brick wall was fairly smooth—there wouldn't be anything for a grappling hook to hold on to, even if I could make one.

I could chop down a tree, maybe. Lean it against the wall and climb it like a ladder. That'd be easier with more people, but no one seemed to be stepping up to the plate to help me, even the V's.

Maybe I could dig under the wall. The groundskeeping sheds had to have shovels. But then I'd have to persuade Havoc to help me. Or break in.

I got out of bed. There was no use trying to sleep anymore. I moved to the window and checked my watch in the pale moonlight. It was just after three o'clock.

There was haze out in the forest, just enough to blur the trees and hills. I wanted it to be smoke. Where there's smoke there's fire, and where there's fire there're people. I thought I'd seen smoke when I was up in the tree—maybe there really was someone out there.

But tonight it was impossible to tell. Maybe it wasn't anything at all—just the darkness and a dirty window.

Mason was sleeping soundly in the top bunk, snoring enough that I could tell he wasn't aware I was up. He'd come back an hour ago. I'd heard all the V's come back from the party, laughing and happy, but there hadn't been any sounds for the last thirty minutes.

I checked the closets to see if anything had been delivered, but nothing had changed. My paint-splattered sweats still sat on the floor, and my rumpled shirts were on the hangers.

My fingers ran along the edge of the closet, trying to feel where the permanent wall ended and the elevator began. There was a tiny gap, and I thought I almost felt a little breeze. It might have been my imagination.

One thing I hadn't done yet was try to leave the dorms at night. I'd checked the rules and there was nothing in there saying we weren't allowed to, but I wondered whether the door would even unlock for me. Like all the other doors, each dorm room had a sensor and a deadbolt.

My room door has to be unlocked, I reasoned. *In case we need to go to the bathroom.*

Sure enough, the knob turned in my hand, and the cooler air of the corridor swept in as I peeked outside. The only light I could see, other than from the window at the end of the hall, was the narrow glowing crack coming from the bottom of the bathroom door.

I left my room, wearing just a pair of gym shorts and a T-shirt. The hardwood was like ice under my feet, but my cautious footsteps were silent—the wood didn't creak or groan at all under my weight.

There were no sounds other than the hiss of a radiator and the occasional snore that was loud enough to be heard all the way out here.

Pausing at the junction where the Society and Havoc hallways branched off the main one, I listened for any others who might be awake, but heard nothing. In the dark, I could barely make out the clutter that hung from Havoc's ceiling.

I shouldn't be out here alone. The thought kept nagging me, but I pushed it away. The other gangs didn't like me, but they were all sleeping.

There was a noise on the Society's side—nothing loud, just a little click. No lights were on under their doors.

I continued down the hallway, passing dozens of empty dorm rooms. They were closed, but not locked. I entered one and walked to its window to see what the view was like. It looked down on the front side of the building. The narrow road through the woods looked black against the surrounding grass. I couldn't see the moon from where I was, but the stars were brilliant, just as they'd been the night before.

Not that a beautiful sky makes up for anything.

I left the window and went back into the hallway.

Something about being out at night felt good. It was what I used to do to get away—go out, walk the streets, be alone. I wished I could go outside now. I couldn't even open the window.

I was almost to the door that left the dorm when I heard the familiar buzz and click. But the sound wasn't coming from just that door—it was loud, coming from *every* door, all at once. I grabbed the nearest doorknob. Locked.

Voices were coming from back down the corridor— angry voices that were trying unsuccessfully to be quiet.

I ran the last few yards to the exit door, but it didn't unlock for me. I was trapped, everything locked all around me. *Except . . .*

The room I'd just been in was still open—I hadn't shut the door, so it couldn't have locked. I ran back, my bare feet silent on the solid floor. I darted inside and swung the door almost closed—but held it open an inch, so that it couldn't lock with me inside. Then I listened.

"Come out, come out, wherever you are!" a voice called, playful and evil.

It was still far away. Someone must have heard me. Oakland wanted revenge, and he knew I was alone.

There were more voices now—muffled shouts. People were pounding on their walls. Oakland couldn't lock all these doors. No one could do it remotely like this.

No one except the school.

The voices weren't getting any closer. I opened the door a little wider and peeked into the hallway.

I could see dark silhouettes at the junction.

"Little pig, little pig, let me come in." I knew the voice. I'd heard it before. Was it Skiver? Oakland?

The shadows were coming out of the Society's side and going down Havoc's side.

"Open up, Walnut," the voice said. It was Dylan. The Society was going after Havoc in the middle of the night. And the school had locked all the doors.

I wanted to get closer to see what was going on, but I didn't dare.

The pounding sounded like an earthquake now, as Havoc tried to break out of their rooms.

"Wallace Jackson," a new voice said. Isaiah. His words were loud and emotionless. "You have broken the rules, and we are here to collect you for detention. We have orders from the school."

Someone screamed something, but I couldn't make it out—it was probably Walnut behind his door.

"We are simply fulfilling our contract," Isaiah continued. "You knew the rules, you knew the consequences, and you chose to disobey. This is not personal."

"You bet it isn't," Dylan cackled gleefully. "I won't enjoy it at all."

Half a dozen kids were laughing, gloating about whatever would happen to Walnut.

There were more muffled shouts, and now I could barely even understand Isaiah over the pounding.

With fingers shaking from fear, I examined the door I was hiding behind. It was heavy, thick wood with steel deadbolts and large brass hinges. These things were like prison bars—they were made to trap people in their rooms. Walnut was on his own—his was probably the only one unlocked.

I wanted to run out there and stop them, to punch in Dylan's laughing teeth and smash Isaiah's head against the wall. We were all prisoners together—why couldn't they realize that?

It was impossible to tell what was going on now. There

was too much noise, too much yelling, too much pounding. I listened and watched, but couldn't see anything.

And then there was a crash, and Walnut's voice was loud and angry. He swore and screamed. Someone was with him—his roommate, whoever that was—and he was shrieking, too. But there were only the two of them, and I'd seen at least a dozen shadows in the hall. The Society had more than thirty members, and I bet all the guys were there now, helping to subdue Walnut.

Sweat was dripping down my face, despite the cold. There was nothing I could do to help. There were too many of them.

A moment later another shadow emerged from Havoc's hall, and I ducked back into the empty room. I closed the door all but half an inch and watched the corridor.

The Society marched triumphantly past me, laughing in frenzied delight. Isaiah was at their head, quiet but proud. They dragged Walnut behind them, screaming. His hands and feet were bound with something, and he had no shirt on—just boxer shorts.

"What did I do?" he howled desperately. "What did I do?"

I wanted to jump out there. I could stop a few of them.

No. It wouldn't be enough.

They passed out of my view, and I heard the buzz and

click of the opening door. Light from outside spilled into the corridor as the mob left the dorm. Their laughter dropped for a moment. Walnut was groaning.

Isaiah said something I couldn't make out. I opened my door again, just enough to peer out. Laura was waiting for them.

Isaiah said something else, but it was lost in a wail from his prisoner.

"She's downstairs," Laura said, her words breaking between Walnut's cries.

The last of the Society guys let the heavy wooden door swing shut, enveloping me again in darkness.

I took a deep gulp of air and realized I'd been holding my breath. I could still hear pounding and defeated shouts from the Havoc hallway, but all of the Society was gone. Standing on unsteady, trembling legs, I stepped out into the hall.

Part of me wanted to follow them, to find out what detention really was and what would happen to Walnut. I wanted to know who "she" was. Was someone else being taken to detention as well?

But I didn't follow. I'd spent all my time here being too cocky, too confident that nothing bad would really happen. A few fistfights, maybe, and a lot of yelling. But that all changed this afternoon at the graveyard, and Walnut's detention was the final straw. The Society was hauling someone away, laughing and gloating while they did it.

I didn't know what I was supposed to feel now. I wanted to escape more than ever, but it felt impossible. When I'd fallen out of the tree it hadn't been a simple matter of talking Laura and Dylan out of punishment—I'd been lucky to have the V's backing me up. I wouldn't always be so lucky.

Just the thought of being a target of the Society made my heart race. I didn't want to end up like Walnut.

As my panic receded, I remembered that he had to have a roommate. I jogged back down the empty corridor and into Havoc's territory. Their doors were still closed and locked, but there was no pounding anymore. They must have known it was no use.

Walnut's door was open, a little pale gray light from his window trickling out into the hallway.

I stepped inside.

There was a body on the floor by the wall, motionless.

I moved to him. He was one of the fatter kids, and his head was shaved with jagged tattoos drawn across his scalp. I didn't know him at all, other than that he was in my class and I thought his nickname was Mash-something. Masher or Mashed Potato, or something like that.

He was breathing. I could hear it, raspy and shallow. His hands and feet were bound with plastic zip ties.

"You okay?" I said.

He flinched, one eye popping open. "Who's that?" he snapped.

"Benson. Everyone else is locked in."

"Why ain't you?" he snapped.

"I wasn't in my room when they all locked."

"Well, then get me out of these damn handcuffs. There's a knife on the desk."

It only took me a minute to find the knife among the clutter. It was a short steak knife, almost certainly taken from the cafeteria kitchens. Maybe that was why Havoc wanted the food contracts. I knelt behind Mash and sawed quickly through the plastic.

"Why'd they take him?" I asked.

He swore and rubbed his wrists. "Why do you think they did? Because the school told 'em to. That's the only reason."

"You don't know what rule he broke?"

Mash stood, and I saw that he was bleeding a little above his right eye. "Why the hell should I talk to you? You're a V." He walked past me into the hall, and I followed, watching as he went down to Oakland's still-locked door. He was limping, but trying to look like he wasn't.

"Hey," he shouted.

Someone in the room replied, but I couldn't make it out.

"They got him," Mash said. "He's gone, man."

I didn't know what to do. I felt weak and trapped and useless.

I walked back to my room. The door was locked, so I sat on the floor, my back against the wall. My head was spinning, and I felt like I was going to throw up. About an hour later, the Society guys returned, but they didn't see me and I didn't say anything.

It could have been me. If the V's hadn't come after me at the wall, I would have been the one hauled off to detention.

I closed my eyes and leaned my head back, but never went to sleep.

The doors remained locked for a long time. The screen on the corridor wall lit up shortly after dawn with the words CLASSES BEGIN AT TEN O'CLOCK.

I was just starting to nod off when I heard the buzz and click of the doors opening. I scrambled to my feet as quickly as my sore body would let me, and opened my room door. Mason was right in front of me.

"Where've you been?" he asked, his eyes wide and bloodshot.

"Got locked out." I walked past him to the closet and started getting dressed. I wanted to get out of this dorm.

"I thought they'd hauled you away or something. I've been up all night."

"Not me," I said. "Walnut."

Mason left the room. I could hear a lot of voices in the hall as everyone was finally allowed out of their locked prison cells and tried to get the news. He returned as I was lacing my shoes.

"Were you out there when it happened?"

"Yeah."

"They didn't see you, did they?"

The screen in the hallway chimed before I could answer, and both of us ran toward the door. The other V guys were already gathering around Iceman when we got there.

Iceman was staring just off center, as though he was looking at something behind the camera. His jaw was set, and his eyes were cold and gray.

One of the V's—a kid named Hector—grabbed my arm. "Mason said you were there."

I nodded, watching the screen. "It was Walnut."

"They took him to detention?"

Iceman looked into the camera. It felt like he was staring right into my eyes.

"Wallace Jackson," he said, his voice calm and low, "and Maria Nobles were sent to detention during the night."

A V gasped and another swore. From down the hall I could hear angry shouts and curses.

I whispered to Mason, "Who's Maria?"

"Jelly," he said.

Jelly. I'd heard the nickname, but couldn't picture her.

Iceman leaned forward slightly, and I almost thought his eyes darkened. "Let me make something perfectly clear. We do not make the decision to send students to detention. You decide that entirely on your own. Make better choices."

"Turn him off," Curtis said, shaking his head and walking away from the screen.

Iceman continued, "The rest of the daily punishments will be delivered in class. And Havoc—do not think that last night's events have lessened your punishment for losing your match yesterday."

I left, heading down the corridor to the exit. As I passed the Society row I could see that all of their doors were still closed. Would Havoc start something? The Society was bigger than Havoc—close to twice the size, but Havoc would be mad. And they had knives.

The school's halls were empty and cold. The halls were always cold, it seemed. I think they only had the radiators on in the dorms and the classrooms.

Jogging down the stairs, taking two or three at a time, I got to Becky's office in less than a minute. No one was there, so I pressed the small RING FOR SERVICE button mounted on the doorjamb. I waited.

Three minutes later Becky came hurrying down the hallway, her hair still wet and a towel hanging around her neck. Without her perfectly styled 1930s hairdo and her usual flawless makeup she actually looked normal. Then again, she was smiling cheerfully, despite everything that had gone on the night before. That was definitely the opposite of normal.

"Hey, Bense! What's up?"

"I just wondered if I could talk to you for a minute," I said.

"No problem at all." She stepped in front of the door and the lock buzzed open. She turned the knob and opened it. "Come on in. What can I do for you?"

"What happened last night?"

She didn't turn to look at me, but walked to her desk and straightened some of the loose papers.

"What do you mean?"

I rolled my eyes. "You know what I mean. Wallace and Maria."

"Why don't you sit down?"

"I don't want to sit down," I said. "I didn't sleep for a minute last night and I'm sore from paintball and I watched a guy get dragged on his back down to detention."

Becky turned, but stopped herself before our eyes met. She was fiddling with the cuff of her sleeve, trying not to look at me.

"I don't know any more about it than you do," she said simply.

"Come on. You have the contract."

"No," Becky said, glancing up at me but only for an instant. She sat on the couch and crossed her legs. She was wearing flip-flops instead of the dress-code shoes and socks.

"I meant the Society has the contract," I said, leaning against the cabinets on the opposite wall.

"I don't do security," she said, finally looking into my eyes. "I promise. I have a deal with Isaiah. I do new-student orientations, and I don't do the other stuff."

"Dylan does both. He's medical and security."

She looked back down at her cuff. "I'm not Dylan."

I rubbed my eyes. I was exhausted, and I didn't have the energy to argue with Becky.

"But the others talk to you, right?" I asked. "You must have heard what was going on."

"We got the message on our computers in the evening," she said. Her gaze had moved from her cuff and now she was picking invisible lint off her skirt. "It told us what time to take the two students downstairs."

"What rule did they break?"

"It didn't say."

"What?" I stood up from the wall, agitated, but the room was small and there was nowhere else for me to go, so I just stood there, arms folded. "It just said to haul them to detention, no questions asked?"

"That's how it works."

I thought of the howling glee that the Society guys had when they'd dragged Walnut down the hall. They didn't even know what rule he'd broken. It wasn't hard to guess, of course. There were only so many rules that got someone sent to detention. But still, for the Society to relish the job that much while being completely unaware of what rules they were enforcing? It made me sick.

I finally sat on the couch, slumped down next to her. "That's ridiculous."

"I don't like having that contract."

We sat in silence for several seconds. Becky had stopped pretending to pick lint, and I just stared at the wall.

"I don't suppose you have any ibuprofen here," I said. "I don't want to go to the infirmary."

She gave a look that was half smile and half frown. "No. You'd have to go see Anna or Dylan."

My hand went to the bruise on my side. "They actually pretend like Dylan is supposed to heal people?"

Becky looked uncomfortable. "If you want, I can see when Anna's on call instead of Dylan. You could go then."

"Yeah," I said. "Okay."

She reached over to the desk and picked up her mini-computer.

"I have to get out of here," I said, staring forward. "This place is crazy. It's a crazy school full of crazy people."

Becky's tour-guide smile appeared, and she cocked her

head to the side. "You don't mean that."

"I do mean it," I said. "Nothing here makes sense, and the place is run by thugs and . . . whatever Laura is."

Becky folded her arms. "Laura's my roommate."

"She wanted to send me to detention."

"Because you were trying to escape," Becky snapped, and then glanced up at the cameras self-consciously.

"Look at you," I said, raising my voice. "You're afraid of people you've never even seen. Do you think this school could run without our consent? What would have happened if you Society guys just refused to take Wallace and Maria?"

Becky opened her mouth, but I kept talking. "What if all of us tried to leave—all seventy-four of us? Let's just build some ladders and go. No one is keeping us in here except us."

Becky sat down at the desk. "It's not that simple."

"It *is* that simple," I insisted. "That's all there is to it. Maybe the only real person on the other side of those cameras is that woman who dropped me off. She's just some rich crazy lady, all alone, screwing with our heads."

"No." Her voice was firm. She stared at me for a long time, not saying anything. I didn't know what she was thinking, but her eyes bore into me, and I couldn't read the emotion on her face.

"What is it?" I insisted. "What's stopping us?"

A tear boiled up in Becky's eye, but it didn't drop. She spoke barely above a whisper, and she had turned her face away from the cameras. "I don't know. Something. Back in the spring four Society kids tried to escape. They were working together, on guard duty. They didn't make it."

"What stopped them?"

She wiped her eye with the back of her thumb and then turned away. "Let me take you to the infirmary," she finally said. She tapped the computer screen with her fingernail. "According to the schedule, Anna is on call."

Becky stood and opened the door. She was all Society. When logic and reason conflicted with obedience, she just ignored them.

I followed her down the hallway. She passed the basement stairs without a look. I'd thought that was the way to the infirmary.

"I think you'll like Anna," Becky said. "She's from Pennsylvania, too. Maybe you guys know some of the same people?"

Yeah. Because it's really small.

She turned a corner and opened a small door. It was another set of stairs, old and narrow. She held the door for me as I went in, and then let it close behind her. As soon as it shut she put her hand on my arm.

"There are no cameras in here," she whispered.

I waited for her to continue—she wanted to say

something, but looked scared.

"What?"

"I—I just wish you would stop," she said. "I don't know a lot of what goes on here. But there are two things that I wish you'd understand."

She took a deep breath. "First, detention is death. We don't know much about it. There's a room downstairs for detention. You get put in the room for the night. In the morning, no one is left in there."

I cut her off. "Then how do you know they kill you? What if it's like the closets in the dorms—like they're secret elevators or something."

Becky was trembling now, and she folded her arms to stop from shaking. "I haven't ever seen it. But there's blood sometimes." Her voice was wavering. "On the floor."

I opened my mouth to respond, but couldn't. She was watching my eyes.

"What's the other thing?" I finally said.

Becky shook her head, like she was trying to clear a thought. "No one ever escapes. People make it over the wall sometimes—the security guys have seen people do it. But they're still caught. Like the ones I told you about. I don't think we're the only ones who guard the wall." She stared into my eyes. "That's why I'm Society. I want to stop people from going to detention and from trying to escape. This place isn't so bad. Why risk . . ." Her voice trailed off.

"What?"

"No," she said, stopping me with her hand. "That's enough. The cameras will notice if we're in here too long." She pushed past me and hurried down the stairs.

"We'll have to get out of here eventually," I said, calling after her. "We're not going to live the rest of our lives in this school."

She refused to turn and look at me. As she reached the bottom of the stairs she threw the door open, seeming almost relieved to be back with the cameras. I had to jog to catch up with her as she sped to the infirmary.

"Here we are," she said, her voice cheerful but her eyes not yet recovered.

"Becky," I began, but she put her finger to her lips.

"I have to get ready for class," she said. She turned to the girl sitting behind the infirmary desk. "Anna, this is Benson." Before I could say anything else, Becky was out the door.

Anna didn't even bother inspecting the welts. She hardly even glanced up—just pointed to a basket of individual packets of medicine on the desk. She said she always had a constant stream of bruises and aches on the day after paintball.

I took the pills and swallowed them with water from the infirmary drinking fountain. When I stepped back into the narrow basement hallway, Becky was nowhere to be found.

Returning to the old stairway, I plodded up the rough cement steps, taking a tiny amount of pleasure in knowing I was out of the school's sight for a few minutes. When I reached the door I paused, not wanting to go back out in front of the cameras.

I was wrong when I talked to Becky. It wasn't seventy-four anymore. It was seventy-two.

I walked slowly back up to class on the third floor. At least it wasn't going to be as hard to stay awake this time; I had something to think about. Why kill people in detention? It wasn't as a warning to others—if that was the goal then wouldn't they display the bodies? Wouldn't they call it something other than detention?

Or maybe the school liked that it was all rumor and hushed conversations. Maybe that kept people more scared than a dead body ever would. A dead body might make people mad, make them rebel.

Back in Pittsburgh I'd always been around gangs. Real gangs, not these cocky wannabes. There was always fighting, always violence. But it wasn't until a kid got shot in the grocery store parking lot on a Saturday afternoon that the community really rallied. People had been dying for years, but it was always in alleys and back lots, in the middle of the night. When people actually saw it with their own eyes, that's what made them want to stop it.

Maxfield Academy wanted us to be afraid. They didn't

want us to ever know why we were here.

I'm going to find out.

I was almost to the classroom door when I heard my name.

"Benson!"

I turned just in time to see Jane inches away. She threw her arms around me.

"Oh my gosh," she said. "Are you okay?"

Confused, I hugged her back. I didn't want to tell her that the only thing causing me pain right now was her squeezing my bruises.

"I'm fine."

She pulled back and looked into my face. She was smiling, but her eyes were red like she'd been crying. "I heard what happened. What were you doing out of your room?"

"Just looking around," I said.

It took a minute for me to realize we were standing in the middle of the hall holding each other, and I quickly let go of her.

"Don't do that again," she said, shaking her head and laughing nervously. Her voice hushed. "What if Isaiah caught you?"

We turned toward the classroom door.

"There's nothing in the rules about being out at night," I said.

"Unless he thinks you're trying to escape."

I nodded. She grabbed my arm and gave it a squeeze. "Just be careful, okay?"

"Okay."

Laura was teaching again, smiling as brightly as she had before, but she never made eye contact with me. We halfheartedly discussed the aesthetics textbook that we were supposed to have read, although no one—not even the Society kids—really got into it. I hadn't even thought about the book since I'd gotten it.

As the bell rang for lunch, Laura read a note from her computer.

"We have an announcement from the school," she said happily. "There is going to be a dance in ten days. As contracts will be renewed next week and points awarded, please note that dance attire is available for purchase. You will also be able to purchase music that you wish to have played during the dance. Whoever gets the janitorial contract this month will be responsible for setup and decoration."

Lily slumped in her seat. "That's more work for the V's."

"The contracts are being changed?" I asked.

"They're being renewed," Jane corrected, turning back to look at me. "Nobody negotiates anymore. We have a truce."

I nodded, listening to the rest of the room chatter about the dance. After my conversation with Becky, this all felt so wrong. I understood what she had meant—that it was safer to follow the rules—but could I really go to a dance know-ing what I did about the school? That the same people who were letting us buy tuxes and music were also murdering kids in the basement?

"You okay?" Jane asked. Shaken from my thinking, I realized that most of the other students were on their feet and heading out the door. She was still sitting in front of me.

"Yeah," I said. "I guess."

"The first week is always the hardest," she said. "Every-one has trouble." Jane put her elbows on my desk and rested her chin in her hands, grinning mischievously. "You're a little more vocal about it than some, but everyone thinks like you at first."

I looked at the people filing out of the room, chatting excitedly about the dance. "How long does it take to get brainwashed?"

"Listen," she whispered. "You're in the V's, and we agree with you. A lot of terrible stuff happens here." There was something in her eyes, some hurt that I couldn't identify. "But have you ever stopped to think about where you'd go if you left? You don't have any family. No one here does."

"I'd have my freedom."

"Freedom to do what? Get a minimum-wage job and live in a run-down apartment—if you're lucky?"

I snatched my textbook from my desk. "So you're here

because you like it."

"That's not what I mean."

"What do you mean?"

Jane pulled back from my desk and took a breath. She tiredly ran her fingers through her hair. Finally, she stood and extended her hand to me. "Let's go get some lunch."

CHAPTER NINE

That afternoon we didn't have classes. Instead, Iceman announced that we had last-minute time to complete our contracts before they were renewed. The V's met in the maintenance room, and Curtis and Carrie handed out our assignments.

In addition to the vacuums and mops, the maintenance room had a wide selection of hand tools—hammers and wrenches and saws—and I immediately thought of how I could use them for escape. I searched the peg board for wire cutters, to get through the fence, but didn't see anything too promising. There was a pair of pliers that might work, but it'd be suicide to get all the way over the wall only to have them fail.

Extension cords, on the other hand, were as good as rope, and there were at least three of them. I couldn't help smiling as I turned back to Curtis for my assignment.

It turned out to be trash duty.

It was interesting, being able to walk the halls of the school in silence, to inspect all the nooks and crannies. I started on the top floor, rolling a large garbage can down the halls of the guys' dorm—another V girl was doing the same on her side—dumping the small trash bins. I peeked around some of the other rooms, but no one had much to look at. A few guys had some books, one had a guitar, and three rooms had TVs and video games. Mason had told me that those took almost six months' worth of points.

I don't know what I was expecting in Oakland's room—a gun collection? A list of people to beat up?—but other than an unmade bed and some smelly socks, nothing was out of the ordinary.

I moved floor by floor, room by room, but the building was so big and there were so few of us that most of the trash cans were unused.

On my way down to the basement I stopped by Becky's office and emptied her bin, but Isaiah was talking to her and I didn't want to hang around.

I searched the basement for the detention room. The infirmary was down there, as well as dozens of small storage areas and a boiler room. I checked every door on the floor—the chip in my watch opened all of them since we had the maintenance contract—but none of them looked like what I expected for the detention room. It was just like the basement of any old building: cramped, dark, and plain.

And then I found it, after I'd almost given up. It looked

like the other storage rooms—cement walls, poorly lit. But I noticed the door was heavy when I swung it open, and as I looked closer I could tell it was metal, painted to look like the other wooden doors. And the floor had a hollowness to it, like I wasn't walking on foundation cement anymore. I was standing in an elevator.

I stepped out quickly, suddenly nervous that it might drop out from under me.

As I stood at the door, I could see scratches in the paint. Doomed students trying to get out before the floor lowered?

My muscles tensed and I wanted to run, but something stopped me. I took a deep breath, looked up at the security camera—its glass, lifeless eye staring back at me—and I spit into the detention room. Then I went back upstairs.

When the garbage bags were all gathered by the outside doors, I peered out the windows. I could see a few Havoc members, one in the distance riding a large lawn mower, and two more close by, trimming the bushes and edging the grass. Curtis had said that even though the rules allowed me to take the garbage out to the incinerator, the doors wouldn't open for me. I'd have to get one of them to open it.

I held up my hand to pound on the window, but behind me I heard someone call my name. Jane.

"Hey," she said, jogging down the hall toward me. She was holding a push broom and set it against the wall when she reached me. "Let me go with you. The V's use the buddy system."

She pulled a few loose strands of red hair from her face and readjusted the elastic that held her ponytail. Her eyes sparkled happily, as though taking out the trash were her favorite pastime.

I turned back to the window so that I wouldn't stare at her.

"So, how do you like being a janitor?" she asked with a grin, as she started knocking on the windows.

Through the glass I could see two people walking toward us. One was Skiver, and the other was a girl I didn't know.

"It's awesome," I said. "That's why I signed up for this school in the first place."

Bringing Jane along didn't make me feel any safer, but I wasn't about to tell her that. And, besides, I didn't feel as nervous around Havoc as I did the day before. I'd refused to turn in Oakland and Mouse to the paintball refs for the overkill, and I'd cut Mash's handcuffs off. I figured they might cut me some slack.

I tried to pick up all the bags, but Jane scowled at me and took two of them.

"So, who's Private Ryan?"

"Huh?"

"You started to talk about him yesterday. Private Ryan at Omaha Beach. Was he a relative of yours?"

"What? No. It's a movie. You've never seen that one, either?"

Jane blushed. "I've been in here for two and a half years."

"That one's even older than *Cast Away*."

"I didn't watch a lot of movies before I got here."

I wondered how old she was, how old she'd been two and a half years ago. But the doors opened before I could ask.

"Well, if it isn't the new kid and his girlfriend," Skiver said. I ignored him and pushed my way outside, turning to make sure they didn't stop Jane.

"Just heading to the incinerator," I said. Jane didn't seem bothered by Havoc, but she didn't look at either of them in the face. When she was past them we headed toward the back of the school.

In the distance, closer to the forest's edge, I could see one of the Society's guards on a four-wheeler.

"You need some alone time?" Skiver shouted. They were walking slowly, following us.

"How old are you?" I asked Jane, trying to get her mind off Havoc.

She looked up at me with a smile. "How old do I look?"

"I don't know," I said. "Seventeen?" I figured it was

probably best to aim high.

"Sixteen," she said. "I'll be seventeen in June."

Skiver wasn't far behind, but it didn't look like he was trying to do anything other than intimidate us.

"So when you got here," I said, trying to do the math in my head. She cut me off.

"Thirteen. Pretty great, huh?"

I couldn't imagine coming into a place like this so young. No one here now was younger than fourteen, and there were only a few of them. I looked over at her. I wanted to say something—it seemed so terrible—but I couldn't think of anything.

"It's okay," she said. "Seriously. That's what I keep telling you. This place isn't that bad once you get used to it."

"It's all you've ever known."

She rolled her eyes and grinned. "That's a little melodramatic."

The incinerator was a big rectangular machine, about eight feet tall, and it smelled terrible. Curtis had told me that I didn't need to do anything to operate it—it was all automatic. A small sign indicated where to put the trash, and I tossed the first bag inside.

Skiver shouted, "Nice job at paintball yesterday."

I lifted the next bag up and in, and then the third.

Skiver turned to goading Jane. "Did you know your little Benson wasn't in his room last night? I think he's cheating on you. But for some reason he was still in the boys' dorm. I wonder what that means?"

I threw the last two bags in the incinerator and then turned to look at Skiver. He was smiling nastily. But the girl behind him had left.

I wanted to punch him in the teeth. Not for anything he'd said or even anything he'd done to me. I just felt like hitting him.

Jane took my hand in hers. "Come on."

I nodded and inhaled deeply. Holding her hand felt comfortable, but I knew I was squeezing too tight—angry about Skiver.

We'd only taken a few steps when I noticed a small door in the side of the building. Judging by the slope of the grass, I figured it had to go into the basement, but I didn't remember seeing any exterior doors while I was down there.

"Do you know where that goes?" I asked Jane. The image of the detention room was clear in my mind, and I knew there had to be more to the basement, something deeper down.

She shrugged.

We walked up to it but didn't hear a buzz, and the knob was locked.

"What are you doing?" Skiver shouted.

I turned to him. "Do you know where this door goes?"

"What do I look like, an architect?"

"No, you definitely do not."

He snarled and walked down to me. I listened for the buzz, but it didn't happen for him either. So, the door wasn't opened for maintenance or groundskeeping.

"Aren't you supposed to get back inside and scrub toilets or something?" he said.

Jane's fingers curled tightly around mine.

I breathed out, long and slow. "I guess we'd better."

That night I went to talk to Curtis. He was lying on his bed, fiddling with his computer.

I knocked on the open door. "What's up?"

He sat up. "Oh, hey, Benson. Just entering the contract bids."

Curtis punched a few buttons, and then closed the computer with a click. "Speaking of which, we get paid tomorrow—you'll have a few points."

"Nice," I said, and leaned against his wall. "Too bad I won't be able to afford a fancy new ball gown for the dance."

He laughed. "Don't worry. Most of the guys will just wear their uniforms. The girls can buy dresses if they want, but I doubt many guys will waste our points on it."

"I was wondering if I could ask you something," I said, looking toward his window. It was dark out now, and the moon was just over the horizon. There wasn't any haze.

"Sure. What's up?"

"How long have you been here?"

"Not as long as some, I guess. Maybe a year and a half. I've stopped paying attention."

"Were there ever more students than there are now?"

He nodded, as if my questions weren't surprising. He clasped his hands together and gazed at the floor. "You mean total numbers? Or do you mean, have people ever left?"

"Total numbers," I said. "I already know people have left. Died."

He glanced up at me. "I've never seen a body, you know. I mean, other than the war."

"Huh?"

"I've never seen a body of someone sent to detention. I always hold out hope. Maybe they're alive."

"But I heard about what happens with detention," I said. "I heard about the blood."

He stood up with a grim smile and moved to the window. "Wow. You really are more nosy than most of us. I'd been here a lot longer than you by the time I learned that."

Curtis didn't make much sense to me. He ran after Ms. Vaughn's car. I thought that would mean he was trying to escape, like I was, but most of the time he didn't seem like he was even interested.

"What about total numbers?" I asked.

"It's never been very high." He glanced at me over his shoulder. "You're wondering why the school is so big?"

"Yeah."

"I don't know. We've all wondered."

On a corkboard above his desk were a dozen pencil drawings—the school building, still lifes, faces I didn't recognize.

"You do these?" I said, leaning over for a better look.

"No. Carrie."

"They're good."

"I'll tell her."

I stood back up and turned him. "Who's the oldest here? I mean, who's been here the longest?"

"That's easy. Jane."

"Really? But she said there were people here before her."

"That's the big mystery," he said with a shrug. "She explained it to Carrie once. Fifteen were here before Jane came. One morning they were gone. I guess it was some kind of mass escape."

"Did they get away?"

Curtis shook his head and lay down. "No one escapes. If any of us ever got out of here they'd tell the police and this place would get shut down. Anyway, those fifteen were the only link to the past, and none of them confided in her. She was all by herself until more students were brought in."

I nodded, but my heart fell into my stomach. She would have been young—thirteen—going through all the same things I was going through now, only completely alone. She must have been scared all the time. It was no wonder she kept saying things weren't so bad. They'd been so much worse.

Looking back up at Curtis, I tried to push thoughts of Jane away. "So," I reasoned, "for all we know, this school's been like this for years—decades."

"Maybe. That's why I'm not Society."

"What do you mean?"

"Some people say that we need to just ride it out. Follow the rules and keep our heads low. I agree a little with that, I guess." He smiled. "I mean, I don't think we need to try crazy escapes and fall out of trees. But I do think that, sooner or later, we're going to have to try *something*."

"Right," I said. "They'll never just let us leave because we'd tell the police. So, what does the Society say about that?"

"I think they're scared," he said. "I know it doesn't look like it, but I think they're just too afraid of punishment. Probably because they know better than any of us what the punishments are like."

Curtis was right—it didn't look like it. Maybe Becky was scared, but Dylan? Isaiah? They couldn't be enforcing the rules just because they were too scared to break them.

I looked out the window, trying to guess where the wall was, but all I could see was trees.

"One last thing," I said, touching the glass and peering into the dark. "Have you ever seen smoke in the woods?"

"The campfires, you mean?"

I turned my head enough to look at him with one eye.

He nodded. "You can see them from the girls' dorm better than here. Just little trails of smoke—sometimes one and sometimes eight or ten. We think they might be guards."

"Or a campground," I said. Could help be that close?

Curtis laughed. "Campgrounds. Now that's an optimist."

Back in my room, I stayed up late on my little computer, scrolling through catalog pages of clothes, gear, jewelry, and games. There was nothing for sale that gave any insight into the outside world. No books, no magazines. Even the music we could buy for the dance was fifty or sixty years old.

"You know anything about computers?" I asked Mason, close to midnight.

"A little, but not really."

"Anyone in here a hacker?"

He laughed tiredly. "People have been trying that for as long as I've been here. Oakland looked into it. He knows computers. He said there's no consistent connection.

The network is only up and running for a few seconds a day—that's when the school downloads our purchases and records our bids. He says there's just not enough time to hack it."

"Oakland?"

"He's not as dumb as he looks."

I nodded. "Okay."

I browsed through the contracts. Each one listed the chores to do, the requirements to fulfill, and each showed the current bid. As usual, none of the gangs' bids were contested. They were all at the max points' limit. I could have entered one if I wanted to, like everyone used to do. I thought about doing it to make Havoc mad, but then all of the V's would be stuck with extra work.

I toggled back to the items for sale. The main page featured a wide array of dresses and a few suits.

Who was crazier? The school, who was putting us through all of this, or the students who were spending their hard-earned points on silk gowns, cummerbunds, bow ties, and flowers?

CHAPTER TEN

As much as I was trying to fight it, I was getting more used to school. Every morning I'd get up, listen to Iceman, shower, and get dressed. That TV screen ruled our life—it told us where to be, when to be there, and what to wear. It had begun showing a countdown to the dance, too, which still struck me as ridiculous.

In class we finished our section on aesthetics—it had only lasted a week—and Laura moved us into a riveting course on Field Surveying Techniques. Whoever was choosing the classes here seemed to be doing it at random. When I was back in a real school, I'd taken enough biology and chemistry to learn the scientific method and the testing of hypotheses. If someone really was watching us on those security cameras, experimenting on us like rats in a cage, the study was screwed up. Nothing they were doing could have been remotely scientific. There were too many variables.

Jane turned to me as class was dismissed. We'd spent the last hour looking at deconstructed diagrams of the optical theodolite, and Jane could barely keep her eyes open. "This almost makes me wish I was back studying the definition of beauty."

She stood up and I followed her to the door. "I'd take this over philosophy any day." I handed my aesthetics textbook to Laura and took the new one. *Applied Field Surveying.* "At least this is a practical skill."

Jane walked at my side in the hall. "There are a lot of practical skills that I never have any intention of practicing. Are you really going to use field surveying?"

I laughed. "When I get out of here, I'm going to open a field surveying business."

Jane hooked her arm through mine. "We could start it together—half surveying, half aesthetics."

"We'll make a billion dollars."

I laughed. I still didn't know quite what to make of Jane. We hung out almost all the time, and it wasn't at all uncommon for her to put her arm in mine or take my hand. And while I was definitely not complaining, I had no idea if it was more than friendly.

All the cultural norms of dating were foreign to me—when should you hold hands? When should you kiss? When were you officially a couple? But those norms had to be even more foreign to her, since she'd been in this school almost her entire teenage life.

The dance was tomorrow night. Maybe that would shed

a little light on things.

When we got to the cafeteria, Mouse was standing at the front of the line, arranging a stack of paper boxes and brown sacks on a table.

I peered down at the handwritten label on one of the boxes. "What's this?"

Mouse picked up the one I was looking at and shoved it toward me. "Schedule changed. Eat it up in your room."

Jane picked up a bag. "What's the new schedule?"

"Paintball," Mouse said. She winked at me. "Maybe we'll meet again out there, Fisher."

"I sure hope so."

We left the table and I followed Jane down the hall. A TV screen, mounted high on the wall above the drinking fountain, showed the change of plans. No afternoon classes, just paintball. We had only forty-five minutes to change and get out there.

Jane sighed. "I already didn't have enough time today." She and Carrie had volunteered to be in charge of decorating for the dance.

"We'll have plenty of time," I said. "I can stay up and help."

She scrunched up her face and looked back at the TV. "It's going to be a late night."

"I don't have anywhere to be in the morning. I can sleep through field surveying tomorrow."

Jane laughed. "I almost slept through it today."

We headed for the stairs.

She held up her fingers at me like a gun. "Try not to get shot a hundred times today. I don't want to hear you whining all night."

"I only get shot so you'll come heal me."

I ate my lunch—a chicken sandwich and coleslaw—at my desk while Mason got dressed. I still had my crummy, non-camouflaged sweats, but I was determined that would not stop me from playing better. Lily and Mason had taught me a little more about tactics, and I hoped to be able to try them out.

"Check this out," Mason said, tossing me a heavy plastic tube. It was about three inches long, and I saw it was actually two canisters taped together and slid inside a larger cylinder.

"I bought two of those after the last game," he said. "Just got 'em this morning. Paintball grenades."

"You just throw it and it explodes?"

"No, they're pressurized. One canister is air and the other's paint. Pull the pin, throw it, and it'll spin around and spray. Wipe out everyone in a bunker."

I smiled and tossed it back to him. "Then I hope we're attacking bunkers."

"They only came up for sale this month. I bet the other

gangs have some, too."

"Is it just a one-shot thing? That's got to be pricey."

"You can refill the paint, and buy new air cartridges." Mason walked to the door. "I've got to find Lily before the game. Do you think you can find your way out to the field by yourself?"

"Is it the same one?"

"No, other side of the school. Just hurry and you'll be able to follow somebody."

I dressed quickly, picturing the game in my mind. Maybe the school was trying to train us to be soldiers and maybe it wasn't, but I didn't care—I felt like paintball was helping me prepare for escape. I was learning how to move silently through the forest, how to hide, how to watch for attackers. Maybe that would come in handy soon. I hoped it would.

I was only four or five minutes behind Mason, but most of the school was already empty. I could hear some voices down the Society's corridor, but I didn't see anyone until I got all the way downstairs.

"Hey, Bense!" Becky was coming out of her office as I passed. She was dressed for the game, too, though she didn't seem to be as enthusiastic about it as some. She wore camouflage, but just the most basic, cheap stuff you could buy, and she hadn't upgraded her gun. That was one of the first things anyone did. Her hair was still perfectly styled, and she held her mask in her hand as she walked.

"Hey," I said. "You heading outside?"

"Now I am," she said with a huge smile. Huge smiles were Becky's default. "Just had to finish up a couple quick things."

We walked out the front doors and down the steps. There were a few people on the edge of the forest, but not many. I checked my watch to make sure we weren't late. We still had ten minutes.

"It's cold today," she said.

"If I was back home it'd be snowing."

"Do you miss the snow?"

I shrugged. "It's better than here. But I bet you have hellish summers."

Becky slung her gun over her shoulder. She hadn't removed the strap—even I had done that.

"It's not too bad, really. We are in the mountains, after all."

I had nothing against Becky, but it felt strange talking to her anywhere other than in her office. The Society didn't like me and Isaiah probably wouldn't want us chatting. Then again, maybe Becky was still trying to recruit me. Maybe her talking to me was an assignment.

"Are you excited for the dance?" she asked.

"I guess. Seems a little ridiculous, though. Don't you think?"

She frowned. "I think it's nice. We're trapped here. They could just as well not let us have any fun."

"Maybe. But maybe if things were worse more people would be trying to escape."

Becky didn't answer. We finished crossing the lawn and entered the edge of the forest. I could see the other students gathered together a hundred yards farther in.

"Then I'm even more glad we're having a dance," Becky finally said.

I started to laugh, but she quickened her pace, hurrying off toward where the Society was gathered.

Isaiah was already standing up on a rock when I arrived. He tore open the envelope.

"The scenario is Fly the Flag," he read. "Each team has its own flag. You have to take it to the pole in the center of the field, raise it, and defend it for five minutes."

"Those grenades will come in handy," I whispered to Mason. "Let them get there first, blow 'em away."

"I don't know, man," he said. "This field is tough. That flagpole is up on a little hill, and there's no good cover to get up there."

"Variants versus the Society," Isaiah continued. "Havoc will be refs. Each team gets a medic."

Jane raised her hand again and got the medic badge. Dylan got it for the Society. I hoped I'd get a chance to shoot him. Then again, the list of people I *didn't* want to shoot seemed to get shorter all the time.

Isaiah continued, "The winners of today's game will get double points for all their contracts this week. The losers will get no points, but will still be required to fulfill their contracts." There were groans from both sides that quickly turned into taunts.

"Game starts in fifteen minutes," Isaiah said, and stepped down from the rock, handing the bullhorn to Oakland. I still didn't like the idea of Havoc as the refs. I wouldn't be surprised if they shot me themselves.

Curtis gathered us as we watched the Society hike off toward the other end of the field.

"Okay," he said, keeping his voice low. "We worked something out for this scenario, and I like it. When the whistle blows, the Society's going to charge the flag— everyone always does. So this time we're going to do the same thing, except it'll be a fake." He pointed to Joel, one of the younger squad leaders. "Joel, you guys are fast. You, Gabby, and Tapti charge that hill as soon as the whistle blows. I mean, run your butts off. The rest of us are going to get right on the perimeter ribbons—all of us—and run as fast as we can for their end. Joel's squad will slow the Society from getting on the hill, and then the rest of us will hit them from behind."

Joel nodded. "So we stay up there till we're dead?"

"Yes," Curtis said, and then laughed. "But it'll be a noble death."

"What if it doesn't work?" Joel asked. "What if we get pushed off and they get up there?"

"If that happens then we'll try to hit it from three sides—Lily from the right, me from the back, and Hector from the left. Got it?" He checked his watch. "Jane, you're with us."

She nodded, and we broke the huddle, heading to the taped-off area. Lily, Mason, and I moved to the far right and waited at the ribbon.

Lily pulled her mask down over her face, her hair pulled into a ponytail behind. She turned to me. "You're pretty fast, aren't you?"

"Not fast enough to not get shot," I said, adjusting my own mask.

She knelt down and grabbed a handful of moist mud from the base of a pine tree. "You sent your clothes to the wash," she said simply, and then began wiping the soil on my arms.

I followed her lead, stooping to get more dirt. "I thought washing clothes was a good thing. Besides, they were splattered with red and blue paint. Not exactly camouflage." Rubbing it into the cotton sweats, I wondered whether it would actually do any good. The tan was so light it almost glowed.

"Still better than bright and clean," she said. "What time is it?"

I looked at my watch. "Two minutes."

"When we start running, just go as fast as you can, but stay at least twenty feet behind me. If I get too far ahead, try to catch up once I stop."

"Okay."

The whistle blew, and Lily took off like a rabbit, darting between the trees and bushes. She was wearing some kind of pack under her ghillie suit—maybe tied around her waist—but it didn't slow her down. I wondered whether she'd bought a bunch of the paint grenades, too. I charged on behind her, but she was easily faster than Mason or me.

To my left I could see Joel, Gabby, and Tapti running straight up the middle, the flag flapping in Gabby's hand. None of them had their guns raised—it was a full-on sprint.

This field wasn't as big as the other, and it wasn't long before I saw the hill. I wanted to watch and see if our squad made it up, but my path was getting rockier and I was having trouble keeping an eye on Lily. Suddenly she dived to the ground. I dropped into a crouch and kept running, my gun ready.

I didn't see anyone as I took up a position behind her. Mason knelt down next to me, panting.

"Man, she's fast," I said, trying to calm my own breathing.

"Best player in the V's," he said, his gun pointed off toward her. "Probably the whole school."

"She been doing this a long time? Or just naturally good?"

He laughed quietly, his eyes still on the forest in front of us. "Works on it constantly. Always practicing. I bet this plan we're using is something she came up with."

"She really wants to be the super soldier, huh?"

Mason snorted. "Something like that."

There was shooting somewhere.

The bullhorn sounded. "The V's have raised their flag. The timer starts now."

Lily looked back at me and motioned to follow her. She lifted into a low crouch and began slowly creeping left. I did the same.

Almost immediately she dropped to her knees, ducking behind a tree. Shots hissed, popping into the ground all around her. Mason was firing behind me, but I couldn't tell what he was shooting at.

Lily was pinned. I met her eyes and she gestured toward her attacker, but her hand signals were too vague.

I watched Mason's shots, trying to trace them to the Society sniper, but I finally figured he was firing blind.

Everything fell silent. Lily peeked around the tree and paint splattered instantly into the trunk and she had to hide again.

Catching Lily's attention, I held up my hand, wishing that I knew sign language. Five fingers, four, three, two . . .

I jumped from my spot, running to the left and diving for a tall bush. The sniper's paint followed me, crashing through the foliage, but there was no hit. I couldn't watch Lily—I was just trying to move fast—but in my peripheral vision I saw her turn and fire.

"Hit!" someone called out. "Medic!"

The distraction had worked. Lily got him.

I expected her to form another ambush around the hit sniper—I wanted to wait for Dylan—but she was in a hurry. She gave me a thumbs-up and then motioned for me and Mason to follow her.

We moved toward the hill slowly and carefully. I was trying to walk the way Lily had taught me—stepping with the side of the foot and heel and rolling onto the flat of my foot. It was a lot quieter.

The shots up by the flag were fast and unending, and I wondered how soon it would be before Joel's squad ran out of paint. We all carried spare packs, but there were hundreds of balls being fired.

Lily moved from tree to tree, and I tried to watch her and scan for bad guys at the same time. Most of them should be attacking the hill. The five minutes had to be close to up, and the game was going to end if no one got our flag down.

She left the cover of one pine and darted to another. Once she was in place, I moved from my rock and—

I never saw him before he shot, but as I ran I moved directly in front of someone in a ghillie suit, hidden in the grass.

"Medic!" I shouted, sitting down on a log. A moment later my shooter called out as well, two blue splotches on his shoulder.

Mason ran over to me and crouched for a moment. There was laughter in his voice. "You still haven't fired your gun, Fish."

"The V's have lost the hill, and their flag has been lowered," the bullhorn blared. "The timer is off."

Lily motioned for Mason. "Sorry, Benson. We can't wait."

I watched them leave. Mason seemed to know what he was doing—much more so than I did. But Lily was a pro, moving as quickly and deftly as a deer through the forest.

When they were far enough from me that I wouldn't risk their position, I yelled again. "Medic!"

There was silence for a moment, the hum of a distant four-wheeler the only sound. The guy in the ghillie suit spoke.

"So, Benson," he said, stretching his back and then leaning against a stump, "are you still happy with your choice?"

I looked over at him, trying to recognize his face under the camouflage. Isaiah.

"What choice is that?"

He pulled a tube of paintballs from his belt and began refilling his gun. "Your choice of gangs. Have the V's been everything you wanted?"

I kept my gaze on the forest around me, waiting for Jane to appear. "It's better than the others."

He closed the plastic cap on the tube and then looked over at me. I avoided his eyes.

The bullhorn blasted. "The Society has raised its flag!"

Isaiah seemed to ignore the game. "Why are the V's better?"

"Because you're crazy. Isn't that enough?" I cupped my hands and yelled again. "Medic!"

"I didn't mean the Society," he said. "But don't you think you fit a little better with Havoc?"

"What does that mean?" I glanced at his eyes, which were still motionless.

"You seem like you'd fit in well there," he said simply. "You're aggressive, you're more concerned about yourself than others, you're—"

I felt my finger almost unconsciously slide onto the trigger of my gun. "I'm more concerned about myself than others?"

His voice was calm and even. "Isn't that true?"

"If anyone in this place can be accused of being selfish, it's you and your Boy Scouts. If you wanted to help anyone, you'd just call off security and we could all climb over that wall."

Isaiah was completely cold—he didn't seem to react at all. "So we'd be over the wall. What would that do? Getting over the wall hasn't helped anyone in the past. Surely by now you've heard that no one ever escapes."

"Has anyone ever tried with a big group? All seventy-two of us? The guards can't kill everyone."

Isaiah paused. "How many of us have to escape to make the deaths of the others worth it?"

"Huh?"

He leaned forward, setting his gun on the ground beside him. "Let's say all seventy-two try to escape. What are acceptable losses? Ten? Twenty? If it means that you're safe and free, how many deaths are too many?"

I shook my head and turned away from him. There were still shots in the distance, and the occasional yell, but the only movement I saw was a fat brown squirrel sitting in a tree, chewing something.

"You're in the Society," Isaiah continued, "whether you want to be or not. This school is a society, and we all have our roles. There are those who want to keep people alive, and there are those who want people to die."

I shot him a look. "Did Walnut want to die?"

"He knew the rules. He knew the consequences."

I cupped my hands again. "Medic!"

There was no sign of Jane.

Without looking back at him, I spoke. "So when does it end? How long will you keep people inside here and alive?"

"Until conditions require us to leave. I really don't know what you're fighting against, Benson. You have everything here you could ever want in a school. Food, education, recreation. I've even heard there might be something between you and Jane. And yet you'd risk your life—and the lives of those around you—because you just don't like being surrounded by a wall? And you say *I'm* the crazy one."

There was a sudden sound of footsteps, and I turned to see Dylan, his medic badge clearly displayed, running toward us.

"Everyone is angry when they first get here," Isaiah said, raising his hand so the medic could see him. "Don't do something you'd regret."

Dylan's hand touched Isaiah's shoulder, and they ran off together.

I watched them go, darting between the trees as they headed toward the flag. I hated him. I hated that I hadn't been able to respond. He wasn't right—I knew he wasn't right. His words made a kind of twisted sense, but I knew he was wrong.

Someone was walking through the forest, but with a

raised gun—someone was dead. As the person got closer I realized it was Lily. She had two bright hits on her shoulders, but her head appeared to be clean. I wondered why she wasn't waiting for the medic.

"Is Jane dead?" I asked, as she got close. That would explain why she hadn't come to heal me yet.

"I don't know," Lily said. "I'm hit." She didn't look over.

I watched her leave, walking toward the ribbon.

As she moved out of sight another set of footsteps broke through the silent forest. Jane appeared, sprinting through the trees. Her head moved back and forth, scanning the trees until she saw me. She changed course, running past me like before, her fingers brushing across my back.

"Hurry," she shouted. "Get to the hill."

I jumped to my feet and set out. I ran, crouched down, gun forward, from a juniper thicket to a boulder, to a tall patch of grass. I was angry, and I could feel adrenaline pumping through my body. I hoped Isaiah was at the flag.

The shooting at the hill continued, and I could hear lots of voices calling for medics.

"One minute!" the bullhorn blasted.

I was in the same situation as before—all alone, hadn't fired a shot, and now I needed to charge the hill.

I took a breath and then ran, ignoring cover. The hill was right in front of me, but I didn't see anyone, and no one was shooting at me. I heard a voice at the top. "Medic!"

Charging forward, I crested the steep hill. Two people turned, looking surprised. One was Dylan. I shot them both—wildly, firing and screaming at the same time.

Dylan swore. He couldn't see it under my mask, but I was grinning from ear to ear.

I dropped to my knees, waiting for someone else to shoot at me, but no one did.

Reaching for the flagpole, I wrapped my left hand around the rope.

"Game over," the bullhorn yelled. "Society wins."

"What?" I jumped to my feet, searching for the ref with the horn. Oakland was standing under a pine at the bottom of the hill, his hand holding a stopwatch. I scrambled down the rocky mound toward him. Curtis was already ahead of me.

"He killed the last two, didn't he?" Curtis said. "Everyone in the Society is dead!"

Oakland shrugged, smug. "That's not how you win. At the end of five minutes, the Society flag was still up."

"That's—" Curtis stopped himself, and then turned away, his hands balled into fists.

Mason appeared at my side. His camouflage was wet with white splatters.

"Nice shots," he said, pulling his mask up onto the top of his head. He grinned. "We're going to have to work on your approaches, though. The suicide charge isn't always the best tactic."

"It worked, didn't it?"

Mason nodded and laughed. "Yep. I just wish you were ten seconds faster."

That night the V's gathered in the cafeteria, doing our best to turn it into a ballroom. Rosa had collected lamps from several of the dorm rooms, and she and a couple others were making new shades out of construction paper. A few of the guys were cutting long sheets of butcher paper into strips for streamers, and Jane and I were working on a banner. It looked like a bunch of little kids had decorated their bedroom.

"So why are you always the medic?" I asked, painting where she had instructed me to.

She smiled. "Because I don't like lying in the dirt."

"Really?"

"No, not really," she said with a laugh. "I don't like being in the squads."

"I get that," I said, leaning back to stretch. "All of my moments of brave heroism have come when I was working alone."

Jane laughed. "I wish I'd been there to see that."

"It was very awesome."

"We still lost."

"That makes it even better," I said, dipping the brush in more paint. "It's not nearly as heroic if you win. I was Bruce Willis blowing up inside the asteroid, or Slim Pickens riding the bomb."

She pushed her red hair behind her ear so she could see what she was doing. "I have no idea what you're talking about."

"There aren't a lot of movies in here," I conceded.

"That's got to be pretty hard on you," she said with a laugh. "All you do is quote movies."

I shrugged. "When you spend a lot of time alone, you watch a lot of TV."

"You have to remember," Jane said, moving the conversation back to the original topic, "that the gangs were formed less than a year ago. Before that it really was chaos in here. Our old paintball teams never used squads. It was just us. I got used to being on my own."

I nodded and then set my brush in a cup of water.

"Jane, what did you used to do before you came here?"

She looked up at me from the side of her eye and then focused back on the banner. "Why do you want to know?"

"Just curious," I said. "I think you're interesting." While that was true—I really did find Jane fascinating— ever since the paintball game I'd been thinking about what Isaiah had said. Maybe he was right—maybe I *was* concerned only about myself. I didn't know how to fix that, but I thought I'd start with Jane.

"What did you used to do?" she asked.

"I moved around a lot," I said. "Foster care. No idea who my dad was. My mom took off when I was five, I think. Left me with a babysitter. Never came back."

She set down her brush. "I'm sorry."

"It's all right," I said. I didn't want Jane to think I wanted pity. "I don't really remember her. Anyway, since then, I've just bumped around. Bluff, Elliott, South Side. Not exactly the hot Pittsburgh tourist spots."

Jane reached across the banner and put her hand on mine. "Isn't this place a little better?"

And for a moment, I couldn't think of a single reason I'd want to leave.

"What about you?"

She frowned. I was worried that she'd move her hand, but she didn't.

"Baltimore," she said, her green eyes no longer on me.

"You said that before," I coaxed.

"I was homeless."

There was a long pause, and I wanted to say something comforting but couldn't think of anything. Homeless. To go from that to here. No wonder she kept saying this place wasn't so bad.

She finally looked up at me.

I spoke. "Will you go to the dance with me tomorrow?"

Jane smiled, the corners of her mouth slowly widening until I could see her white teeth and a look of pure joy.

Her fingers curled around my hand and I squeezed them back.

CHAPTER ELEVEN

Tapping.

I opened my eyes. The room was pitch-black. I could barely see Mason's bunk above me. No light was coming in through the drapes, and even the gap under the door was dark.

There it was again. Tapping, far away. I sat up and listened. It was persistent, somewhere down the corridor.

Standing up, I saw that Mason was still asleep. It was chilly, and I pulled my Steelers sweatshirt on and opened the door.

The hallway was dim, but I could tell that no one was there. I had expected to see someone trying to get into another guy's room, but the corridor was empty. I checked my watch: 3:34 A.M.

The noise was coming from the far end, and I hurried down after it, even though I knew it was foolish going anywhere alone at night. I was well aware of the enemies I'd made.

As I got nearer, it was clear that the sound was coming

from outside the dorm. Someone was pounding on our door. I quickened my pace and as I reached the door the lock buzzed and opened.

Carrie was there, alone.

She grabbed my arm. "Benson."

"What's wrong?"

"Lily's missing. Go get Curtis."

I nodded and turned, running back down the hall. Had she tried to escape? Or was it detention? Carrie had said she was missing, not that she'd been taken. But maybe she hadn't heard? As I ran I could picture Laura and the Society girls dragging Lily away just as the guys had done to Walnut.

Curtis must have heard something because he opened his door almost immediately after I knocked. In seconds, we were back down with Carrie.

"She's nowhere in the dorm," Carrie said. "We've searched all the rooms, even the other gangs'."

Curtis's face looked grim in the dim light. "When was the last time anyone saw her?"

"We were all down in the cafeteria doing decorations last night," Carrie said. "But no one remembers seeing her."

The last I was sure I'd seen Lily was when she walked off the paintball field, with the two hits to her shoulder. Had she been in the cafeteria? I couldn't remember.

"What about her roommate?" I said.

"Tapti didn't get back to her room until after midnight, and the lights were off. She said she assumed that Lily was already there, asleep. Lily has the top bunk."

Why hadn't Lily waited for the medic? Did she want to leave the field?

Curtis put his arm around Carrie's trembling shoulders. "Lily's smart. She's probably just . . . I'll get everybody up. We'll search the school."

"Okay."

I finally spoke. "I think she tried to escape."

Carrie gasped. "What?"

"Did you know about this?" Curtis snapped.

"No," I said, holding up my hands in my defense. "I don't know anything about it. But Lily's one of the few people in here who I've heard actually say that she wants to escape. She says it all the time."

Curtis sighed and rubbed his hands over his face. "Other people say it, too."

They obviously didn't want to listen to me talk about escape attempts, but things were starting to click in my brain. "She left during the paintball game. Listen, I was hit and sitting there waiting for Jane, and Lily walked past me. She'd been hit in the shoulder, not the head, but she wasn't waiting for the medic."

Neither Curtis nor Carrie said anything, but they

exchanged a look.

"I don't know," I finally said. "Maybe she did, maybe she didn't. Let's go look for her."

Twenty minutes later, all the V's had been roused out of bed and were gathered on the first floor. Jane was standing at the doors, staring out the window. I was about to go talk to her when Curtis got everyone's attention.

"Just for simplicity," he said, "let's just break up into our paintball squads. I don't want anyone going alone."

"What's the deal with the lights?" I asked. I'd tried the switches, but they weren't working.

Curtis shook his head angrily. "I don't know. They won't come on."

Mason, rubbing his eyes, whispered, "Rats in a cage, man."

"Joel, you have the third floor," Curtis said, handing out assignments. "Hector, second. John, first." He paused, looking at Mason and me. Our squad was missing a member. "Mason, Benson, take the basement. If you find anything, meet back here. I'm going to go talk to Oakland and Isaiah and see if they know anything."

"Isaiah probably did it," Hector grumbled. "Put her in detention or something."

"Don't say that," one of the girls said. "She's going to be fine."

Curtis clapped his hands, just as he did before every

paintball match, and we all split up. Mason and I walked in silence, heading down the main stairs into the blackness of the basement. I checked the switch at the bottom, but it didn't work, either.

"Hang on, Fish," Mason said quietly. I could barely see his outline in the dark but heard him fiddling with something. A moment later a tiny round light turned on.

"Reading light," he said, the blue glow illuminating his skin. He looked like a ghost. "I bought it a couple months ago but ran out of good stuff to read."

I called out Lily's name and then listened. The narrow cement walls muted the sound and it disappeared almost instantly. The two of us stood there, waiting, but there was no response.

Without a word, Mason headed for the first door. The lock buzzed and opened. He shined his light inside. The room was empty and small. It had one of the deep basement window wells, and the little bit of moonlight spilled on the floor.

I moved to the next door. We repeated the process up and down the hall, sometimes finding storage—mostly old desks or textbooks or scraps of lumber and pipe—but a lot of the rooms were empty, just as they'd been when I'd gone through here looking for trash. Our janitorial and maintenance contracts let us go almost anywhere we wanted—we searched the infirmary rooms, including any closets or cabinets she could possibly fit into—but there was no sign of her anywhere.

I had high hopes for the back stairs that Becky had shown me. If Lily had wanted to hide, that could have been a good spot. But, like everywhere else, they were empty. Besides, why would she want to hide?

"Did you see her on the field after she'd been shot?" I asked, as we opened another door. This room had several rows of boxes, stacked to the ceiling, and Mason peeked around them with his light.

"No," he said. "We left you. I got hit and she kept going." His voice was cold and tired.

"She passed me," I said. "She'd been shot but could have waited for a medic."

"You think she went over the wall?"

"Maybe. Don't know."

He turned his gaze back to the boxes and opened one. It looked like lab supplies—rubber hoses and Bunsen burners and all kinds of bottles and jars.

"I hated chemistry. Be glad you missed it," Mason said absently, like he felt he ought to make a joke but had no desire to laugh.

"Do you think she was serious about escaping?" I asked as we moved to the next room. "I mean, really considered it? She talked about it all the time."

He just pointed at a security camera.

"About a year ago I worked for a hospital," I said. "I was just a janitor and I was only there for a month, but I knew the security guys and I hung out in their office sometimes. They didn't even have TVs to watch their cameras. They were just there in case some crime was committed. Then they'd look at the tape."

Mason sighed. "So what?"

"I think we're all too afraid of these cameras. There have to be a thousand cameras. They can't watch all of them all the time."

"But people get punished every day," he said. "Someone must be watching."

I nodded, unconvinced. Did they really catch everything? The students were usually all in the same place, weren't they? All in class or all at lunch or all in the dorms. The school didn't even have to watch all the cameras.

Of course, sometimes the school punished people for no reason at all, cameras or not.

I changed the subject. "I wonder if we could make something with those chemistry supplies. Maybe some acid to burn through the fence?"

Mason spun, glaring at me. "What is wrong with you, man?"

"What?"

"Lily might be dead, and you don't even care. All you

ever talk about is escaping and trying to figure stupid things out."

I paused, stunned. "Well, don't you want to figure it out, too?"

"Not when we're looking for Lily," he said, turning and opening a new door.

In another ten minutes we met up with Tapti, Gabby, and Joel. I could tell from their somber faces that they hadn't had any more luck than we'd had. We left the basement and returned to the main floor to join the others. Depression hung like a cloud over the gang. Curtis was sitting on a bench, his elbows resting on his knees. I sat beside him.

Mason's words kept running through my head. He was right. My escape could wait.

I hadn't been treating the V's like friends. They were just people, just part of the school that I hated. My chest felt heavy and tight. I wished now that I'd said something to Lily, that maybe I'd . . . I don't know.

"What about outside?" I asked Curtis, my voice low. Maybe, like me, Lily hadn't been able to get over the wall. Maybe she'd gotten hurt and was out there somewhere.

Curtis shook his head. "I woke up Isaiah and Oakland. Isaiah insists that they didn't take her to detention— and you know he'd be proud of it if they did. He'd say something. Oakland even offered to open the outside doors for us to go out there."

"Really?"

"Yeah. I think he was doing it just to piss off Isaiah."

"So let's go," I said. "Even if she didn't try to escape, maybe she just twisted her ankle in the forest or something."

"No," he said. His face was ashen. "Oakland came down here but they wouldn't open for him. He said they usually can't get out until dawn."

With nothing else to do, we all split up and headed back to our dorms. The schedule was already posted on the TV. Class today would be early—7:00 A.M. I had to wonder whether it was a punishment; they weren't giving us the chance to go back to sleep.

Mason opened the closet when we got back and started getting dressed.

"You all right?" I asked.

He shrugged.

"Just . . . I thought maybe you guys, you and Lily, might have been . . ."

He shook his head. "No."

It had to be a lie. They were always together.

"Oh." I sat down on my bed. My head ached from stress and lack of sleep.

Mason turned to look at me as he buttoned his shirt. His face was tight and cold. "I decided early on that I wasn't going to do that, get attached, I mean. Like with Curtis and Carrie—I think they're nuts."

"But isn't that part of surviving this place?" I said, thinking of Jane. "We're stuck here, so let's make the most of it."

"If you say so," he said, his face stony and emotionless. "But what if one of them gets it? What if the school decides one day that Curtis has been too much trouble and they toss him in detention? What'll that do to Carrie?"

I didn't say anything. Images of Jane filled my mind— her hair, her eyes, her smile, her hand on mine.

"You know that old saying," Mason continued. "'Better to have loved and lost than never loved at all'?"

I nodded.

"Complete horsecrap. Especially in here." He put his tie around his neck. "One day you're going to get it. You know it and I know it. One day you're going to do some fool thing and get caught."

He waited for me to say something, but I couldn't. Was he right?

"I stay quiet," he said, making the knot in his tie. "I stay out of everyone's way."

I felt like hitting him, though I tried not to show it. "Why aren't you Society then?"

"I don't care what other people do," he said. "If other people want to try to get out of here, then good for them. If you want to go to the dance with Jane, and screw up your life—and hers—then do it. I'm not going to stop you."

He and Lily *had* been together. He wasn't telling me about what might happen; he was telling me about what had just happened to him.

I lay back on the bed and stared upward.

"One dance is going to screw up my life?" I said with a little laugh, trying to lighten the situation.

Mason's voice was serious. "Becky had a guy. She wasn't always screwed up. She was a V. Helped start the V's, actually."

"You're kidding." I rolled onto my side to look at him.

He pulled his red sweater on, and his eyes met mine. "Do what you want, man. But if you're going to get killed next week crossing the wall, stay away from Jane. She doesn't deserve that."

CHAPTER TWELVE

At seven o'clock we filed into class. The Society and Havoc kids were all chattering in whispered voices and pointing over at Lily's empty seat. Some of them seemed concerned, others self-righteous, giving one another I-told-you-so looks. I tried to ignore them and looked straight ahead.

Everything about this school was wrong. Lily was missing, maybe dead, and yet here we were, about to have a lesson on field surveying, and later we'd go to a dance. I needed to get out. I needed to run, get help, tell someone about the school, and get the police.

And yet, in some ways, escape felt wrong, too. Yes, I needed to do all of those things, but should I do it on my own? Could I really leave the others behind and just hope they'd be okay and that I'd be able to get them out later? Could I do that to Jane?

She was sitting in front of me now, hunched forward, her arms propped on the desk. Her hair really was beautiful. The rich red wasn't quite copper, but more the shade of autumn leaves. It made her red uniform sweater look garish and cheap.

Maybe Mason was right. I needed to concentrate on getting out of here, not on girls. Jane should be the least of my worries.

Laura came in the room quietly and fiddled with her computer for a few minutes.

"Welcome to class," she said. Her expression was serious, but there was a kind of brightness to her eyes, like she was hiding a secret. "Before we begin, I have an announcement that was delivered with today's lesson plans." She tapped her keypad and the class quieted instantly.

Laura's eyes didn't move from the screen as she read. "We regret to inform you that Lillian Paterson was killed last night, hit by a car on the highway."

"Murdering bastards," Mason whispered. Jane dropped her head, burrowing her face into her arms. My muscles tensed, and my hands clenched under my desk.

Laura continued, "Please remember that crossing the wall is cause for detention."

I raised my hand. "I have a question."

She looked surprised and unsure of what to do, so I just went ahead.

"We all drove in here, and I only saw one road within fifty miles, and the only place it goes is here. So how did she get hit by a car?"

Laura frowned. "We don't know the circumstances, but—"

I interrupted, anger swelling in my chest. "There are only two possibilities: She was hit by a car on our road—but that makes no sense because no car came here—or she walked all the way to the main highway in one night. Which is it?"

Other kids were chattering around me, but I stared at Laura and waited for her to answer.

"We don't know the circumstances," she repeated.

"Yes, we do," I snapped. "The note says she was hit by a car. So, Laura, explain it to me. Take a guess."

She seethed, her lips tight together. "Maybe there are other roads in the forest."

Without even realizing what I was doing, I stood up and began shouting, "You know what pisses me off the most about this? If you'd caught her *before* she got over the wall, Laura, she'd be just as dead as she is now."

Before I could finish the room erupted in chaos, some people shouting at Laura, but most of them yelling back at me. The Havoc kids were on my side, barking angrily at the Society. I glanced up at the security camera, actually hoping someone was watching this time.

"Take your seat, Benson," Laura was yelling, trying to be heard over the crowd.

I touched Jane's back and coaxed her up. As she stood, I

could see her wet, red eyes.

"Take your seats," Laura shouted.

"No." I took Jane by the hand and led her out into the hall. As soon as we got outside she stopped and wrapped her arms around me, sobbing and shuddering.

The classroom door fell closed, but I could still hear the muffled shouting on the other side. No one came after us.

I held Jane, my left hand on her back and my right cradling her head while she cried into my chest.

I wanted to tell her that everything would be fine, that I'd get us both out of Maxfield Academy, but I couldn't bring myself to say it. And she wouldn't want to hear it anyway. It wasn't true.

No one could make it out of this place alive.

She was trying to calm herself, taking deep breaths between sobs. "I am so sick of this, Benson."

"I know."

"Two and a half years."

"I know."

CHAPTER THIRTEEN

We stood in the hallway for a long time. The noises from the class died down, and I listened to Jane breathe and felt her body slowly grow calm. I wasn't worried about punishment for missing class. We'd lose points, but right now I didn't care about that at all.

Finally, Jane looked up at me. Her eyes were bloodshot, and her mascara streaked down her cheeks. "Come on."

She took my hand and we walked in silence, heading down the large staircase to the first floor. The corridor was quiet, all the students still in their classrooms. She led me to the cafeteria, and we let ourselves in. It was dark and empty.

Once again I wished we had the groundskeeping contract. We could get outside and run. I was surprised the Havoc kids hadn't already tried it. Actually, since the Society had the security contract, it was just us V's who couldn't leave the building. Maybe it was time the V's bid for one of those contracts.

The decorations were already in place, though they looked strange and shoddy without any lighting. The lunch tables were still set up as usual. We had planned to move them later, before the dance.

"We should cancel," I said. "I know that they want us to have a dance, but how can we?"

Jane shook her head, her face set. "No. We're not going to cancel. Here, help me." She climbed up on a chair to reach one side of the banner we'd painted and hung the night before. I went to the other side and helped take it down.

We'd had trouble coming up with a good slogan for the banner. This wasn't a regular high school, so this dance wasn't like a regular dance. There was no theme. It didn't have a name—it wasn't homecoming or junior prom—so our sign just said MAXFIELD ACADEMY DANCE.

I laid the banner down on a lunch table while Jane rummaged through the decoration supplies. She came back with a smaller sheet of butcher paper, glue, paint, and two brushes.

Following her lead, I trimmed the paper and then glued it to the banner, covering the words *Maxfield Academy*. Jane sketched new words in pencil, and we finished them with paint. Ten minutes later we stood back and looked at our work.

"'Lily Paterson Memorial Dance,'" I read. "The Society's going to be pissed."

Jane smiled and took my hand. "I hope so."

Chapter Fourteen

I waited on the fourth floor by the unused common room, absently staring out the window as night fell. The windows faced east, and the pine forest below me was glowing orange, reflecting what must have been a magnificent sunset in the west.

Nothing had been scheduled after class, and dinner was postponed to be included with the dance. We'd had nothing to do but sit in the dorms. Fortunately, anticipation seemed to quell the earlier unrest. I hadn't seen Isaiah all day, and even Havoc was calm.

Almost all of the V guys were just wearing their uniforms to the dance, though most were a little more cleaned up than usual. Curtis had bought a sports coat and wore it over his usual shirt and tie.

I didn't want to spend my few points on clothes, but I'd got my tie as straight as I could, and I'd borrowed Curtis's polish kit to shine my shoes. Now, standing and waiting for Jane, I kind of wished I could have done more.

I heard the click of footsteps behind me.

It was Jane, and she was gorgeous. Her dress was brown and lustrous, like melted chocolate, and it gave her skin a golden hue. Her red hair was pulled up on top of her head, and she wore heels, emphasizing her slender legs. She put the sunset to shame.

"Hi," I said.

"Hi."

"You look good."

"You too."

I exhaled and glanced down at my uniform. "Yeah. Sorry. I didn't have anything else."

Jane stepped toward me and I caught a scent of her perfume. It was sweet and subtle, almost like vanilla or honey, but more floral. She didn't always wear it, but I loved when she did. "I think you look great."

"Thanks."

She kissed my cheek and slipped her arm through mine. "Can I hang on to you?" she asked with a giggle. "I've never worn heels before."

I laughed. "You can definitely hang on to me. And you should wear them more often."

We descended the stairs slowly. Feeling Jane on my arm made me forget about my problems.

That feeling was shattered when we got to the cafeteria. As expected, the banner was a major source of controversy, and just as we were walking in the door Isaiah was standing on a chair to tear it down. He was too late, of course—almost everyone was already at the dance and had seen it. Jane and I smiled and walked into the room.

Music was playing, loud enough that it was a little hard to hear each other. I didn't know most of the songs, but I didn't care. Jane and I walked out onto the dance floor and she put her arms around my neck.

"I've never been to a dance back in the real world," she said. To be able to hear her I had to keep my cheek almost against hers. "Is this anything like those?"

"Not sure," I said. "I went to a few of the casual dances, but never anything like prom."

"How come?"

I shrugged. "Never had a girlfriend."

As I said it, I wondered what that sentence implied. If I'd never been to a dance because I didn't have a girlfriend, but I came to this dance . . .

It suddenly struck me that there was no way the security cameras or microphones could hear what we were talking about. We could say anything. We could plan an escape or talk about what detention really was. She could tell me about those fifteen people who had been here when she'd come—I'd never asked her.

It could wait. I held her a little tighter.

Even on the dance floor, all the students stayed with their gangs. The V's hung out at the back by the outside doors—someone had propped them open to let the cool night air inside. The girls had all spent points on dresses, and they all looked completely different without their usual uniforms. Gabby wore something blue and shimmery that showed off her legs. Tapti's clothes were traditional, from whatever country she was from; I had no idea which. Carrie was gorgeous, all smiles and laughter. No one could have guessed we were all prisoners.

The other gangs were dressed up, too. The Society, which always looked a little overdone to begin with, now looked like characters in an old black-and-white gangster movie. The girls wore long elegant gowns and perfect, intricate hairdos, and the guys were all in tuxedos. It must have cost a lot of points.

Havoc wasn't as uniform in their style, but almost all of them had new, intricate tattoos and too much jewelry.

But the longer we danced the less I cared. I wasn't looking around the room anymore, nervously watching for Oakland or Skiver or trying to count Isaiah's guards. It felt less important now. My arms were around Jane, my hands on her soft, warm back. I could feel her breath on my neck, her cheek brushing mine.

When the lights turned up a little brighter and dinner was announced, we didn't move. Even when the music was shut off, Jane and I stayed on the dance floor, not wanting it to end.

Jane sighed, and I squeezed her tightly, pulling her against me.

"Time to eat," I finally said.

"Do we have to?"

"I think they're waiting for us."

Dinner was served on a long table at the side of the hall. Understandably, Havoc hadn't wanted to spend time in the kitchen, so most of the food had been pre-prepared and was served cold—several kinds of salads, finger sandwiches, fresh fruit, cheese plates. It didn't seem like a typical formal dinner, but we weren't going to complain. As I looked up and down the table, I hadn't ever seen this many Maxfield students looking this happy.

After dessert was served, Curtis stood and shouted for everyone to be quiet.

He raised his drink. We were all drinking soda, which was a luxury. "I'd like to propose a toast," he said, as the group quieted. I glanced at Isaiah, halfway down the table. Not surprisingly, he looked suspicious.

"To Havoc for this awesome dinner," Curtis began. After a moment of astonishment, cheers erupted up and down the table.

"To the Society, for handling the administration of all this," he continued. I had no idea what he meant, and I don't think anyone else really did either, but people cheered. Maybe it was the best compliment he could give them—something vague.

"And to Carrie," he said. There were cheers and laughs, and Skiver made a gagging noise.

Mouse stood up, raising her cup. Her dance attire was somewhere in between a dress and lingerie. I definitely hadn't seen it in the catalog—she must have made it. "And to the V's for the decorations." More applause.

Jane was on her feet before I knew it. "And to Lily Paterson."

The table exploded, many standing and cheering, and others booing and yelling. I stood and put my arm around Jane's waist and joined her in the toast. It was too chaotic now for anyone to drink in unison—many in the Society section had put their cups down—but Jane and I clinked our glasses. A few moments later, the relative calm of the dinner lost, the table was pushed back to the side of the hall and the music resumed.

I was helping shift chairs in the crowd when someone touched my arm. I turned to see Becky. She was wearing a floor-length black dress, her hair curled and twisted like springs.

"Hey, Becky," I said, as I continued to move the chairs.

"Hi, Bense." She took my arm to stop me.

I looked back at her, waiting for her to say something, but she seemed reluctant.

"What's up?" I said, having to shout a little to be heard over the music.

She leaned in. "I just wanted to say that I agree with

you and Jane. Some people think that Lily deserved it, but I don't."

I looked into her eyes and she stared back.

She stammered. "I—I just wanted you to know."

Before I could reply, she'd turned and left, pushing her way through the crowd.

I watched her for a moment. She'd been a V, Mason had said. She'd helped start the V's. And now she was so . . . broken. Lonely. I felt a sudden ache—I wanted to go after her and say something. I wanted to hug her.

I'd find her tomorrow. It could wait until we weren't surrounded by other students. I couldn't imagine that the Society liked seeing me talk to her.

I finished helping with the chairs, then hurried back across the dance floor to where Jane stood, laughing with two of the V girls. When she saw me, she excused herself.

"Hey," she said, taking my hand. "Want to go for a walk?" She motioned toward the door.

"Won't you be cold?" I asked, looking at her bare arms and neck.

"You'll have to put your arm around me."

"How could I say no?"

We stepped out the patio door and were met with a cool breeze. I slipped my arm around her and pulled her tight against me.

"Hang on," she said, bending down. A moment later she

stood back up, her shoes in her hand. "I hate these things."

"But they look so good," I said with a laugh.

"I'll give them to you and you can look at them anytime you want."

The moon was out and we could see the dim traces of the track, the forest, and the groundskeeping sheds. A few other couples were out on the lawn, strolling and talking. A deer stood out beyond the track, cautiously watching us.

"What would you do if you got out?" she asked. We were walking close to the building—I hoped it would keep some of the breeze off her.

I was about to answer but she stopped me. "I know what you're going to say, and that's not the answer I want. Skip all the stuff about calling the police and freeing everyone from the school. After that."

"I haven't really thought that far ahead," I said with a smile.

"What about a job?"

"I told you. I'm going to be a field surveyor."

Jane laughed. "For real."

"I honestly don't know. I've always thought I'd like to own my own business, be my own boss. But I don't know what I'd do."

We turned the corner toward the front of the school.

"I think I'd like to be a doctor," Jane said.

"What kind?"

"No idea."

We walked in silence for a little while, and she had me move my arm from her waist to her shoulders, to keep her warm. I offered my sweater, but she said she didn't want to cover her dress.

I formed a question in my head, and tried to think of different ways to ask it. *I know you hate it when I bring this up. . . . Let me just ask one thing and then I'll shut up. . . . I'm only asking because I really like you. . . .*

What if we ran away?

But I couldn't force myself to say it. At that moment, it just didn't feel right. I didn't want to think about climbing walls and cutting razor wire and starting forest fires. Even if Jane was totally willing. It was dangerous. Lily had died.

If we followed the rules, no one would die. Jane and I could walk like this all the time, every day. Of course, eventually someone would have to do something. But I could worry about that later. For now, things were good.

She turned toward the building and led me to the wall, to a small alcove between a short manicured pine and a window well. I felt my blood pressure surge as she turned to face me. She slipped her arms around my neck, just as she had on the dance floor.

Her green eyes were locked on mine.

"Thanks for asking me to the dance." Her voice was

barely above a whisper, her lips curling up in a tiny, uncertain smile.

"Thanks for saying yes."

I could feel her breath on my face.

"I'm glad you came to Maxfield," she said.

My heart was thumping in my chest. She smelled so good, like fresh roses. "Me too."

She leaned toward me, and I wrapped my arms tighter around her back.

Her lips were cool and soft, and every other thought disappeared from my head. There was only Jane.

I didn't let go, didn't want to ever let go. I didn't want to go back to normal life.

Why couldn't this be normal life?

She pulled back. She was beaming, her eyes sparkling in the starlight.

We stared at each other for a moment. The scent of her perfume still hung on my lips, and I wanted to kiss her again. But I could see from her smile that she wanted to say something.

"What?" I asked, unable to hide my own grin.

Jane stepped up to me again, her face an inch away. I could almost feel her lips on mine, but instead of kissing me she spoke.

"You don't still want to leave, do you?"

I smiled. "Well, not tonight."

Her eyes narrowed and she moved back slightly. Her arms hung around my shoulders. "You're still planning on it, though."

"Of course," I said, confused. "We'll go together, you and me."

"But . . ." Her voice trailed off, and she looked up at the stars.

"I can't stay here."

Her hands fell to her sides. "But this is good," she said. "Can't you see that? We can be happy here."

"If we stay here we'll die."

"If we stay here then we'll have more of this," she insisted with desperate eyes. "We can be together. We can be happy."

I took a breath, wishing we could rewind the conversation and go back to where we were a minute before.

"I'm not saying that we have to escape tomorrow."

She clutched my arms, her face again close to mine. "Then let's just not talk about it. Let's wait. Let's just be like this, you and me. Think about it."

"Think about it?" I said, my voice raised. "No, you think about it. What do you think is going to happen a year from now, or two years from now? This is some weird prison—it's not a resort. No one grows old here."

Her eyes flashed as she stepped away from me and folded her arms. "Don't tell me what this school is like. I know it better than you do."

I yelled, "Then what do you think is going to happen?"

Jane spun away from me, facing the cold rough stone of the school's walls.

I could feel adrenaline pumping in my veins, and I tried to calm down. I didn't want to act like this, not tonight. But Jane, of all people, should have realized that the school was a death trap. Every day we stayed was a day closer to detention or worse.

I reached out with one hand and touched her shoulder.

She shrugged me away. "Don't."

"Jane . . ."

I could tell she was crying now. It didn't have to end like this. But maybe it was better if it did. Mason's words rang through my head. *If you're going to get killed next week crossing the wall, stay away from Jane.*

I touched her shoulder again. "I'm sorry." She didn't shake me off this time.

Her hand reached up and touched mine. She was ice cold. She turned toward me.

Suddenly her eyes went wide, looking over my shoulder. Her mouth opened in a scream, but it was knocked out of her—something hit me in the back and I smashed forward into Jane, knocking her into the wall.

I stumbled and turned just in time to see Dylan swinging a pipe. I wanted to duck but turned my back to the blow to shield Jane. Pain rocketed through my body, and I collapsed to the ground. I could hear Jane screaming above me, and then she let out a yelp, and I felt her fall next to me.

My lungs weren't working. I desperately sucked at the air.

"You couldn't leave well enough alone," a female voice shrieked. I turned my head just enough to see it was Laura, standing behind Dylan. He was holding the pipe like a bat.

I couldn't breathe.

I turned to look at Jane. She was dazed but awake, lying against the wall. Her neck and chest were splattered with blood.

"You, Benson," Laura spat, "think that you're the big man because you don't care about the rules. Do you think that Lily would have tried to escape if you hadn't been goading her on?"

I didn't even care about arguing. I just wanted to protect Jane. I forced my aching lungs to breathe the word "stop."

"Stop?" Dylan mocked. "I shouldn't have stopped last time. I should have finished you off at the wall." He raised the pipe and there was nothing I could do. He swung it down like an axe, smashing my raised arm and pounding down into Jane's leg. She groaned, low and soft.

I could barely move, but they were going to kill us, and I couldn't let them. He took a step back, preparing the heavy pipe again. I started to stand and got up on one knee before Dylan's swing caught me in the stomach. I reached for something, my fingers dragging across Jane's bleeding leg, but I couldn't stay up.

I plummeted down into the deep window well.

Blackness was gathering all around me. Above me, silhouetted against the sky, I saw Dylan raise the pipe and hack it down onto Jane.

I watched him do it again. And again.

CHAPTER FIFTEEN

I woke.

Silence. Pitch-black.

I tried to move, and sharp, terrifying pains pierced my body.

There was a patch of gray sky above me. As I stared, I could see specks of light. Stars.

The almost-rectangular sky was interrupted by a small black spot. I tried to focus on it, tried to see it.

It was a hand. A hand reaching over the edge of the well. No—*hanging* over the edge.

Jane.

I pushed myself up, trembling with pain. I remembered what had happened. Laura's grotesque screaming. Dylan's swinging pipe. Jane's silence.

I reached for her hand, and the stretch made me gasp. My ribs were on fire. Tears ran down my face as I touched her fingers with mine. They were cold. She didn't move.

"Jane!" I shouted, desperately looking around me for some way to climb out. I put my foot on the corrugated metal, and it slipped off.

"Jane!" I yelled again. My voice was hoarse and dry. "Jane, wake up!"

I stretched for the top and discovered that the fingers on my left hand wouldn't grip. They wouldn't even respond. I crumpled back down to the bottom of the window well, scorching pain wracking my entire left side.

"Jane! You've got to wake up!" I moved to the far end of the well and then tried to run and leap for the top, but the sudden movement seemed to cripple me. I couldn't force my body to jump.

"Come on, Jane," I said, spinning in a circle, looking for anything I could find. The ground was thick with dry leaves. I kicked through them.

My foot caught on something and I dug it up—a short two-by-four.

"I'm coming, Jane," I said through the tears. I jabbed one end of the board into the dirt and leaned it against the side of the well. "I'm coming. Don't worry." I stepped up onto the high end, and my head was over the side.

Jane was motionless. She was dead.

I grabbed at the grass with my good hand and scrambled up onto the lawn, panting for air and fighting the pain.

I moved to Jane, brushing her hair from her face. She was bleeding.

No, the blood was dry.

"Jane!" I yelled. "No!" I grabbed her neck, pressing with my fingers, searching for a pulse. There was nothing.

I was crying now. I knelt over her, my face bent down to her lips, trying to feel a breath against my cheek. Nothing.

Blood was everywhere—face, neck, arms, legs.

Gripping my useless left hand with my right, I pressed down onto her chest, over and over. I bent over her lifeless face and breathed into her mouth.

Nothing.

What could I do? Where could I go? We had no 911. No ambulance.

I looked at Jane and touched her face. I touched her hand and touched her dress, ripped at the waist where the rough pipe had smashed against her.

She twitched.

"Jane?" I stared at her arm, wondering whether I'd seen something real.

It twitched again.

"Come on," I shouted, feeling her neck again for a pulse. My fingers were throbbing so much I couldn't tell.

Her head moved.

"Jane, can you hear me?"

Her hand lifted and fell.

"Stay there," I said, struggling to stand. "I'll get some guys."

She kept moving, pushing herself up.

"Are you okay? Can you hear me?"

She didn't respond, but moved to her knees. I offered my hand, but she climbed to a standing position without it.

I put my arm around her waist to help. "Come on," I said. "Can you walk? Let's get inside." My body was screaming with pain. Adrenaline must have been keeping me up.

She looked back at me, but her eyes were slightly crossed.

"You're in shock," I said, trying to be calm. "Lie down. I'll go for help."

But she didn't listen. She took an unsteady step, and then two more. She was limping severely on her right leg.

"What's going on, Jane?" I said, trying to hold her up the best I could. "Talk to me."

She kept walking.

I moved in front, trying to stop her. She was delusional. I grabbed her in a hug, but she didn't respond.

She took another step in spite of me, and I stumbled and fell. As I hit the ground, daggers of pain stabbed my ribs, hip, arm, and chest. I gasped for breath. Jane kept walking.

"Stop it," I shouted, trying to get back up. "Jane, just sit down!"

But she kept moving, limping slowly but deliberately around to the back of the building.

I shoved myself up, gritting my teeth against my injuries.

She was almost around the corner when I was back on my feet, and I hobbled after her, yelling.

There were no lights close to me. I didn't know how much time had passed, but the dance must have been long over. Turning back, I could see a dim glow high above me, coming from one window of the girls' dorm. For a moment I thought I should run there and try to throw a rock, try to get someone's attention, but Jane was already out of view around the corner and I couldn't leave her. She would fall at any minute—on the sharp stone steps or down into another window well. She could die. *She might die anyway.*

I pushed through the aching and throbbing, running with one leg and trying not to buckle on the other. As I turned the corner I saw her disappear around the back. That was good—she was getting closer to the cafeteria doors. Maybe they'd still be open.

"Jane, wait!"

When I saw her again she was almost in front of the cafeteria, which was now dark. The doors were closed.

The moon was on this side of the building, giving me a little light. Jane was moving awkwardly; I could see now that both her legs were probably injured, not just one. Given my pain, I didn't know how she was still standing.

I also noticed for the first time that my left hand—the one that wasn't working—was black with dried blood.

Jane was moving in spurts now, slowing, stopping,

taking a few sudden steps, over and over. I was gaining on her.

She ignored the cafeteria and was now limping past the incinerator. I was twenty steps behind her. I called again, but it was like she couldn't hear me.

Dylan must have hit her in the head. She had a concussion—or worse. I wasn't going to spend another day in this school—I'd get sent to detention for killing Dylan. And Laura. And I didn't care.

Jane turned after the incinerator. I followed.

She was heading for the door. The door that no one could open.

I reached her and grabbed her arm, but she shook me off.

"Jane, what are you doing?" I pleaded. "You need to lie down."

Ignoring me, she stepped in front of the door.

Buzz. Click.

Her hand, crippled and stained with blood, took the knob and opened it. I grabbed the door behind her, not letting it shut.

She was limping down a cement-walled hallway, like the others in the basement, except that this place smelled cleaner—like ammonia. A dim blue bulb hung from the ceiling, and as Jane passed beneath it her skin looked pale and dead.

The hall opened into a long, narrow room that reminded me of an old hospital. There were cupboards along one wall and empty shelves above them. On the right side was a row of steel floor-to-ceiling cabinets, and on the left was a metal table and a computer.

I had my hand on Jane's waist, following her helplessly as she walked to the steel table. I tried to help as she climbed up onto it, but she ignored me. Worse than ignored me— she moved as though I wasn't there at all.

My face was wet, but I didn't know whether it was tears or blood. Probably both.

"Jane," I whispered. "What's going on? Are you okay?"

She sat on the table, her legs stretched in front of her. I noticed a huge black bulge in her right leg just above the knee. Her bone was broken, but she'd been walking on it. Her injured hand was tugging at her ear, and her eyes stared blankly ahead.

I held her hand, but she didn't acknowledge it.

"What is wrong with you?" I shouted. "I'm trying to help!"

She tugged at her ear again, and this time it came off in her hand. There were lights behind it, and metal.

Where her skull should be. Metal and lights.

Jane pulled a cable from the computer and plugged it into her head.

I stumbled backward.

No. No, no, no.

The computer lit up and lines of text began appearing one at a time on the screen.

```
EMERGENCY DAMAGE REPORT
AUTO RETRIEVE MODE
MODEL: JANE 117C
SEARCHING FOR DAMAGE . . .
DAMAGE CODES:
WA 24584
MG 58348
OC 32111
     . . .
```

The numbers went on and on. Dozens, then hundreds.

I stared at her.

"Jane." The word was barely audible.

Her lips didn't move, but she spoke. It wasn't her voice.

"You shouldn't be here."

CHAPTER SIXTEEN

I ran.

I scrambled back down the hallway, struggling to balance as my hip kept trying to give way. I was terrified that the door wouldn't unlock for me, but the knob turned without a noise. I threw it open and charged outside, finally collapsing on the grass by the track.

I curled into a ball, the pain of my chest and leg and arm all overwhelming now. But worse was my heart, which felt like it had been ripped from my body and run through a shredder.

Model: Jane 117C

Jane had a model number. She was a . . . I had no idea.

An android? A robot? I thought I was going to throw up.

No. She couldn't be a robot. Jane had feelings and she had ideas and she had a personality.

I had kissed her. She had kissed me.

I tried to picture her, the Jane from before—happy, beautiful, alive Jane. But all I could see was her hobbling down the blue hallway, tearing off her ear, plugging into the computer.

There were no more lights on in the building. The school was silent, and no one knew. No one knew, and how was I going to tell them? How could I explain something that I didn't understand? I needed to get them in that door and show them, but I couldn't imagine going back in there. I couldn't see her again, not like that.

She was a computer program. I'd been falling in love with a computer program. When she smiled it was because some algorithm had commanded her to. When she kissed me it was because a complex chain of ones and zeros made her do it. She wasn't real, and she never had been.

But this was impossible. Computers couldn't think, and they couldn't act the way Jane acted. Machines couldn't look like Jane looked. Her skin felt real. There was life in her eyes.

I closed my eyes as a sharp wave of pain wracked my chest. I needed a doctor, but the infirmary was run by Dylan. And even if he hadn't been the one who'd beaten me, what could he do? He was a teenager, just like me.

Or was he?

Jane had a model number. And her number was 117C. Were there 116 others? There weren't even that many students in the school. But with the way people came and went, maybe there had been 116. Maybe the others died, like Jane.

Jane was dead.

No—she was never alive.

Was everyone a robot but me? Maybe they were watching me, testing me. How will Benson Fisher respond if he's in a fight? Will he try to escape? Will he make friends? Will he fall in love?

Breathing hurt. Lying on the ground hurt, but I couldn't do anything else.

Jane could have been the only one. She'd been in the school longer than anyone else. Maybe her stories about the fifteen others who had disappeared weren't true. She was the first, and she was here to watch everyone else.

I suddenly realized that everything else must have been a lie, too. She wasn't from Baltimore. She hadn't been homeless. She didn't want to be a doctor. Her freckles were paint, her hair was dyed.

I yelled, a visceral angry cry. Jane had tried to make me think that I could survive in this place, that I shouldn't kill myself in a crazy escape. That there were good things in this life. But it was all fake.

Maybe that was why she'd become my friend in the first place. I was getting ready to run, and her programmers wanted me to stay. They knew I needed a reason to keep me here, so they activated some "flirt" command in Jane's circuitry.

But it couldn't just be her. There had to be others in there—in that building right now. Why else would people follow all these stupid rules? Isaiah had to be one, running the Society and giving orders to keep everyone in line. But were there others? What about Carrie and Curtis? Maybe one of them was in the same situation as I was—trying to escape and in need of a reason to stay.

What about Mason? Someone to keep an eye on me, since I was the new guy.

Laura and Dylan for sure. They were too concerned about enforcing the rules, too strongly allied to the school. But then why would they attack Jane? It didn't make sense. Why would a robot kill a robot?

Nausea swept over me.

Becky, I wasn't sure about. At first I would have thought yes, definitely. She was fake. Too cheerful, too obedient. But there was sadness in her eyes, and loss. Fear.

No. Jane had emotions, too. Becky's sadness wasn't any more telling than Jane's happiness or mischievousness or rebelliousness.

I rolled onto my back and looked at the school. Anyone could be like Jane. Everyone could be like Jane.

I had to escape. I had no option anymore to try to take someone with me, to try for a mass exodus and hope for strength in numbers. I couldn't trust anyone anymore.

I struggled to get to my feet, fighting the pain but unable to fight the hopelessness. Jane had become my best friend, and now she was gone. But it was worse than death—she had never existed. I wasn't a boyfriend mourning for a lost love; I was a dupe, mourning my own blindness.

I limped across the track, heading for the trees. My hip

was burning with every step, and I couldn't breathe. Still, I'd find some way to climb the wall. The paintball flagpole had at least twenty feet of rope—I could cut that and use it for something. Or I could knock down a tree. Or take some of the lumber from a bunker. There had to be a way.

I was light-headed, and I began swaying with every limp. I coughed, and the pain was so bad it nearly knocked me to my knees. And then I coughed again and couldn't stay up. Blood dripped out of my mouth.

I have to keep going. I gritted my teeth and stood again. I was almost to the tree line. It would be harder walking in the woods, but I had to do it. I had to get out tonight.

The thought struck me that someone might already be coming. I'd seen what Jane was. There had to be repercussions. Whoever was keeping it a secret would know what I'd seen. They knew I could ruin it all for them.

I was moving so slowly, forcing every step.

The school was wrong, though. I couldn't ruin everything, even though I'd seen Jane and the metal under her ear. I couldn't tell anyone because there was no one to trust. And there was nothing I could give as proof.

And tomorrow Laura and Dylan would just finish the job, anyway.

The woods around me were spinning. It was so cold. I stumbled and then fell.

CHAPTER SEVENTEEN

I do not want to find these guys making out in a bunker."

My left eye opened slowly, like it was struggling under some heavy weight. I could only see dirt and rocks.

"Benson and Jane I can understand," another voice said, "but Dylan and Laura? The Society won't put up with that—they'll be kicked out."

"All four of them will get detention anyway. Whose dumb idea was it to open the doors? Did you see Benson and Jane leaving together all gooey eyed? I wanted to throw up."

The voices faded away and I closed my eye again.

I could tell that I was breathing because it hurt to do it, but my brain was foggy and sluggish. My muscles weren't responding.

I was cold.

Two four-wheelers were out in the forest, one far and one close. I could hear their engines.

Footsteps somewhere nearby. Someone was running.

"Hey, guys!" someone shouted. "I think they tried to escape."

"What'd you see?" It was Curtis.

"Blood, and lots of it. Around the front of the school. The Society just found it."

"I knew it. Benson ran."

"But Jane?"

Curtis's voice was hard and angry. "He talked her into it."

There were more footsteps crunching in the loose rock, and the voices disappeared.

I opened my eye again and found the strength to move my head slightly. I was in the forest, but I wasn't sure how far. There was a patch of dry grass a few inches in front of me, and bare dirt. A lone intact paintball lay among the pebbles.

My left hand was in view. It was swollen, caked in blood, and purple.

I could hear more voices now—not clearly enough to understand what they were saying, but I knew that there were lots of people outside. Probably all the students.

Dylan, Laura, Jane, and I were missing. They were searching for us, just like when Lily disappeared. But the Society must have been able to unlock the doors to check outside this time.

What would the announcement say about Jane? Hit by a car?

Grunting, I moved my right arm underneath me and

began to lift myself off the ground. It felt almost impossible, like I had an extra hundred pounds of weight strapped to my body.

I coughed and nearly fainted.

I could see the students now. They were spread out across the campus, some in groups and some alone. Most were over at the school, and more were heading around to the front, to where the blood had been found. Jane's blood.

Why would an android have blood?

I raised my right hand, hoping to signal someone, but I couldn't keep it up. It was too heavy.

"Hey," I croaked, but even I could barely hear myself.

I watched them as they searched. It wasn't organized, not like how Curtis had set things up yesterday—*was that only yesterday?*

It would be a tough search. If they were assuming we were in the woods somewhere, they'd have a huge area to scour. Still, if they quit ogling the blood, it wouldn't be hard to find me.

Did I want them to find me?

I raised my hand again and managed this time to give a little wave before dropping it. Still no looks in my direction. I was wearing my red uniform sweater. That had to stand out.

My mind was numb now. I wasn't angry, wasn't sad. I

was nothing. I would die in this school, today or a year from now.

There were footsteps behind me, but I couldn't muster the energy to turn.

"Hey," a voice said. "Hey, what's that?"

The footsteps sped up, getting louder and louder, and suddenly they were next to me.

"Benson? Oh, wow."

Someone stepped in front of me and then darted out onto the track. I tried to identify her. My brain was moving so slowly. I knew her. Gabby—one of the V's. She was screaming for the others to come, jumping and waving her arms.

"Oh, Bense," a voice beside me said, and I felt arms around me in a hug. "Hang on, okay?"

I nodded.

"Do you know where Jane is?" the voice asked.

I turned to look, rotating my head slowly and shakily. Brown hair, curled. Becky. I stared at her, not sure what to say.

"Jane," Becky said again. "Do you know what happened?" Her gaze was moving around my injured body, from my hand to my face to the bloodstains all over my clothes. Not all the blood was mine.

"It was Dylan," I said. "And Laura."

Becky gritted her teeth and looked down at the

ground for a moment, tears forming in her eyes. After a moment she spoke again. "Do you know where they took Jane?"

I stared. Was Becky friends with Jane? I didn't know. What would Becky think if she knew the truth? Maybe she already did. *Maybe she's one of them.*

"No."

Becky bit her lip and nodded. "You're going to be okay, Bense," she finally said, her voice quivering, but her smile appearing. "The infirmary's great. You'll be okay."

Others were almost to us, and Gabby came back. She asked the same thing about Jane, and Becky answered for me. A moment later Isaiah arrived, two younger Society guys in tow.

"What happened?" he asked accusingly.

Becky stood, stared at him, and then walked away.

"It was your stupid goons," Gabby said quietly. "Laura and Dylan did this."

The two Society guys flinched, stepping forward like they wanted to shut her up. Curtis appeared and jumped in front of them.

Was this real? Were they humans? Or was I watching an elaborate play designed to make me think they weren't all in on it?

Curtis turned on Isaiah, jabbing his fingers into Isaiah's chest and speaking in a low growl. "I don't care what you think happened here, but you have the medical contract, and you'd better get someone over here this minute."

Isaiah opened his mouth to say something, but Curtis grabbed him by the sweater. "And if I find out that Dylan was doing this under your orders, I will break every bone in your body. One at a time. Slowly." With his last word he shoved Isaiah backward.

One of the Society kids threw a punch, but Curtis easily dodged and then knocked the kid to the ground. Isaiah barked out a harsh order, and the fight was over as quickly as it started.

A crowd was forming around us now, and almost all of the V's were there. Mason stood quietly at the edge of the crowd, his face stoic. He'd been right. I shouldn't have gotten involved with Jane. Did that mean that he wasn't one of them? He'd tried to get me to not fall for Jane—he was working against her.

Or was this all an act?

Carrie, Jane's roommate, was on her knees at my side, tearfully pleading to know where Jane was. I told her I didn't know.

"Were you together?" Curtis asked. They thought she was still out there somewhere. Maybe they'd find her, like they'd found me.

I tried to nod, but even that hurt. "Yeah," I said. "We'd left the dance. We went around the front of the building . . ." Everyone's eyes were glued to me as I spoke, even the Society's. Oakland and Mouse stood at the edge of the circle, listening to every word. "It was Laura and Dylan. He had a pipe."

There were murmurs in the crowd, then raised voices, and then people began shoving each other again. Curtis bellowed at everyone to shut up.

"Go on," Carrie said, her face red.

Jane's face was like that when she cried. Then again, so was everyone's.

"They attacked us," I said. "Dylan knocked me into the window well." I paused, wondering what I should say. How would I explain how I got over here?

Carrie touched my hand. "And Jane?"

I shook my head. Pain. "I don't know."

I should be crying, I thought. *I should be sobbing. Why can't I?*

A moment later Isaiah broke back through the crowd, with Anna following him. She looked terrified as she knelt beside me.

Everyone grew quiet as Anna fumbled with her first-aid kit. She opened it uncertainly, looked at me, then looked back at her kit. She pulled out a gauze bandage and with trembling fingers tore the plastic shrink-wrapping off. But then she paused, staring back at the various items. She pulled out a little bottle of something, then set it down and chose another.

"Come on," Curtis snapped, motioning to Mason and Joel. "Let's get him down to the infirmary. The rest of you get out there and find Jane. She could be anywhere."

Chapter Eighteen

I spent five days in the infirmary. Anna was out of her league. She could take X-rays, but never saw the results. Instead, she'd put the undeveloped films in a locker—an elevator, like my closet—and then get back a list of things to do. In the end, I was surprised to find that the only serious injury was a concussion. I had bruises and contusions from head to toe, a nasty cut on my forearm (Anna said it would normally have had stitches, but too much time had passed before they found me), and two dislocated fingers. My arms and hands were bandaged like a mummy's, both my wrists in braces, and I was on a heavy dose of pain medication, but that was all. She said I probably felt worse than I was. I felt terrible.

Some days I was the only person in the infirmary, and other days the entire gang was there with me. I heard it was different now—things had been shaken up. For a while Curtis worried about another gang war, like before the truce, but that had blown over. In the end, four people left the Society. Three had gone to Havoc, and Anna joined the V's. Since Dylan was gone and Anna was now a V, the medical contract was automatically transferred to us, which infuriated Isaiah.

The strangest news, however, was Iceman's explanation of events. Jane was dead, though we got no explanation about how or where. But Dylan and Laura were sent to detention. Curtis had asked Isaiah about that, and Isaiah insisted he wasn't involved. Someone else must have taken them.

On the fifth day, knowing that I was about to be discharged I got out of bed and looked around the infirmary. I couldn't face the idea of going back to my room, back to the normal routine. I needed to find a way out of here. I needed escape plans and weapons and tools.

I inspected the elevator through which Anna sent X-ray film and received instructions. It was short and built into the basement wall. I would have assumed it was just a cupboard if I hadn't known better. There were no buttons or controls.

The other cabinets had about what I expected: gauze and tongue depressors and latex gloves. There were syringes but no needles. Nothing that looked like a weapon of any kind.

I took a bottle of rubbing alcohol because I vaguely remembered something from a cop show about how to use it as a weapon. At the very least, I figured it was flammable. And I hoped that whoever was watching on the cameras would assume my theft was a dangerously moronic attempt at getting drunk.

"Hey, Bense." I spun from the cupboards to see Becky standing in the doorway. I did my best to look innocent as I put the alcohol bottle on the counter.

"Hi."

She was holding a clipboard against her chest, her arms folded. "I just need to ask you a couple of questions before you're released. Stupid forms I have to fill out." She made a fake grimace and laughed.

I nodded and moved to sit. I was wearing a pair of white flannel pajamas Anna had taken from a closet, and I felt like a kid as I climbed up onto the too-tall hospital bed.

"There's paperwork in this place?" I asked.

"That's ninety percent of my contract," Becky said.

I lay back onto the raised pillows. My head still ached, though the pain was duller now.

"Shoot," I said, staring at the ceiling. I didn't want to look at her. There were plenty of people in this school that I strongly suspected of being robots. Becky was on the list. All of the Society was.

She clicked her pen. "First, how would you rate the care you received while you've been in the infirmary?"

I rolled my head to look at her. She smiled.

"You're kidding."

Becky glanced down at the clipboard. "Scale of one to five, one being excellent and five being not good at all."

I looked back at the ceiling and then closed my eyes. "This school, where we're prisoners and people die, cares about good customer service?"

"We don't know that people—" Becky stopped.

There was silence.

I cracked open one eye. She was wiping her cheek.

Her voice trembled. "I'm sorry."

"It's okay."

We sat there for several seconds, Becky staring at her paper and me looking at the white cement ceiling.

It was never going to be normal here. I'd been fooling myself before, back when I thought that I could actually enjoy myself. I had liked paintball and the good food and the guys in my gang and . . . Jane. But it was all a lie.

Becky held up her clipboard. The paper was blank.

"There's no paperwork," she said, and wiped her eye again. "I just wanted to check on you."

"I'm okay."

I returned to my dorm that afternoon. A few people had made get-well cards for me, and some girls collected plants from the gardens and put them in a vase on my desk. I thanked them all, but things were different now.

I hid the bottle of rubbing alcohol in my pillowcase.

I needed more ingredients before I could make it into a weapon, but that could wait. In my five days spent lying in bed I'd come up with a theory.

My logic went like this: First, we were in the school for a reason, either to be tested or to be trained. I couldn't guess which because neither really made sense. If we were being tested then the test was extremely broad and abstract. If we were being trained then you'd think there would be more focus on what we were learning—better teaching, stricter testing, higher expectations. Even the people who thought we were being trained as soldiers because of the paintball didn't have any answer for why we weren't being taught tactics. We were just making everything up.

Anyway, if I assumed we were in the school for a reason then I should also assume that the presence of Jane and any other androids—I still hated using that word for her— would be to aid in the training or testing.

So, if androids were the basis for the experiment or training, then it would make sense that they had been here since the beginning of the experiment. Jane was perfect evidence—she was the first of all of us.

I decided to chart all of the students, all sixty-eight of us who remained, and figure out who came first. If my reasoning held up then they should be the androids.

Unless they all were.

And, of course, I had no idea where to draw the line.

Were there five of them? Ten? Thirty?

I made a chart in a notebook, and then walked down the dorm hallways, with Mason's help, asking how long people had been there. I didn't tell Mason why I was doing it, and I think that he might have thought I'd lost it. Maybe he wasn't too far off.

The V's all offered up their info easily enough, and most everyone else did, too. When I got down to Oakland's room, Skiver opened the door. Oakland was sitting in his chair, his feet up on the desk while he scrolled through his minicomputer. He glanced up long enough to see who I was and then looked back at the screen.

"Hey, guys," I said. "I have a couple questions for you."

Skiver started to close the door in my face, but I stepped forward and it hit my shoe.

He scowled and puffed out his chest. "What's your problem?"

"Just have a question," I said. "Humor me. I'm trying to chart the whole school and see who's been here the longest."

"What do you care?"

"I'm curious."

He gritted his teeth and narrowed his eyes in what was probably supposed to be a threatening face. "You got me out of bed for that?" Skiver acted tougher than his size warranted, but ever since the fight on our first day he'd taunted me as though he'd beat me in the Ultimate Fighting Championship.

"I realize that it's a long way from the bed to the door," I said. "And I apologize."

He stared back at me, with more of his semi-threatening expressions.

I pointed to the chair. "If you want, you could sit and catch your breath."

Skiver opened his mouth, but Oakland spoke. "What's the question?"

"How long have you guys been here?"

"Why do you care?" Skiver snapped.

"You already asked me that," I said calmly, watching Oakland.

He looked back at me, thinking. Skiver seemed to be confused as to why he wasn't hitting something.

I decided to ease the tension. "I'm trying to figure something out about this stupid place," I said. "But I need to talk to the people who've been here the longest."

Oakland stared at me for a long time, and then finally spoke. "Jane was the oldest, wasn't she?" His words weren't sympathizing, but they weren't his normal jerk self, either. It was a simple statement.

I nodded. "Yeah."

"About a year and nine months," Oakland said. "I think. Not totally sure. Skiver's less than a year."

Skiver looked confused that Oakland would help me and stared as I wrote the dates down in my notebook.

"Thanks, guys," I said.

As I was turning to leave, Skiver spoke. "Nice job taking care of your girl, Fisher."

I paused, rage building up in my chest. Taking a deep breath, I looked back at Oakland. I stared at him long enough for Skiver to wonder what was going on, so that he looked back, too. Then I sucker punched Skiver in the jaw.

He dropped straight to the floor. Oakland's eyes met mine for a moment, paused, and then he turned back at his computer.

By the end of the night, I had gotten answers from almost all the guys. Two Society guys refused to answer, saying that they needed to ask Isaiah before they helped me. I wanted to hit them, too.

Isaiah didn't answer either, but I was able to find out about him from several others. Not surprisingly, he was one of the oldest. I knew it. He had to be an android.

Over the next two days I was able to gather the information from the girls, in class and in the cafeteria. In the end, I found that there were five of them who had arrived at school together, including Isaiah. They all claimed to have been in the school for just over two years, and they remembered driving in together in a van. In addition to

Isaiah, there was another Society kid, Raymond, and two girls from Havoc—Mouse and Tiny. And Rosa, one of the V's.

I didn't know Rosa very well. She was one of the oldest girls. She had the best paintball gun. She had asthma. She didn't seem to go out of her way to talk to people.

I was going to have to keep an eye on her.

Of course, the entire list was a guess. It was still all based on the assumption that the androids came first. And it was based on the even greater assumption that there were more than just Jane.

That night, lying in bed, I wanted to say something to Mason. Based on my chart, he was among the newer half of the students. Hopefully that meant he wasn't part of . . . whatever this all was.

It was dark, and I could hear him in the bunk above me, quietly tapping on his minicomputer.

"Hey," I said.

He yawned. "What's up?"

I paused. Dim light glowed from his screen, and it reflected off the smooth lens of the security camera in the corner.

"Nothing, I guess," I said.

"'Kay."

It would have to wait until we were outside, away from the microphones.

I got up from my bed, too awake to sleep, and took my computer from the closet. The contracts were coming up for renewal again soon, and I was curious about the medical one. There had been talk that the Society might try to take it back from us. The gangs were supposed to get together to discuss it soon. It sounded like a silly thing to fight over to me, but I'd heard that the contracts disputes often got violent—that's why everything had been settled with a truce.

I read the medical requirements, but there wasn't much of interest there. The points were relatively low, compared with the big contracts like groundskeeping and the cafeteria—the two huge ones that Havoc owned.

Bored, I toggled over to the purchase screens and looked at what new items were being offered. It wasn't much—a few new kinds of snacks, a few new outfits (all for girls), and a new video game.

The paintball stuff was enticing—page after page of camouflage clothing, and eight different kinds of ghillie suits. There was even a white-and-gray one, for when the snow started to fall. Looking at the paintball pages, I wanted one of everything—not because I wanted to excel in paintball, but because escape would be so much easier if I could do it in full camo.

But it'd be a while before I could afford anything good. Breaking the rules probably hadn't been beneficial to my points, and I only had payment for part of a month. I clicked on a few menus to try to check my account—I hadn't fiddled with it much—and it took me a few minutes to find it.

That's not right . . .

"Hey, Mason," I said, confused. "How many points do you have?" I knew he'd been saving up for several months for a ghillie suit, only splurging on a few things like the paintball grenades.

"Hang on," he said sleepily. I could hear the tap of his keyboard. "Looks like . . . a thousand eight hundred thirty."

That was good—1,830—he could buy most anything in the catalog except the most expensive things.

"I only need forty-five more," he said. "Hey, did you see they finally added winter camo to . . ."

I wasn't listening to Mason anymore. Something was wrong.

My point total read five million.

The school was trying to buy me off.

CHAPTER NINETEEN

I didn't want everyone to know about my points—the Society would have been suspicious if I'd ordered a ghillie suit with only a few weeks' worth of points. But I'd bought a pair of cargo pants and I filled the oversize pockets with several expensive purchases—paintball grenades, binoculars, a flashlight, and, most expensive, a pair of two-way radios.

I also started building a stockpile of supplies: granola bars, crackers, beef jerky. Hopefully the school thought that I was enjoying their bribes, but maybe they knew the truth: I was preparing for escape. Either way, whoever was on the other end of the security cameras must have been pretty confident in the school's walls; the gear they sold practically taunted me into trying to run.

I hated class now. Hated sitting there, day after day, staring at the two empty seats in front of Mason and me. Lily was dead. Jane was gone. Every day I'd sit in my desk, staring at her chair, remembering her hair, remembering her lying on the table in the basement.

I noticed Becky was the same way, sitting alone now in her front desk. Laura always sat beside her, and Laura was gone. Good riddance.

After several days of monotony, Iceman announced that we were to head outside for paintball. I tried to hide my excitement as I changed my clothes and packed up my gear. I wasn't excited for paintball itself, but I wanted to use the time in the woods—away from the cameras—to work on something.

Mason had already left the room by the time I finished dressing. I was purposely being slow, and as soon as the door closed behind him I moved to my bed and pulled out the bottle of rubbing alcohol.

I shook it and looked at the color. It was completely reddish brown now. The night before I'd poured an entire can of cayenne pepper into it. I'd bribed a kid from Havoc to steal it out of the kitchen by telling him that it was for a prank I was playing on Isaiah, and giving him a three-hundred-point gold chain in exchange.

And, when I'd gone back to the infirmary this morning to get another day's dose of pain medicine from Anna, I'd stolen a syringe and gauze pads.

Now I'd find out whether it all worked. I'd seen it done on TV, but that didn't always mean anything.

I dropped the bottle into a pocket of my cargo pants and headed down the hall.

I could feel my extra gear weighing me down, thumping against my legs as I hurried for the stairs. I didn't know who, if anyone, would get my second two-way radio. Of everyone left in the school, Mason was the one I trusted most, but he wasn't eager to escape. Maybe no one would come with me.

But that didn't matter today. For now, I was just experimenting.

Curtis found me as I was crossing the track. "Might get snow," he said, looking up at the low clouds.

I shrugged. "It's been doing this all week."

Curtis was one I wasn't sure of. He'd come six months after Isaiah, but he was still among the ten oldest students. I had to wonder whether all of the gangs were run by androids: Oakland and Mouse, Isaiah, and Curtis. The only one that seemed out of place was Carrie, who had only been in the school for a year. While she didn't seem to be a co-leader of the gang, like Mouse was, Carrie had become a kind of second in command after Curtis.

I wondered whether she was a human in love with an android. *Just like I'd been.*

"Are you okay to play today?" Curtis asked me while we walked.

"I think so," I said. "My head's feeling better, and I can do most things with these braces, no problem."

"And your ribs?"

"Hurt like hell," I said with a laugh.

"Well, we'll try to keep you in one spot if we can. Defending something, maybe. With any luck, we'll be reffing today and you can sit out."

The paintball field that we were heading to was one of the biggest, I was told, with dozens of small plywood buildings arranged like we would be fighting in a city.

As usual, Isaiah stood at the head of the crowd.

The crowd was a little quieter than usual and more somber. This was the first game we'd played since everything had happened—the teams had changed, and key players were missing.

"The game today is Bodyguard," Isaiah announced through the bullhorn. "Society on offense, the V's on defense."

Curtis patted me on the back and gave me a smile. I'd be able to defend somewhere without a lot of running around. That wasn't what I planned on doing, but I gave him a nod.

"The Society will designate one player as the VIP," Isaiah continued. "That player has to touch the flag in the center of the town square. The offense will also have five more players than the defense. Both teams have a medic, but the VIP cannot be healed."

I turned to look at the V's, gathered together in a group behind Curtis. Everyone seemed hesitant, like no one wanted to take Jane's place. I could see her in my mind, standing right with us, cheerfully raising her hand.

She'd said it was because she liked being alone. Someone had programmed her to like that, I guess.

Timidly, Carrie volunteered. "I'll do it."

A few in the crowd nodded their heads in approval, but no one looked very enthusiastic.

In some ways, I think that I was getting over Jane faster than any of them. They hadn't seen what I'd seen. To them she was still their good friend who was brutally murdered. To me—well, I didn't know what she was. But every time a good memory of her appeared, it was followed by one of her sitting on that table, her torn ear in her hand, and a voice that didn't belong to her.

The Society's medic was Vivian, someone I didn't really know, but Becky was chosen as the VIP.

Isaiah made sure the medic sleeves were handed out and then read the rewards and penalties for the game. He raised an eyebrow and stared for a moment before reading the words aloud. It was obvious he didn't approve. "The team that wins today will receive decreased punishments for any rules infractions that take place this week. The team that loses will have increased punishments."

There were murmurs among the crowd, especially in the V's. "This is bull," Mason said. "The defenders always lose here."

Isaiah looked at his watch and announced that we had fifteen minutes to get in place before the game started. I lifted up the ribbon and let the others go under.

"Okay," Curtis said as we all walked together. "We don't have everyone we used to. Mason and Benson, take up defensive positions in the town. Joel, you've got front perimeter, and Hector, you've got back. John, I want you guys to split up and work independently as snipers on the streambed. Anna, you're with them. Find cover and wait for them to come to you. Carrie, stay in the city and heal defenders as they get hit. Society outnumbers us, and they're probably going to hit us from all sides at the same time."

He clapped his hands and wished us good luck, and we split up. Mason and I headed for the city, walking slower than the others for my sake. My chest hurt.

With the buildings of the city in sight, we had to drop down into the deep, dry streambed that Curtis had mentioned and then climb back out.

The city was even bigger than I expected—maybe thirty or forty small buildings made of plywood, a third of which were two stories tall, and one a skinny three-story tower. They were clustered together and stained with old paint splotches.

"It's a mess," Mason said. "They always give the offense more people here. We get slaughtered."

"What do they do when the V's are offense? The other team would only have ten or twelve guys."

"We're *never* the offense here. Always defense. We always lose. Which, I guess, means that we'd better not break any rules this week. I want to eat."

Mason placed me in a good defensive position on the second story of a plywood building with two windows— one facing the woods and the other facing one of the main entries into the town.

"Good luck, man," he said, and gestured to the paint-splattered walls. They were coated with layer after layer. "You won't last long."

With that, he turned and left, hurrying deeper into the city.

As soon as he was gone, I pulled supplies from my pockets and set them on the floor in front of me: the bottle of now-red alcohol, the syringe, a stack of gauze pads, and a bottle of water.

From another pocket I took out three paintball grenades. I hadn't used them before, but they looked simple enough: a canister of paint and another of compressed air. I pulled the pin on the first and threw it down the stairs, and then did the same with the other two.

There was a loud hiss, and the sound of skittering and scraping as the pressurized grenades spun and sprayed the room below. When the noise stopped I hurried down the steps. The room was streaked and speckled with neon green, white, and yellow.

I picked up the grenades and ran back to the second floor.

I unscrewed the top of the water bottle and poured it out, not caring where it spilled. Then, after laying two gauze pads over the mouth of the bottle, I gently strained the alcohol through the gauze.

The smell was already overwhelming, and my eyes began to water.

The cayenne pepper was supposed to infuse with the alcohol—that's what I'd seen on TV. It seemed to be working, because as the water bottle filled with reddish rubbing alcohol, all of the bits of pepper remained on the gauze and the liquid below hardly had anything floating in it.

From somewhere in the distance I heard the pops of a few shots.

I dipped the syringe down into the alcohol and drew back on the plunger.

The sound of paintballs hitting the perimeter buildings was coming from two different sides of the city—loud, resonating *thwacks*. I peeked out my window but didn't see anyone.

Carefully, I turned the syringe to the first grenade, refilling the paint canister. I spilled a little on my hand, and it stung and burned the tiny hangnails on my thumb and index finger.

I gingerly replaced the pin and then hurried to fill the other two.

There were shouts, people calling for the medic. They were close.

I attached new air cartridges to the grenades.

They were done. Three pepper spray grenades.

It wasn't a gun, but I suddenly felt much more in control. I had weapons. They wouldn't stop an android, but they'd stop an idiot Society kid.

I wanted to try one now, throw it out the window when I heard someone coming, but there'd be no way to not get caught. It was better to know that I had the grenades—that they *might* work—than to risk being caught.

There were no cameras out here. The school had no idea.

I gently put the grenades back in my pants pockets, picked up my gun again, and looked out the window.

I couldn't keep the smile off my face.

I stood and positioned myself at the window, trying to get my mind back on the game. I couldn't see anyone, but from the noise I could tell that our forward defenders— the guys at the streambed—hadn't been very successful.

A thought suddenly popped into my head. A deep streambed cut through this paintball field. There was no way that the origin of that stream was contained within the walls of the school; it had to pass through the wall somewhere.

Noise came from the first floor of the building—muffled voices—and I instinctively turned to aim at the stairwell. A moment later a grenade skittered across the floor. It hissed and spun, spraying a mist of blue around the room that splashed across my mask.

I called, "Hit!" and stood up to leave, wiping my mask. Out the window I saw Becky enter the city protected by five others.

There had been no way to hide from that grenade. I imagined throwing one of mine into Isaiah's dorm room.

I laughed as I left the building.

I headed off the field, my gun pointed toward the sky to show I was dead. A few refs lingered in the forest, but most of them were following the action into the plywood buildings.

When I got to the streambed I followed it uphill, walking casually and not trying to hide. I'd gone only a few hundred feet when Mason appeared at my side. He had at least seven neon green hits on his arms and chest.

"You're not running now, are you?" he said.

I didn't look at him. "What makes you say that?"

"You're going the wrong direction."

"I just want to see where this stream goes," I said.

He nodded and walked next to me in silence for a while. As we plodded along the dry bed I wondered whether it had ever had water in it. Maybe it was dry because the wall blocked it.

The cold stung my fingers, now that the excitement and adrenaline were wearing off.

"Is it December yet?" I asked.

"No idea. I don't keep track."

Near the base of the wall, the stream disappeared into a culvert pipe, about two and a half feet wide. As we neared it, standing in the well-worn tracks of the Society's four-wheelers, I bent over to look through.

"It's clear all the way," I said, confused. "You could crawl straight through, be out in a minute."

"No," Mason said. As I stood back up I saw him pointing. There were two cameras flanking the pipe, about forty feet to either side. They were both pointed at us.

"Oh," I said, and gave a little wave to the cameras. "Well, that's that, then."

It didn't dissuade me. If I was going to escape, I'd have to do it fast anyway. And maybe these cameras were like the ones back at the hospital where I'd worked—they weren't being constantly monitored. They could just be recording, in case someone had a question later.

"What do you think's on the other side?" I asked.

He shrugged. "Guards."

"You'd think we could hear something. Those four-wheelers are loud—wouldn't the guards on the other side have those, too?"

"They have campfires. You've seen the smoke."

"Or maybe those are actually campers. Maybe it's a campground."

Mason snorted. "Well, if I ever get out of here, I'd rather take my chances in the forest than walk into a group of guards."

I nodded but didn't say anything. A Society girl, killed with a bright blue head shot, was walking through the forest and watching us. Mason slapped my shoulder and gestured for us to head back.

The school was just barely coming into view when I spoke again. I pointed across the track.

"You know what that door is?" I asked, as casually as possible. "The one by the incinerator?"

"No idea."

"Groundskeeping can't open it and neither can we. Maybe it's a security thing?"

"Maybe. I think I saw Rosa go in there once." Mason's tone was matter-of-fact and disinterested, like he was just making conversation. I tried to match it.

"You did? Recently?"

"No. A year ago, at least. Rosa." He glanced at me. "Isn't she one that's been here a long time?"

"One of the five, yeah."

"It was before the gangs. She wasn't a V then."

I nodded but inside my heart was racing. Rosa. She'd been here since the beginning. She had to be one of them.

CHAPTER TWENTY

During the next few days I made a point of looking for Rosa, but watching her only added to my confusion. If she really was an android—and she had to be since she'd been in that room—then why was she always so quiet? She wasn't influencing anything, wasn't trying like Jane to prevent me from leaving. She was just there, shy and in the background. You'd think that if someone went to the trouble to build an android, they'd give it something to do.

After class I went down to Becky's office and rang the bell. It took her a little longer this time to come down from the dorm, but as usual she was smiling and happy.

"Hey, Bense. What's up?"

"I had a couple questions," I said, as she opened the door and let me into the office. I sat down on the couch, and she leaned on the edge of the desk.

"Go for it," she said.

"Okay. You have all the records for all the students, right?"

"What records do you mean?" She folded her arms. "There aren't any grades."

"I meant that letter you have—the one Ms. Vaughn gave me to give to you."

"Oh," Becky said, suddenly blushing. "You want to see what it said about you?" She turned from the desk and walked to a file cabinet. I stood to watch, hoping to get a glimpse of what else was in there. There weren't many records, but everyone had a thin file.

She pulled out the folder with my name and opened it. The envelope was inside.

"Take a look," she said, almost laughing.

The envelope had been opened very neatly, cut with a knife. Becky seemed like the organized type.

Inside was one sheet of folded paper. I pulled it out. It was blank.

I looked up at her.

"Seriously?"

Becky nodded, grinning sheepishly. "I think that she does that so that you'll have to find me and won't get side-tracked. But none of the letters ever say anything. Just pieces of plain paper."

"So, if I wanted to find something out about some-one—where they're from, how old they are—then you have nothing like that?"

"Nope," Becky said. "Not in the files. But I've been here for a while and I think I know everybody. What's your question?"

I almost wanted to tell her everything. Looking at her standing there—her smile, her hair, her skin—she was real. And I knew a little about her past. I knew that she'd had her heart broken.

But everything I could say about Becky I could have said about Jane. I'd talked to Jane far more than I'd talked to Becky. Jane had emotions and sadness. I'd kissed her, for crying out loud. If that wasn't enough to tip me off that she wasn't real, I don't know what would have.

"Do you know Rosa?" I finally asked.

Becky looked surprised and a little deflated.

"Yeah," she said. "I guess."

"It's for something Mason and I are doing," I lied. "You know how I was making that chart of when everyone came to the school?"

"Oh yeah," she said, lightening a little. "Can't you just ask her that?"

"She told me. But you know how she is—so quiet. Now I'm trying to figure out more—where she's from."

I had meant for this to be easy and quick. I'd hoped that Becky could have just looked in her files and rattled off some quick information and I could be done. But now I felt like I had to soothe Becky's feelings, for some reason.

She sat up on the edge of the desk and crossed her legs. "I think that she's from somewhere in the South. I want to say Georgia, but I'm not sure. What's this project for, anyway?"

"Just curious," I said. "Boredom, mostly. And I figure that someone ought to be keeping some kind of record of this place, just in case we ever get out of here."

Becky nodded. "I write in a journal. Every night."

"Really?" I sat back on the couch.

"Yep. I did before, too. I wish I still had those."

I was watching her face. She seemed to be deep in thought.

"Where are you from?"

It seemed to shake her back. She sat up a little straighter and looked at me again. "Not far from here. Arizona. Flag-staff."

"Really? How far away is that?"

"Five or six hours."

"And you don't have any friends there? Someone you could contact?"

She laughed softly and shook her head. "I lived with my grandma, on an old ranch. Homeschooled. She died when I was fifteen."

"I'm sorry."

"It's okay." She looked down at her skirt and smoothed it with her hands. "I like that you're collecting this stuff. When you're done I'd like to see it. Maybe we'll have some real records here for once."

I nodded and smiled. "Sure." There was so much more I wanted to say. I wanted to trust her. I wished I could.

By the way, Jane was an android.

I stood up to leave but didn't step toward the door.

Becky watched me expectantly—or was she trying to say something to me? I couldn't tell. Her eyes looked intense, but distant.

"I'd better go," I finally said.

She looked into my eyes. "Okay."

I turned and had almost touched the doorknob when she spoke.

"I'm sorry," she said. "About Jane. All of us in the Society aren't like Laura and Dylan."

A flare of anger sparked, but I tried to keep it down.

Without turning around, I nodded.

"Don't . . . ," she began, but stopped. I waited, my hand tightly gripping the doorknob and squeezing it until my knuckles were white. She was still one of them. Anna had become a V. Others had joined Havoc. But Becky was still in the Society.

She stammered out her words. "I'm only trying to . . . I just . . . I just want everyone to be safe."

"Okay." I opened the door and left.

For the next few days I tried to find a way to talk to Rosa, but nothing presented itself. We'd stopped eating lunch on the bleachers—it was too cold—and lots of the girls retreated to the dorms to eat, rather than be in the cafeteria.

I was lonely.

Every day was getting worse. I'd spent my entire life without anyone I could talk to—that was normal. I was almost always in a foster home with six or seven other kids—all of whom were as screwed up as I was—and I never stayed longer than a few months. By the time I was twelve or thirteen I'd stopped unpacking my bag altogether. I was never part of a team, never in a study group or a clique. I was always the new guy.

But at Maxfield I'd had friends. I'd had people who talked to me. Jane was a weird case—she'd never actually been my girlfriend, and I'd only known her for a few weeks, but we were definitely friends. We talked all the time. And now she was gone.

She was never real. I don't know why I had so much trouble remembering that.

My other friends seemed to be drying up, too. The same distrust that was ruining things with Mason had wrecked my friendships with the rest of the V's. I was just there, in the background.

I missed people. I missed Jane. I missed Mason and Lily. I missed being able to sit in a group and think they were my friends. Now, every time I was in a class or the dorms or the cafeteria I was looking around at the faces. *Was that leg movement mechanical? Do people really blink like that? Is she breathing?*

I'd spent my whole life alone, but I'd never felt as alone as I did now.

I finally had my chance to seek out Rosa. As we filed out of the classroom, the TV screen in the hallway was running announcements—contracts were going to be renewed that night, so everyone would have the afternoon to finish job responsibilities. When the V's met, I was once again assigned to garbage duty, but I kept listening when Curtis doled out the assignments. Rosa was sent up to the third floor to fix a broken radiator.

I kept to my routine, starting with the dorms on the fourth floor, with plans to work my way down to the classroom where she was. I wanted it to look normal, not like I was stalking her. As I picked up each garbage bag, I planned what I'd say to her when I got down there.

Unfortunately, Isaiah was in the dorms, too, and as I passed his door he came out to talk.

"Benson," he said. "Question."

"What?" I didn't look back at him but continued with my job, opening each door and taking the trash.

"I heard that you and Mason went to the wall."

"We did indeed," I said, dumping a basket into my large can.

"That's against the rules."

I glanced at him for a moment and then looked back at my work. "It is not against the rules, actually. I would think that you of all people would know what the rules are."

"True," he said. "Going to the wall is not against the rules. Attempting to escape is against the rules, however. And, as you know, the V's lost the last paintball match and have increased punishments."

I feigned innocence. "Did I attempt to escape?"

"I think you are, even this very minute. Planning is part of the attempt."

I pushed the can down the hall to another door. "Then you'd better lock up half the school." The painful part was that it wasn't true. Isaiah knew as well as I did that hardly anyone was seriously trying to get out.

"So you admit it?"

I opened the next door and stepped inside. Isaiah had to be a robot. He was too strict, too obedient. Was anyone actually like this?

When I reemerged from the room I was looking at him, and he stared back at me. "What if I were to tell you," I said, dumping the basket, "that Jane was an android?"

Without waiting for his response I went back into the room and set the basket down. I wasn't worried. If he was an android, part of the school experiment, then he'd already be aware that I knew about Jane. If he wasn't, he wouldn't believe me anyway.

"What?" he said as I reappeared.

"She was an android," I said. "A robot. C-3PO."

He stared at me. I took another basket and then another.

"There's no insanity defense here," he finally said. "You can't wear a dress and get sent home for being crazy."

"Okay," I said. "But if you ever want to talk about it, you come see me."

I opened another door and stepped inside to get the basket.

"I don't think you know what you're dealing with here," Isaiah said, still standing in the hall by the large trash can.

I came out of the room and rammed my finger into his chest. "I'm the only one in the whole damn place who knows what he's dealing with." I tossed the garbage in the bin and then yanked it down to the next room. The last thing I needed right now was to deal with Isaiah and his self-righteous Society. It wasn't about keeping anyone safe—it was about keeping himself safe. He did what the school wanted so that he'd be fine, not so that other people would be. I picked up a few wadded papers off the floor and stuffed them into the small can before heading back to the hall.

Two other guys were with Isaiah now. I quickly dropped the trash in the large can and went back into the room, trying to think of something to do—some way to get past them or talk my way out of this—but it was too late. They'd followed me in.

"This is what the Society is all about, huh?" I said, as the two thugs walked toward me.

I took a swing at one, missing, and then tried to run past them. But there was no way. In an instant I was on the floor. My good arm was being twisted behind my back and someone's knee was pressing down on my spine. The more I struggled, the more pain shot through my body.

Isaiah calmly knelt down beside me. I tried to swing at him with my bad arm but the angle prevented anything more than a weak swat.

"If you want to escape," he whispered, his lips almost touching my ear, "then do it and die already. I keep this school healthy, and you're a cancer. Jane was a cancer, too. And Lily. Two down, one to go."

I threw my head against his, but didn't have enough power behind it to hurt him and the pain in my own head flared. I struggled against the two on top of me, but it was useless.

Isaiah stood, and in a moment he calmly ordered the two thugs to do the same. "Let him up."

"The cameras saw all of this," I said, trying not to show how much pain I was in. "You'll be punished."

He smirked and moved close to me, his face only inches

from mine. His voice was barely a whisper, not loud enough for his guards to hear. "This school has four rules and one punishment—detention. All other rules and all other punishments are dispensed by the Society. The school has learned it can trust us."

"What?"

"You can try to tell the others," he said, "but they won't believe you. Very few in the Society know."

I was stunned. When I could finally find strength to say something I murmured, "I bet the school loves you." I looked at the guards. "Did you guys know he's the one who makes up the punishments?"

His goons' faces didn't change at all.

Isaiah walked toward the door.

"The school can still love you, too. Or it can hate you."

And with that, he was gone.

I ignored the rest of the garbage on the fourth floor and headed down to the third. I didn't know what to ask Rosa, if I should ask her anything at all. Maybe I should just forget about trying to find out who was an android. No one would believe me. No one else was trying to get away. Everyone seemed so maddeningly complacent. Granted, they'd been here a lot longer than I had, but if a month of my prodding hadn't spurred any of them into action, I doubted that another month would, either.

I entered a classroom and saw Rosa kneeling by the radiator, her hands splotched with black grease. She looked up at me.

"Hey, Benson," she said quietly, and then focused back on the radiator.

"Hey." I pulled the trash bag from the room's small basket. "Where did you learn to do that?"

"Here," she said.

"Oh," I said, trying to figure out how to stretch the conversation. "Someone taught you?"

"No. Some directions came with the contract."

"But you're at least mechanically inclined." I tossed the bag into the big can.

"I guess."

This was going nowhere. It was time to be bold.

"So, if you do a lot of maintenance stuff, have you ever worked on the incinerator?"

Her face was still down, and she was fiddling with a wrench. "Why? Is it broken?"

"No," I said. "I was just wondering if you knew anything about that door—"

Before I had a chance to finish the sentence she looked up at me.

"You do?" I asked.

"Oh," she said, frozen for a moment. "I—no. No idea. Maybe it's for groundskeeping?" She looked back down.

What was that? It was definitely a reaction. Was it nervousness? Fear? Surprise?

"So you've never gone in there?" I asked.

"No." She bent down to get a closer look at the pipe. Or, to make it look like she was too busy to talk.

"You're one of the oldest here, aren't you?" I said, trying to draw the conversation out. I slowly unfolded a new garbage bag and placed it in the basket.

"Um, yeah," she said. "I guess so. I'm eighteen."

"So you got here when you were, what, sixteen?"

"Yeah," Rosa said, turning her head in my direction but not looking directly at me. "Listen, I've got to finish this up and then there's a broken light switch in the girls' dorm. I need to concentrate."

"And you're sure you've never been in that room, not even a long time ago?"

"Very sure."

"Okay," I said. "Good talking to you."

"Yeah."

I pushed the large garbage can back out into the hallway and headed for the next room.

I needed to take things to the next level.

CHAPTER TWENTY-ONE

I sat alone at dinner. I ate almost every meal alone now.

I took my plastic dinner tray and sat on the fourth floor, in the common room that no one ever used. It was already dark outside—sunset was earlier and earlier now. I watched as a few people walked past my door. Three Society girls were somewhere down the hall, talking and laughing about something that had happened in class that morning. I still couldn't fathom it—how could they be so calm? How could they be *laughing*?

One thing I hadn't figured out was where I'd go when I finally broke out. Of course, I'd go to the police first, and if they didn't help I'd go to the newspapers. But after that, I didn't know. I guess, up to now, I'd kind of assumed that escaping would be the happy ending—it'd be so much better than inside Maxfield Academy that it didn't really matter.

But it hadn't been that long since I'd left my foster family, and I hated it there. I didn't want to get shipped back. I didn't want to return to Pittsburgh at all—I wanted something better. I wished that I actually was in a private school, like the scholarship had advertised. Real teachers, real learning—real *people*. A real life.

I left the room and walked to the broad windows that overlooked the grounds in front of the school. I'd stood at these windows and waited for Jane the night of the dance.

I cupped my hands around my eyes and leaned against the glass, trying to see past the glare of the hall lights and into the darkness. There was fog or mist that hung over the trees in the distance. Could it be smoke from a guard camp? There didn't seem to be enough moisture here for fog.

I heard soft footsteps padding up behind me.

"Hey, Bense." Becky.

"Hey." I kept my eyes on the forest.

"What are you looking at?"

She leaned beside me and peered outside.

"Just the woods. Do you ever see the campfire smoke out there?"

She pulled back from the window and so did I. She was wearing thick green flannel pajamas and flip-flops, but her makeup and hair were still flawless.

"Yeah," she said. "Not very often. It's not far."

I looked into her eyes for a minute. Was she real? And if she was, was she one of the Society members who doled out punishments? Had she been lying to me?

I turned back to the window.

"What do you think it is?"

"I like to think that it's a town," she said. "But it's probably too close. Some people say it's guards."

The stars were almost entirely blotted out by clouds, but there was one dark patch of sky where a few bright lights twinkled through. I wished I could get out of the school and see them.

"You said you don't do security, right?"

"Right."

"But you have the contract, so your necklace can open doors, right?"

"Sure."

I turned to look at her—stared. I gazed into her eyes, studying the iris and the color and the eyelashes. Up close her eyes were bluer than they looked from far away, and right around the iris they were tinged with reddish brown. Everything about them—the delicate blood vessels, the streaks of color, the pink of her tear duct—seemed so real. So *human*.

Becky smiled awkwardly. "What?"

"Come with me," I said, and started toward the stairs.

She didn't move, so I turned back and grabbed her hand. "Come on."

We hurried down the empty stairs and made our way to the first floor and the big open foyer. I led her to the front doors.

"Can we go outside and look at the sky?" I asked.

A flash of concern crossed her face, but she hid it quickly. "Why?"

"I like being outside at night," I said. "I promise—we won't leave the front steps."

She looked at me, her lips pursed in thought.

"Listen," I said. "When I was back home, I was always outside at night. That's where I'd go to think. And I can't do it here."

Becky took a deep breath. Her eyes were suddenly somber and intense. "You promise? Don't lie to me."

"I promise," I said. "All I want to do is stand out there— we'll be right next to the door."

She moved toward the door. It buzzed and clicked, and she pushed it open.

We stepped out and stood side by side, looking at the forest.

It was colder than it appeared from the window. Becky folded her arms tightly, her shoulders raised as she tried to fend off the chill.

It smelled good out here. Completely different from inside the school, but also unlike the cold nights back home. Fresh and earthy. For a moment I thought I got a whiff of wood smoke, but couldn't be sure.

Freedom. I felt free.

"I need to ask you a question," I said.

Her arm touched mine as she stood beside me. "Okay."

"Who decides the punishments?"

There was a pause. She seemed like she'd been expecting something else.

"The school," she finally said, as if it was obvious.

"Does Isaiah have anything to do with it?"

From the corner of my eye I saw her shake her head. "No. We get the list of punishments every morning, and then the teachers read them in class."

"They come on your computers?"

"Well, no. They come on Isaiah's computer," she said. "So, I was wrong. He distributes the list to the teachers to make the announcements. At least, that's what would happen with Laura, back when . . ."

Her voice trailed off.

I wanted to believe her. But she'd never believe me.

"What if—" I stopped myself. What was I going to say?

Becky turned to me. She was shivering now, but didn't move back toward the door.

"What if," I continued, "things here aren't what we think they are?"

She smiled, but it seemed sad. "What are they?"

"I don't know."

I looked down at her, her face pale in the dim light. I wanted to put my arm around her.

"We can go back inside," I finally said.

But Becky just stared at me, the smile gone from her face. Her eyes flashed out to the forest and then back to me.

"What time is it?" she finally asked.

I checked my watch. "Seven thirty."

"It feels later," she said, staring out at the cold, dark forest.

"We can go in. Your feet have to be freezing."

She nodded absently and exhaled long and slow, her breath a puff of gray in the cold air.

"I want to show you something," she said, and motioned for me to follow her. Before I could say anything she was down the steps and heading across the lawn. I jogged after her to catch up.

"Where are we going?"

"I want to show you something," Becky repeated. We were going around the front of the school, walking past the deep window wells. The last time I'd been outside in the dark, I'd been right here, with a girl. I could see it all, replaying over and over.

I tried to push it away, to focus on something else. The distant hum of a four-wheeler engine. The crunch of the frosted grass under my shoes. The swirling clouds of frozen breath that escaped Becky's lips.

She led me to the corner of the school. Directly above us was the boys' dorm, but no one could have seen us. We were too close to the building.

She stepped into the garden and crouched down. I didn't see anything. Just the foundation—bricks and cement and dirt. It was too dark to make out any details.

"I had the groundskeeping contract once," she said, her voice trembling slightly. "A long time ago, before the gangs. A bunch of the girls bid on it together—me and Laura and Carrie and . . . some others you never met."

She took my hand and pressed it against something at the base of the wall. It was ice cold. Metal.

"Sorry," she said. "It's too dark to read it, but can you feel the numbers with your fingers?"

It was some kind of pipe jutting out of the cement, and I could tell there were raised bumps, but they were rough and uneven with rust and age. I couldn't guess the numbers.

"What is it?" I asked.

"Eighteen ninety-three," she said. "Around the bottom side of the pipe it says Steffen Metalworks, but you have to lie down in the garden to read it."

"What does it mean?"

Becky stood, shivering now. "Let's get back inside."

I followed her. "Does that mean this place was built in 1893?"

"The pipe is from 1893," she said.

"What was in New Mexico in 1893?"

"No idea," she said, rubbing her arms to stay warm.

"But there wasn't much. There wasn't much in Arizona in 1893—mining towns and Catholic missions and Native Americans. Probably the same for here."

"Maybe they just used an old pipe when they were building this."

We climbed the stairs, and the door unlocked for her. Warmth poured out of the foyer as we stepped inside.

"Maybe," she said, turning to look at me. Her cheeks were red from cold. She lowered her voice, even though no one was in sight. "But either way, this building is really old, and it seems designed to be Maxfield Academy. Even the elevators don't look like a recent addition."

"What are you saying?"

"People have been here for a long time. A really long time."

I shook my head. "That doesn't make any sense."

Becky's trademark smile came back. "Since when does anything here make sense?"

I almost told her, right there. I almost spit it all out.

But there's a difference between believing that the building was really old and believing that one of our friends was a robot.

I needed to show her. I had to find a way.

I lay awake that night, staring at Mason's bunk above me. I wasn't going to be able to convince anyone with words. I knew that. And I wasn't going to be able to figure things out by just observing.

I looked at my watch. 11:56 P.M.

Jumping out of bed, I hurried to my closet and pulled out my minicomputer. Bidding on the contracts ended at midnight.

I'd never bid on anything before. That was done by Curtis for the gang. But we all had access. I clicked on groundskeeping and entered a bid of one point. Then I clicked on security and did the same thing. I waited until 11:59, and hit Save.

There was going to be hell to pay in the morning.

CHAPTER TWENTY-TWO

I was shaken awake. Curtis and Carrie were standing over me.

"What did you do?" Curtis whispered, his voice harsh and angry.

I looked to the window. It was still completely dark outside. My head was foggy from too little sleep.

"What's going on?" I said.

"Benson, do you realize what you've done?" Carrie said, her arms folded across her chest. She was still in her pajamas. Curtis was just wearing a T-shirt and shorts.

"The contracts," I said, coming out of my sleepy daze.

"Yes, the contracts." Curtis glanced toward the door.

"I bid on some contracts."

I heard Mason shift on the upper bunk, and then his feet swung over the side. "You did *what*? Which ones?"

"Security," Carrie said, "and groundskeeping."

Mason whistled. "Please tell me he didn't win the bid. Fish, you're an idiot."

"Of course he did," she answered, taking a deep breath.

"He bid one point for each."

"Tell me it was an accident," Curtis said, though in his voice I could hear that he knew it wasn't. "Tell me that you hit the wrong thing, or you were goofing around and accidentally pressed Save."

I stood and walked to my closet. I'd ordered more supplies last night, figuring this was my last chance. They hadn't come. *Crap.*

"Well?" Carrie said.

I looked at her and shook my head. "No. Not an accident. How did you get in here?"

Curtis stepped toward me. "Benson, you don't understand what you've done. Hasn't anyone told you about the truce we have with the gangs? Haven't they told you why we needed one?"

"I had to do it," I said. "They can have the contracts back later. Heck, I have lots of points. I'll buy them whatever they need."

"No," Curtis said again. "The truce wasn't just like we got together at lunch and flipped a coin. There were fights. Riots. You've seen the graveyard."

"People died," Carrie said. She turned from me and walked to the window.

I looked up at Mason, but he just shook his head, his lips pursed.

"We have to get all the V's up," Curtis said. He pointed

to Mason. "Start going around, but be quiet. I don't even want to think about what would have happened if Havoc or the Society had checked the bids before Carrie."

Mason nodded and rubbed his face. "Where are we meeting?"

Curtis looked over at Carrie, but she was still staring out the window.

"Downstairs," he finally said. "First floor, maintenance room."

Mason understood something from Curtis's words that I didn't—his eyes went wide and he paused, thinking, before he hopped down from the bunk.

As Mason was pulling on a pair of socks, Curtis spoke. "Make sure they all get dressed. Jeans or something, not uniforms. And good shoes." Mason nodded.

"What could happen?" I asked. I wanted to tell them what I was planning, but it was too soon—I had only one chance, and I didn't dare blow it. I had to wait until the outside doors were unlocked—until I could open them. I had those contracts now.

Carrie turned back to me, her eyes burning. She didn't say anything.

"We'll go get the girls," Curtis said. "You get to the maintenance room, Benson. We have to find a way to fix this."

The two of them went for the door, but he turned back,

looking me in the eyes. "If any of the V's get hurt because of this it's going to be on your head. Got that?"

I nodded.

I got dressed quickly, wearing my Steelers sweatshirt and the cargo pants—stuffing the pockets with everything I could. The radios, a little bit of food, the binoculars. The three pepper spray grenades. I wished I had more. As I quietly headed out into the hall, a few of the other V's were groggily getting out of bed. Hector's eyes met mine as I passed his door, but he didn't look upset. Mason must not have told him.

Honestly, I hadn't expected this. I knew that the other gangs would be mad, and I figured that I'd probably get a beating for it, but I wasn't expecting gang war.

The door at the end of the hall was propped open with a book, so I didn't make any noise as I opened it and left.

There were no lights on anywhere, only the faint glow of obscured moonlight coming in the windows. I hurried as quickly as I could in the dark and jogged to the front doors. They were still locked, even now that I owned the contracts that would let me outside. I held my watch up to the window to read it. It was almost five. I'd seen Mouse jogging on the track as early as six.

There were footsteps above me as more of the V's came down. Leaving the front doors, I headed for the maintenance room. I assumed Curtis wanted to meet there because only the V's could access it. It would be safe, but it wouldn't give us any way out.

I was the first there. The door buzzed and unlocked, and I went in and flipped the light switch. The room was mostly empty, with a few folding chairs on the wide cement floor. On one wall hung dozens of tools—wrenches, hammers, and saws of all shapes—and the other wall was taken up by three large cabinets filled with paint, cleaners, and glues. A big red metal tool chest sat near the door. I set my bag and backpack behind it.

The guys were the first to arrive, dressed but bleary-eyed. Joel was wearing sandals—I wondered whether he would regret that later.

Hector sat down against the wall. "Do you know what's going on?"

I looked over at Mason. His face was flat and emotionless as he stared back at me.

"I'll tell you," I finally said. "But let's wait till the girls get here."

"I'm not running," Joel said. "Not now. Not without a plan."

"That's not what this is about," I said, only telling half the truth. If everything went well we might run, but that was a long way away. First I had to persuade my gang not to feed me to the wolves, and then hope we could survive until six.

"Are we at war again?" Hector asked.

I didn't answer, but stepped to the doorway and looked out. I heard Mason say yes. Hector swore and reached above him, taking a hammer off the wall. He held it in his hands tightly, staring at the floor.

A few minutes later the girls appeared at the end of the hall. They were carrying backpacks, so Curtis must have given them more direction than Mason gave the boys. I stepped back from the door as they entered, but the glares on their faces as they passed me were evidence enough that they'd been told about the contracts. A few refused to even look at me. When they were all in the room, Curtis took a final check of the hall, paused to listen, and then closed the door.

Curtis looked at Mason. "Everybody know?" Mason shook his head.

"Well." Curtis took a deep breath, watching the nervous, tired faces around him. Almost everyone was standing, waiting for an explanation. "I guess we'll start with what we know and then we'll figure out what we can do about it." He glanced at me, and then back at the V's. "Last night Benson made one-point bids on grounds and security."

Immediately, the guys who hadn't heard the news began talking. Curtis cut them off.

"I'm going to give him a chance to speak in his defense," Curtis said, "but first we should know what's coming. He's pissed off both gangs. They probably won't be working together, but they'll both be after us."

"After him," Hector said, pointing at me. "Why should they be after the rest of us?"

Curtis nodded, his mouth shut tight. "Well, that's what we need to figure out. The V's take care of their own." He looked at me. "We'll give you a chance to explain." He turned back to the group. "But first, how many of you were here before the truce?"

All but five raised their hands. Anna was one of the five, and she looked terrified. I'm sure she now wished she'd never switched sides.

"For the benefit of those who weren't," Curtis said, glancing again at me. "It was bad. We had the truce to end the fighting, and all of us knew what would happen if the truce was broken."

Anna timidly raised her hand. "How bad is bad?"

Mason spoke. "You've all seen the graveyard. People died."

Curtis's face was ice cold. "Four died. Three in fights and one stabbed while she slept. Twelve others were sent to detention. Two haven't ever been accounted for. Just disappeared."

Anna lowered her head and started to cry.

Curtis turned to me. "Talk."

I looked around at the faces of my fellow V's. Some were

scared, others angry. Carrie stared at the floor.

"I bid on the contracts last night," I began, my heart pounding. I'd expected to feel like I was standing in front of a firing squad, but it actually felt the other way around, like I held their lives in my hands.

"I bid on those contracts because they're the ones that have access to the outside doors." I paused, watching their faces. I'm sure that some of them expected that I meant I was going to make a run for it and wanted the Society guys locked inside. It might come to that.

But as I watched them my eyes caught Rosa's, and I was suddenly gripped by fear. Any of the people in front of me could be androids. What would they do? Stop me? Kill me? Send me to detention?

"Anyway," I said, taking a breath and trying to get my thoughts back. "I know that ever since I've gotten here I've been a real pain in the butt. I know that a lot of people blame me for a lot of things—and I blame myself for a lot of things, too."

My eyes darted from face to face, hoping for some kind of understanding, but I didn't see any. I looked at Mason. His expression was somber and cold.

"I don't expect you people to trust me, because I don't think that I've earned your trust. I've acted stupid and stubborn." I looked over at Hector, and then to Curtis. "And I know that you guys think I'm still doing it."

Carrie finally interrupted. "Will you just tell us why already?"

I turned to her. Her hair was uncombed and there were dark circles under her eyes. I expected anger but saw only fear.

"No," I said, and the group immediately began grumbling. "But," I shouted over the noise, "all I want is an hour. Just help me until the outside doors unlock. I promise that I'm not going to run. If, after I'm done, you don't agree with me, then I will leave the V's. The other gangs can have their war with me, not you."

"They'll kill you," Gabby said. "Everyone needs a gang."

I shook my head. "If I fail at this, then I'll be going to detention anyway." I looked at Curtis. "But I promise—I promise—that two hours from now the V's will not be the target of anybody."

He stared at me, his face still tight and serious. He was almost like the father of the group, and he had to be feeling a tangle of emotions: fear for the others, anger at me, maybe even a yearning to be free himself.

"We'll put it to a vote," he said. "I'm not going to decide this for anybody." He looked at the group and then checked his watch. "Do we give him two hours, or do we turn him over now? All in favor of giving him time?"

I held my breath. I felt nauseated and dizzy. And, for a moment, no one moved. Finally, Carrie raised her hand.

She still didn't look at me, but she spoke. "What's wrong with you people? You know what'll happen to him."

Hector raised his voice. "But what about us?"

It was Curtis who answered next, his words slow. "We can stall for two hours, I think. We can talk that long."

The room was quiet, and breathing felt a little easier, though my muscles were still tense.

Carrie spoke. "You said that in two hours we'll either turn you over or agree with you. What happens if we agree with you?"

I paused. "I don't know. We'll see. But if you can agree with me, then hopefully everyone else will, too."

There was a knock on the door—a pounding fist—and everyone flinched.

Curtis pointed at the wall of tools. "Grab something, guys. But don't start anything. Let's see if we can keep it calm." He moved to the large toolbox and shoved it over to the door, almost blocking it completely.

He touched the doorknob and then looked at me. "You need to get outside, right?"

"Yeah."

"Okay." He motioned for the V's to move to the other side of the room, away from the door. Most of them were armed now, some with hammers, others with wrenches. I'd taken a crowbar from the wall.

Curtis turned the knob just enough that it unlatched,

and the door immediately slammed into the toolbox. The box was holding, but three of the guys put their weight against it, just in case. The door was only open about three inches.

"What the hell are you doing?"

It was Oakland.

I looked at my watch. 5:40 A.M.

Curtis was helping hold the box, and standing out of the way of the door so no one could hit him through the opening. "Oakland? It's Curtis."

"We had a truce," Oakland said. Behind him, the rest of Havoc screamed and swore.

"I know we had a truce," Curtis said. "Give us a minute to figure out what happened."

"Is he in there with you?"

"Who?"

I looked at Curtis and shook my head. "I'm here."

Oakland let out a string of profanity and pounded on the door. "That's our contract, Fisher. You stole it."

"We're going to sort this out," Curtis said. "But you have to give us some time."

"There's nothing to sort out," Oakland yelled. "You broke the truce. You're going to pay."

"Give us an hour."

"What's going to change in an hour? The V's are the smallest gang. You've pissed off the Society, too."

"Let's meet," Curtis said. "You, me, Isaiah."

There was a sudden surge against the door, and the toolbox slipped an inch. Five more V's jumped to brace it. The others stood poised, nervously holding their weapons and hoping Havoc didn't break through.

"Hold on," Curtis shouted. "Is Isaiah out there? Get him over here."

A chunk of something flew through the crack in the door, smacking into the peg board with a crack. A handsaw and T square crashed to the floor.

"Curtis," another voice said.

"Isaiah." Curtis's voice was still even, but he had a look of desperation in his eyes. "Let's meet. You, me, and Oakland."

"And me," said a girl angrily. Mouse.

"Yes, of course. Let's talk and figure this out."

Isaiah's face was close to the crack, probably so he could speak without shouting. "What is there to talk about? You broke the truce."

"So that's it, Isaiah? What about the no-fighting rules? Don't you care about those, or do you only care about the truce?"

"The truce is what keeps order around here. Do you want to go back to the way things used to be?"

"I know," Curtis said. He motioned for me to take his place holding the toolbox. As I did, he cautiously moved over so he could see out the door. "I want to keep the truce, and I want to keep the order. Let's talk about this and see what we can do."

The shouting didn't stop on the other side, but Isaiah, Oakland, and Mouse didn't answer for a minute. I watched the door. I didn't want to look at anyone; I didn't want anyone looking at me. I hadn't expected this to be so bad.

"You come out," Oakland finally said.

Curtis looked back at the V's. "Okay. But here's the deal. You guys back away from the door. The V's are safe until we're done talking. Got it?"

The noise died down as the other gangs talked. "Fine, but here's *our* deal. Carrie comes, too."

"No." Curtis was staring at her now, horrified. Tears spilled down her face.

"Yes," Oakland said. "I don't know what crap you're trying to pull, but I don't want you playing the martyr while everyone tries to run. Carrie comes with us, too, and if your gang tries anything stupid . . ." He didn't finish, but he didn't have to. Curtis was glaring at me now, and I wondered whether he was just going to throw me out into the hall. Finally, Carrie stepped forward.

"I'll go."

Curtis grabbed the front of my shirt. His voice was a low, animal-like growl. "I am not going to let anything happen to her, got that?"

I nodded.

He stared at me, his eyes boring down into mine, and his teeth clenched. Carrie reached over and took his hand.

"Okay," Curtis called over his shoulder, his gaze still on me. "We're coming." Finally, he turned toward the V's, his eyes going from face to face. "Hector, you're in charge. Keep 'em safe."

Hector nodded solemnly. His fingers were tight around the claw hammer in his hands. He looked just as ready to attack me with it as defend me.

Curtis stepped to the door. "We're all coming out. All the V's. Gangs'll stay away from each other, and we meet in the foyer. That work?"

There was a pause. "That works."

"Okay. Everybody back away."

All of us were tense, watching Curtis and Carrie as they waited at the door. This could all be a trick—they could attack as soon as we came out—and all of us knew it. Curtis's and Carrie's hands were tight together, their knuckles white.

Curtis motioned to us, and we pushed the toolbox away from the door. Hector moved up right behind our unarmed leaders, and the rest of us followed as they slowly opened the door. The hall in front was clear. They stepped out.

I glanced down the back hall. I could see the outside

doors. No one was blocking them.

"We're coming," Curtis said. "You have Carrie and me as collateral. The V's are going to wait outside." He motioned to Hector, who immediately began hurrying us down the hall toward the doors.

Shouting swelled behind us, and I heard Curtis yell over the noise. "They're not escaping. They're just going where you can't get them while we talk."

We ran to the doors. I checked my watch. 5:51 A.M.

Mason was the first to reach them, a pipe wrench hanging in his hand. There was a buzz and click, and he pushed the door open.

Chapter Twenty-three

Hector waited as the rest of the V's ran outside. I was at the back of the group, and when I reached him I paused.

"Well?" he said, scowling. "Whatever you're doing, you'd better hurry."

"Yeah." I hefted the crowbar in my hand and then sprinted for the incinerator and the door. I hadn't been back to it since everything had happened—I hadn't wanted to touch it, or relive it. I'd been replaying the whole thing in my mind enough as it was.

I stopped in front of it, the incinerator to my right. The door didn't look like anything special. It was metal, painted a warm brown to match the building's brick. The knob was silver, round and smooth, and one of the unlocking sensors was fastened to the brick above the jamb.

Behind it was a scene I didn't want to revisit, but I knew I had to. It was the only way to persuade them to run—the only way to get anyone to believe. They had to know what was going on. They had to be scared.

"So what do we do?" Hector was standing beside me now, his breath puffing in cold clouds.

"I'm going to break in."

"What do you need me to do?"

I looked at him, surprised. "Hector—"

He interrupted, gesturing back toward the doors we'd just left. "Just tell me what to do. We only have an hour."

I nodded. He didn't want to help me; he wanted to help Curtis and Carrie.

I stepped up to the door, which fit snugly into the jamb; there was hardly any gap between. I tested putting the wedged tip of the crowbar in the crack, but it didn't go far.

"Here," he said, holding up his hammer.

I held the crowbar in place and he tapped it with the hammer, trying to push the edge into the gap. But it wasn't going far. After a dozen taps, he shook his head. "It's not working."

I knocked on the metal, and it resonated. The door was hollow. That was something. My worry had been that the door wasn't a regular door, that it was some kind of reinforced vault. But, it seemed perfectly normal.

"Stand back," I said. He moved away.

I swung the crowbar down at the knob. It clanged loudly and bounced off. The vibrations in my injured arm stung viciously, but I tried to ignore them. I looked down at the knob. A small dent, but that was all.

"Keep trying," someone said. I didn't look to see who.

I hit it again and again, banging down on the metal handle until it was bent and scratched.

I had to get inside. I didn't even care about the consequences of going back to face the other gangs now—I needed to show them this.

"Mason," Hector called. "Get over here."

I stopped for a breath. I was sweating now, overheated under my sweatshirt even though it was freezing outside. As I watched Mason approach, I saw the others. All the V's were standing behind us.

Hector directed Mason to the door. "Your turn."

He looked surprised, but he couldn't have been more shocked than I was.

"You won't be in trouble," he assured him. "They'll think Benson did it."

He pointed up at the building. "Did you see them?"

On the floor above us a dozen faces were pressed against the windows, trying to look down and figure out what we were doing.

"Just do it," Hector said, looking back at the door.

A little smile appeared on Mason's face. He raised his heavy pipe wrench and swung it onto the knob. His first blow skidded a few inches down the metal door, scraping a silver gash in the paint. I watched him as he pounded it again and again, raising his arms, taking a breath, and then slamming it down.

And suddenly I was watching Dylan with his pipe, relentlessly beating Jane. I bent in half and then fell to a crouch, trying not to throw up.

Gabby jogged over from the rest of the V's. While Mason worked, she spoke to Hector.

"They're trying to force the door," she said. "They're coming out here."

"Who is?"

Gabby's eyes were wide, and her chin was trembling. "The other gangs. I don't know who. But I can hear them."

Hector turned to the others. "Tapti, you and Gabby watch the door. If they break through, get back here as fast as you can." He directed two others toward the far corner of the building to watch for someone coming that way, and then sent two more fifty yards back from us to watch the windows. "Benson's turn again."

I took the pipe wrench from Mason—it was heavier and he was having more luck with it—and began smashing the knob again. He'd done a lot of damage—it was bent down at a forty-five-degree angle. I hit it three times but then asked for the crowbar back. I'd noticed the bent knob had folded away from the door—there was a half-inch gap.

Mason helped me position the bar, jamming in the sharp wedge, and then we both pried with all our strength. It felt so close.

Hector jumped in and then called for Joel.

I heard a shout somewhere and for a moment all three of us stopped to look. We couldn't see anything.

I reached in my pocket and pulled out the grenades.

"Here," I said, shoving them into Hector's hands. "They're filled with pepper spray."

A smile crossed his face for an instant, but then he pointed at the door again. "You'd better hurry."

He left in a run.

"Come on," I said, turning back to the knob and yanking again on the crowbar. The strain was sending bolts of pain across my chest and ribs, but I continued. Maybe I was imagining it, but it felt like it was moving ever so slightly.

"They're coming," someone behind us said. I felt the pressure in the bar lessen as Joel turned to look.

"One more time," I urged. "Come on."

Dozens of voices were yelling now, and I was suddenly aware that all of the V's were close, surrounding us. Guarding us.

I pushed with all my strength, my arms and legs quivering as I struggled to move the bar. Joel put a foot on the door for leverage and Mason grunted.

With a pop, all three of us fell, the crowbar flipping and launching the broken doorknob in the air.

The door was still closed, leaving a hole where the knob used to be. Unfortunately, a horizontal bar crossed through the hole—the door was still locked.

I heard Skiver's voice, and he was close. It didn't sound like anyone had started fighting yet, though.

I picked up the crowbar and looked at Mason and Joel. They didn't know what to do.

Just as I had raised the crowbar to ram into the hole, I heard someone say, "Benson. Wait!" I lowered the bar and looked.

Rosa was behind me. I felt my body tense, and my grip tightened on the crowbar.

"If you smash it you'll bend the locking mechanism and you'll never get it open," she said. Pushing past me, she knelt at the door, peering in the hole. She pulled out a pocketknife and unfolded the screwdriver.

I looked back at the crowd around us. It was mostly Havoc, but there were a few Society kids there, too. No one had started fighting yet—none of the leaders were there— but they all were screaming at one another.

Rosa had only been fiddling with the knob for thirty seconds when I heard her say, "All done."

She stood, pulling on the door with two fingers. It swung open.

I stared at her. Wasn't she supposed to stop me? Was she an android setting a trap, or was I wrong about her?

At the movement of the door, the mob dropped into low murmurs. Even the V's, who had been ready for a fight, turned enough to see what was behind the door.

I suddenly felt completely overwhelmed. I couldn't walk down there alone.

"Mason," I said, motioning him over.

He stood in front of me, peering cautiously down the half-open door. His voice was quiet and trembling. "What's down there, Fish?"

I stared. Everything was silent.

I glanced at him. "Give me a second?"

He took a long, deep breath. "Yeah. But not much more than that. They're not going to stay calm for long."

"Okay."

I stepped around the door, almost not wanting to touch it. The hallway was lit like before, with the dim blue glow of an old fluorescent bulb. The concrete walls seemed wider than before, and the ceiling higher.

It was terrifying.

I walked slowly, the noises of the students behind me vanishing as my mind focused on what I might find. I needed some sign of what had happened, but I knew the best I could hope for was the computer. There were computer experts in the school; even if they could only pull up information about MODEL: JANE 117C then I might be able to convince them.

But part of me suddenly didn't want to find anything. I could barely breathe as I walked, the memories of that night pouring through my mind. The awkward way she'd limped on obviously broken legs, the deadness of her eyes, the voice that wasn't hers.

The hall was coming to an end, and I stopped, not wanting to enter the room.

But the V's couldn't hold the others off forever. I needed to get back there. I'd promised no one would get hurt.

I stepped into the room.

"Jane," I gasped.

She was still there, exactly where I'd left her. How long had it been? Two weeks? Three? More?

I couldn't walk to her. There was no way my legs would carry me.

I was suddenly aware of tears running down my face.

There was the scuffle of footsteps behind me, and I felt a hand on my arm.

"Benson." Hector spoke, but he was behind me in the hall and couldn't have seen her body. It was Mason who entered first.

He inhaled sharply. When he finally spoke, his voice was barely a whisper. "What the hell . . . ?"

I heard more people enter the hallway above us and felt compelled to get to Jane before they did, so we crossed the room to her body.

Jane was lying down now. She wore the same dress, torn and stained with blood. With the exception of the blue lighting that cast a deathly pall on her skin, she looked asleep.

I caught a lingering scent of her perfume—vanilla and roses—and had to turn away.

The other V's were just coming into the room, and the noise from the hall was getting loud. Mason swore. He'd seen the ear. Maybe the cable was still plugged in. I didn't want to look.

The crowd was staring and quiet, and as new people came into the room they almost immediately froze.

"This is Jane," I said, talking through my tears. "Laura and Dylan killed her, like I told you. But she came down here that night." My chest was tight and I could hardly get air to speak. I gritted my teeth and looked down at the concrete floor, not wanting to see the horror on anyone else's face.

"Is she dead?" someone asked. I knew what he meant, but I could hardly bring myself to respond. I'd tried to convince myself that this was simple, that I could think about it rationally, not emotionally, but I couldn't.

"Yes," I breathed. "And no." I raised my hand and motioned them over, and the group—probably forty students by now—slowly crossed the room toward her body.

I forced myself to look.

Someone had been there. Half of the skin and hair on Jane's head had been peeled back revealing a steel skull.

Half a dozen cables now ran to the computer, and a tray of tools—scalpels, tweezers, tiny screwdrivers, and others I didn't recognize—lay on the table next to her head.

I stood there, not moving as they passed around me. One by one I heard the gasps and shrieks as they saw the exposed metal of Jane's android skull. Whispers bounced through the crowd as the ones at the front passed the news to the back and ones in the back refused to believe.

One of the girls pushed past me and ran up the hallway and out of the building. I wanted to follow her—to run away and never think of this place again—but instead I moved to the back of the room, crouched down, and leaned against the wall. I closed my eyes. Things would be different now.

Chapter Twenty-four

More people were entering the room now, but many had already left. Gabby ran for the door but didn't quite make it out of the hall before throwing up. Most of the V's were still there, standing near Jane's body defensively, like they had to protect her from the onlookers. Like she was still one of us.

She was never one of us.

I closed my eyes and put my face in my hands. No one could argue anymore that things here were pretty good and that we should make the most of it. Things here were a lie. We couldn't trust one another. No one could have friends. No one could be in love.

A hand touched my shoulder, and I looked up to see Gabby gesturing over to the hallway. The gang leaders had arrived.

The five of them—Curtis, Carrie, Oakland, Mouse, and Isaiah—all stood together, cautiously surveying the room.

I stood, moving to the crowd around Jane's body. "Hey, guys, clear out for a second."

Slowly and numbly, the group filed toward the door. Some of their eyes lingered on Jane while others simply stared at the floor. Mason moved to the far side of the room, by the tall cabinets, and leaned against the wall.

Isaiah was the first to move, leaving the four others behind and striding up to Jane's body. "What's the big deal? We already knew she was dead."

I grabbed him by the arm—harder than was necessary, but I wanted him to feel it—and yanked him to the other side of the table. Then, my hand on the back of his neck, I shoved his face close to Jane's torn ear.

I couldn't see his eyes, but all his struggling suddenly stopped.

The metal was as visible and gleaming as it had been that night, but the small lights I'd seen by the cable ports were now dark.

I shoved Isaiah away and then motioned for the other four. Curtis's and Carrie's hands were clenched tight. They walked ahead, while Oakland and Mouse followed behind. I moved out of the way to give the four of them a clear look.

Oakland swore, almost inaudibly. Mouse's eyes jumped from Jane's body to me, back to Jane. Carrie timidly reached her hand out and touched Jane's arm with her fingertips.

Curtis looked up at me. "How long have you known about this?"

"Since that night."

"Why didn't you tell anyone?"

I opened my mouth to speak, and my voice cracked. "It was Jane," I managed to say. "Who would have believed me?"

"You should have said something," Mouse snapped. "We deserved to know."

I took a breath. "You would have trusted me about this?"

"What's that supposed to mean?" she said, but her voice was weak.

Oakland's fingers had followed the cables from Jane's head to the computer beside her. The screen was dark.

I stepped closer to the table. I wanted to touch Jane's hand but couldn't bring myself to. "It means that if I was fooled by Jane—and I was *completely* fooled by Jane—then who else in this school might be a . . . like her."

Oakland's eyes met mine, his face pale. No one said anything, though I saw Oakland steal a quick glance at Mouse.

To cut the silence I began talking. I told them the entire story—Laura and Dylan coming out to find us, the attack, my attempts at resuscitation, and then the awkward and terrifying trip down into this room.

"What did the computer say?" Oakland asked. "When she plugged in."

"It was some kind of damage report. It listed a bunch of code numbers—I don't know what they meant."

He turned to the computer and touched one of the keys. The screen flickered and then lit up, as though it had only been on standby.

I stepped closer to read it, looking over Mouse's shoulder as the five leaders clustered around the screen. Hector, behind us, asked what it said.

"Just numbers," Curtis answered. "A list of codes."

The entire screen was filled with the same types of numbers I'd seen before, when Jane had first plugged herself in. Except for the last line. "At the end," I told Hector, "it says 'Recommended Action: Transfer and Permanent Deactivation Due to Extensive and Irreparable Damages.'"

Carrie breathed a soft, heartbroken moan and put her hand to her eyes.

Suddenly Mason gasped. "Holy—Guys, you'd better look at this."

We all turned.

He was facing the tall cabinets, staring at something inside.

Mouse was the first to cross to him. "What is it?"

He swung the door open. "See for yourself."

It was dark, but the shape inside was unmistakable. It was a person.

Dylan. He was strapped against a board, almost

vertical, with thick nylon belts holding him up—wrapped at his knees, waist, and chest. His eyes were open, but they were as lifeless as Jane's. A cable ran from his ear as well, plugged in to a small digital panel on the side of the cabinet. However, unlike hers, his ear looked as though it had been cut away carefully.

Oakland swore again, but it was Isaiah who seemed the most distraught, stepping forward and peering closely into Dylan's face, inspecting the hole in his head.

Mason, suddenly shaken into awareness, began throwing the other cabinets open. There were four of them, and two had the same board inside, with leather straps ready to hold another person—another android. The other two cabinets were locked.

"What about Laura?" Isaiah asked, looking at us, dumbfounded. His mouth hung open slightly, and his eyes were wide and expectant.

"Maybe she wasn't one of them," I said. The presence of Dylan destroyed my old theory. Dylan was relatively new to the school. I'd have to check my chart, but I was pretty sure he'd only been here eight or nine months. "Not everybody is, I don't think."

Mouse's lips curled into a disgusted snarl. "Well, I'm not." She slammed the cabinet closed on Dylan and spun to face the other leaders. "What about the rest of you?"

They began to protest, but I shouted over them. "There's

no way to tell," I said. "I've been thinking about this for weeks. Jane could bleed. I mean, I kissed her and never had any idea that she was . . . like that. It's not like we can cut off everyone's ears just to check."

We stood in silence for several seconds. I thought I saw Carrie's eyes flick nervously to Curtis, but then she just stared at the cabinet.

"Anyone know how to make a metal detector?" Mason asked.

No one answered.

"There are all those old textbooks in the basement," I said. "Maybe there's one on electronics."

"What about the X-ray machine?" Curtis asked.

I shook my head. "We have to send the film off to get developed. The school does that."

Isaiah nodded absently, deep in his own thoughts. Mouse's eyes were fierce, her teeth clenched. Oakland just looked mad, like he wanted to hit something. Carrie seemed dead, no emotion at all, and Curtis's face was contorted and distraught. As I watched him, he stared back at me for a long time. Finally, he spoke.

"We need to talk to everyone."

Isaiah looked up. "But what do we tell them?"

"The truth," Curtis said.

Isaiah took off his glasses and rubbed his eyes. "No one is going to trust anyone now."

Oakland snorted. "Like they really did before."

Curtis's eyes met mine. "The V's trust each other," he said. I nodded, even though it was more hope than truth. Oakland was right. No one could trust anyone anymore.

I went back up the hallway. Outside, the sun was beginning to rise. Most people were out on the track, having moved out of the building's shadow and into the warm light.

We walked in silence, everyone but Carrie and Curtis separate and alone. And even the two of them, though their hands were still together, seemed farther apart.

Becky came toward us, speaking in an injured whisper. "The school's locked. Even the V's can't get in." She looked at me, her eyes swollen and red. She wanted to say something. I wanted to say something, but didn't know what.

I turned away and looked back at the door. The brown paint now bore long white scratches and dents. It swung in the gentle breeze, closing but then bouncing open again without anything to latch it shut.

Mouse emerged slowly, gazing at the waiting students. After a moment, she walked over to us.

"Oakland's trying to work on the computer," she said blankly, not really directing her words to any one of us in particular.

Isaiah seemed to be waiting for something, but when no one said anything, he turned to the group of students.

"First of all," he began, "there is no reason to panic. What we've seen is strange and different, but it doesn't—" He was cut off by the shouts and jeers from the crowd.

"Shut up, Isaiah! You're probably one of them!"

Mouse and Curtis looked at each other, and then Curtis pointed at me. "You might as well go ahead."

I frowned, but Mouse seemed to have no objection. Isaiah was obviously annoyed.

I stepped forward. "We don't know much about what's going on. When I first found out about Jane, I thought she might be the only one. But, just now, Mason found Dylan. He was one, too."

There were gasps from the crowd, and a few people began talking. But the conversations seemed to stall and end quickly, as though they were wondering whether they were actually talking to friends or enemies.

"We don't have any way to tell if there are other androids among us," I said. Several visibly flinched at the word. "I don't suppose anyone knows how to build a metal detector?"

I scanned the crowd, but no one raised a hand.

"We can't tell," I said, "but I don't think we can let that stop us. I think it's time that we got out of here for good. I've always thought that we could do it if we worked together. Let's all go, now, today. We can get over the wall easy enough—through the culvert or knock down some trees." I looked over at Isaiah. "I've got the security contract right now and I promise you it will not be enforced."

No one seemed to jump at my suggestion, but no one protested it either, so I continued, "The highway is maybe fifty miles from here, and if we keep moving we can cover that in a couple days. From there we should be able to flag down some help."

Skiver shouted, "Any one of you could be robots. The minute we try to leave, you'll kill the rest of us."

Joel was next. "What about water? Fifty miles without any water—that's suicide."

Others were yelling, but I waved my arms to shush them. "Our only other option is go back inside, if they let us. Don't you guys get it? Whatever we're here for is ruined. We've always said they're either training us or testing us. Now we know about the androids, and that screws up whatever experiment they're doing. Do you think they're just going to let us go back to normal?"

Isaiah turned. "But what about once you got over the wall? They kill people out there. They killed Lily, didn't they? They've killed everyone who's gotten over."

"But not if there's all seventy of us," I insisted. "We need to go together, all of us at the same time."

His voice grew louder. "You haven't been here long enough to know, but there were fifteen who all left at the same time. They were all killed."

"Were they the fifteen who were here when Jane got here?" I asked. "We only know about those fifteen from Jane. She's the one who told us about them, and it might have been a lie. Besides, that was fifteen and we're seventy."

I let my words hang in the air, watching the faces in the crowd as they thought about what was said. All of their fears were legitimate—I knew that we needed water, and I knew that there had to be something out there—but we couldn't just go back to the school and pretend everything was normal.

"Wait a minute." It was Mason, his face twisted in confusion. "Why did Dylan attack Jane? Why would an android kill an android?"

I didn't have a good answer, but I guessed. "Maybe it's all part of their script—for whatever they're trying to do— they wanted to see what would happen if Jane was killed."

He listened, shaking his head, obviously not convinced. "That's weird."

Hector spoke. "It doesn't matter. I vote that we get out."

"No," Isaiah said, swinging both arms in front of him. "Listen. Whatever we're here for, there's a reason for it. The school needs us for something. Now we know the school's little secret, and maybe we can use that for leverage."

"You want us to negotiate?" I knew Isaiah was insane, but this was crazy even for him.

"Yes," he said. "Absolutely. Think about it. First, it's

313

safe. We can go back to the school, we can have food and water, we'll still be able to protect ourselves. Second, do you think it's easy for the school to bring all of us in here for their experiment? Maybe their plan isn't actually spoiled, and they can still use us—but now we can make some demands."

"Has the school ever responded to any of us?" I asked. "Has anyone ever asked a question and gotten an answer?"

"They'll have to now," Isaiah said.

I looked out at the crowd. "Let's put it to a vote. Who wants to go now?"

Nearly all of the V's raised their hands, and a handful from Havoc. No one from Society moved. There were only twenty-two total.

I couldn't believe it. After everything I'd shown them, they still couldn't take the risk. "We can get out of here if we do it together! If half of us leave and half stay then we're all dead. You people think you're keeping yourselves safe, but you're just keeping the rest of us in prison."

I spun on my heel and stormed off. They'd been in the school so long that they were afraid to leave, afraid to take any risks. And now they were condemning me to their same fate.

I walked to the edge of the woods, staring into the vast expanse of the trees. I could hear birds chirping as they warmed in the early sunlight. For them, this forest wasn't a prison but a home.

I stepped off the grass and into the brush. I'd tried to do everything right. I was trying to help everyone, but no one wanted my help. They were all too scared.

Without making a conscious decision, I trudged slowly into the forest and away from the school.

How were they going to negotiate? The idea was so stupid I should have hit Isaiah for it. We couldn't make demands on the school. All they had to do was cut off the food. How many missed meals would we endure before everyone broke? Or, how long would it be before the school decided that we were all useless now and they needed to get rid of us all and start over? How would they kill us? Poison the food? The air? Have a few of the androids slit our throats in our sleep?

I walked through one of the paintball fields, passing speckled trees and bunkers. It was the first one I'd played, back on my second day here.

We were their playthings. Somewhere, they were taking notes as they watched us follow their every order. *Benson Fisher reacts violently under stress—physically assaulting his classmates, damaging school property. How will he react if we lock the doors? If we cut off the food? If we kill his friends?*

I crossed the ribbon at the back of the field. It was rockier here, and the ground sloped upward sharply. I had to run, sliding backward in the loose rock with every step. A minute later, panting and exhausted, I reached the wall.

It was the same here as it was everywhere else—more than twice my height, with the nearby trees cleared so no one could climb over. I touched it. The brick was cold under my hand.

I sat on a rock and stared at the wall. There was no way over it without supplies or help. I could try to knock down another tree, but I knew they were right about crossing. I'd end up just like Lily.

I heard a rattle of stones behind me. Someone else was struggling up the slope. I listened without turning to look.

"Hey." It was Becky.

"Hey."

She walked to me, taking quick shallow breaths, and sat beside me on the rock.

"You're not running," she said.

I stared at the wall, and shook my head.

She didn't say anything, just sat there next to me. The sun hadn't hit this spot yet, blocked by the trees, and the air was cold. I was glad I had my sweatshirt. I hoped the school wouldn't decide to punish us by leaving the doors locked all day and all night. Though if they did, we could just go back into the room with Jane. They couldn't lock that one after what we'd done to it. At least we'd be out of the cold.

"I'm sorry," Becky finally said. "I wish you would have told me, but . . ."

"No," I said. "It's okay. I wouldn't have believed me. Some new guy shows up and starts telling you crazy things about a person you've known for a year. It's okay."

For a long time she sat next to me. Sometimes she'd take a breath like she was going to speak, but then stopped herself.

I stared at the wall. I was going to leave. I just had to figure out how.

"No one can trust anyone anymore," Becky said. She was rubbing her hands to keep them warm. "It's probably been like that for you for a while."

"Yeah." *And it sucks.*

"That's why you were making the list," she said.

I exhaled slowly and then rubbed my face. "Yeah. I figured that the androids had to have been here since the beginning. Like Jane."

She nodded.

"But now we've found Dylan," I continued. "So, that makes everything different."

"Right."

I looked at my watch. It wasn't even eight o'clock. It was going to be a long, cold day.

Becky shifted, turning her body toward me. I took my eyes off the wall and looked at her. She didn't have her usual perfect style—her brown hair was still skewed and flattened from sleep.

"I know that you can't trust me, Bense," she said, and then paused, looking down at her hands. "I just want you to know that I trust you."

"Does that mean that you're leaving the Society? Are you a V again?"

She exhaled and then looked into my eyes. "I'm whatever you are."

We sat in silence, staring at each other for what seemed like several minutes. Then Becky broke down, her body suddenly wracked in sobs. She fell against me and I held her. "I'm sorry," she cried, brokenhearted. "I really thought I was helping people."

"It's okay," I said. "It's okay."

Chapter Twenty-Five

We buried Jane as the sun was climbing the cold morning sky. Becky, Mason, and I went to the maintenance sheds—which thankfully still opened—and got some shovels. The rest of the V's soon joined us, and even a few people from the other gangs. We dug a new grave in the cemetery, and then Curtis and I lowered Jane's body into it.

Most of the flowers around the school had died weeks ago, but Becky gathered some pine boughs. And, instead of a headstone, we made a pile of rocks at the head of the grave, each mourner adding one.

Yes, Jane wasn't a real person. But she'd been real enough that we'd all loved her.

In the wintery silence, Oakland found me. I was sitting on the grass in the graveyard, my shovel still lying across my lap. Becky and a few of the other V's were with me, but no one had spoken for a long time.

"Did Jane have trouble with pop culture?"

Oakland's lips were tight together, and he was looking

thoughtfully at the ground as he spoke.

"You know," he went on, "like music and TV and stuff."

Gabby replied before I got a chance to. Her voice was trembling. "I used to make fun of her for it. She didn't know any of the bands I used to like."

I was going to add that she'd never heard of any movies, but Oakland spoke first.

"I couldn't get much out of that computer. I don't think it's networked, either. But I was able to get some system info from . . . from Jane. Most of it I didn't understand—mechanical stuff. But there were a couple memory upgrades in there. Some programmer made a note about uploading a patch to fix the 'pop culture problem.'"

So that was it. Whenever I quoted a movie to her, she didn't know about it because she hadn't been programmed to know it.

"The 'pop culture problem,'" Curtis repeated, staring at the freshly covered grave.

"They were trying to fix her so we wouldn't notice," I said, and then wished I hadn't spoken. It sounded too mean when it came out.

The group was quiet for a minute, and then Joel spoke. "So, who can name all the Harry Potter books?"

"Shut up," Curtis snapped. "That's the last thing we need."

"They said they fixed it," Oakland added.

The sun still wasn't quite at its peak when someone called us from the school steps. The doors were unlocked, and a meeting was about to begin.

The main foyer inside was ringed with students, mostly sitting against the walls or on the stairs. There were a few cardboard boxes of food that Havoc had dragged up from the cafeteria. Without any clear idea of what was going to happen, they didn't really feel compelled to fulfill their contracts, so they just left the unprepared food—some still frozen—for us to fend for ourselves. I don't think anyone complained.

It was Isaiah who had called the meeting, and he sat on a stone bench by the front door, a notebook in hand. We were going to be discussing our negotiations with the school. The room was silent, everyone determined to hear every word.

Isaiah raised an eyebrow when he saw Becky and me sitting together on the floor. She looked away.

"So what's the most important thing that we want?" he asked. He wrote a heading across the top of the paper and underlined it.

"We want to get out of here," Curtis said. "All of us."

Isaiah drew a bullet point but didn't continue. "We can't just take that to them. This is a negotiation. All of us leaving gives them nothing."

"What?" Carrie leaned forward. "We can't make a

compromise about that. We can't say 'let half of us go.'"

Isaiah shook his head. "Then all we're doing is making a demand, not negotiating. And call me crazy, but I don't think that we want to make demands of a school that kills people."

One of the Society girls raised her hand. "What if we start with something simple, like ask them why we're here?"

Isaiah nodded enthusiastically. "Yes. That's better."

"I think it's obvious why we're here," Oakland said. He was slouching in his chair, wearing a hooded sweatshirt instead of his uniform. "We're being researched. This is some big stupid psychological experiment."

Isaiah raised an eyebrow. "This is obvious?"

"Of course it is," he said. "Why do you think that all this weird stuff happens? Why do they lock the doors and leave us outside? It's all just to see what we'll do. And these robots are part of it." He pointed over to me. "Maybe they wanted to see what he'd do if he had a girlfriend, so they programmed Jane to like him, and then they wanted to see what would happen if the girlfriend died, so they sent Dylan."

No one said anything, but Isaiah looked unconvinced.

"I'm serious," Oakland said. "Why else would they have one robot beat the crap out of another one? Those things can't be cheap."

Mason spoke up, but quietly. "If they wanted to see what happens when someone's girlfriend—or boyfriend—dies, they didn't need to make robots do it."

I didn't look at Becky. She was perfectly still and silent.

"What about being trained?" Hector asked. "Why else would they make us play paintball? There aren't any cameras in the woods, so it can't be part of a research experiment."

Curtis spoke next. "I think it's safe to say that wherever there are androids there are cameras."

"Yeah," Oakland said. "And here's another thing. If we're being trained for something, then what is it? No one ever leaves here, and no one is getting any better at anything. If this is a training program then it's got to be the most expensive, most worthless training ever."

Mouse nodded. "And if they just want to train a bunch of super soldiers, why not program the androids to do that?"

Isaiah jumped in, loudly, to stop anyone else from talking. "I think this is why we need to ask them why we're here. Let's just ask."

Rosa stood. She was carrying a worn notebook and a small bag. Isaiah continued to speak, but Rosa interrupted.

"Can I say something?" Her hands were shaking.

A few people nodded.

"I need to explain," she said. Our eyes met for an instant,

but she looked away, staring at the floor. Tears were flowing down her face now. Carrie stood, but Rosa waved for her to stop.

She opened her notebook. With a quivering voice, she spoke.

"I've been in that room before," she said.

Whispers erupted around the room, and Rosa glanced up, fear and guilt in her eyes. "I promise I didn't know that anyone was a . . . robot. I didn't know, I swear." She looked back at her notebook. "It was more than a year ago, and I was doing maintenance. I was in the library, all alone, and I had all the tools with me. I decided to open a vent and see where it went. I thought maybe it would go down into wherever the closets go."

Everyone was silent, hanging on Rosa's every word. Her fear seemed to be increasing, though.

"I came out in that room. There weren't any people in there then, but there were a lot of other things. Lots of computers. I looked all over but then I heard something, like someone was coming. I got scared and ran."

Mason spoke. "I saw you leave there."

Rosa didn't look up. "I didn't have time to look at the computers, but I grabbed the only thing I could find before I ran. Just one piece of paper. I wrote down what it said in my notebook."

She held up the notebook and then read. "'I understand

your concern about the slowness of the process. However, it is not in the interests of the experiment to instruct them in tactics. Our goal is to have them develop strategies on their own, not to see how well they can learn existing strategies. The fact that they're still behaving poorly on the sports field should not be viewed as failure of the experiment, but as valuable data to be studied.'"

Rosa finished reading and looked up. The foyer was silent. When someone finally did speak, it was Curtis, asking her to read the words again.

I didn't know what to think. This was an experiment, like so many had guessed. And we played paintball so that we could figure out strategies ourselves. But the rest still didn't make sense. That paper only explained paintball, and paintball was only a tiny portion of our time here.

"What happened to the paper?" Isaiah asked.

Rosa's eyes fell again. "The school asked for it back."

All of us were stunned, but it was Isaiah who jumped to his feet. "What? The school actually contacted you?"

She nodded.

"What did they say?"

"They just asked for it back—a message on my computer—and they told me I wouldn't get detention. I gave it back, but I memorized it. I wrote the words down in the notebook later."

Carrie finally stood and walked to Rosa. "We won't let

them send you to detention now."

Mouse wasn't as compassionate. "Why didn't you tell anybody?"

Rosa wiped tears away with the back of her hand. She looked up at the security cameras. "They were paying me," she said, hysterical now. "Millions of points. Anything I wanted." She opened her bag and dumped the contents into her hand. Out spilled every kind of jewelry I'd ever seen on the catalog—necklaces, rings, bracelets, hair clips. There were at least a hundred pieces, falling from her hand and clattering across the marble floor.

Isaiah jumped to his feet. "You were hiding this all because of that?"

Curtis stood. "Shut up, Isaiah."

"No," he snapped. "She knew why we were here, and she didn't tell us because she wanted a lot of cheap chains."

Rosa was sitting again, shuddering with tears, and Carrie had her arms around her. Isaiah and Curtis were right in each other's faces. I decided to step in.

"We still don't have any leverage," I said, finally speaking up. "I think this whole thing is ridiculous. The school has all the power here and they know it." I pointed up at a camera twenty feet away. "They're listening to everything we're saying right here. They control everything. They can cut off our food if we don't follow their rules."

Isaiah spun to me, jabbing his finger into my chest.

"That's why we're just asking a question. They know that we know there are androids here—and they know that Rosa told us what she saw—so now we're asking them a question."

"What do you think they're going to do? I've known about the androids for days, but it's not like that made them give me answers. They just tried to shut me up—they tried to bribe me, too."

All eyes were on me, even Rosa's.

"They gave me five million points," I said. "I've been trying to stockpile supplies in my room ever since. I don't have much yet. I haven't checked today, but what do you want to bet my balance is now zero?"

The room was quiet for a minute.

"But doesn't that prove it?" Isaiah asked. "They were willing to give you and Rosa special treatment because you knew the truth about them."

"You're an idiot," Oakland said, rolling his eyes. "They *were* willing to give special treatment, but they're not anymore. They didn't want him to tell us."

"Right," I said, happy for once that Oakland was around. "I had some leverage because they didn't want you guys to find out what I knew. But, there's no leverage anymore."

"Not unless they know that we're serious about leaving," Oakland said. He pointed a finger at Isaiah. "And they'll always know we're not serious about leaving, because their cameras are watching all the time, and all they see is the Society—a bunch of pansy Girl Scouts—too scared to do anything."

Isaiah's face was tight. "That kind of talk isn't helping. Are we going to send them a message, or not?"

Oakland stood up. "You can kiss their butts all you want. But if you keep me in this place because you're too chicken to stand up for yourself, the school's not going to be the one to kill you." He smacked the notepad from Isaiah's hand and it spun onto the floor. Isaiah and Oakland stared at each other for a moment, and then Oakland left.

Mouse stood, and then Curtis and Carrie. Mason, Becky, and I were next, and then most of the student body was on its feet.

"I'm trying to keep everyone alive," Isaiah said, not moving.

We left, climbing the stairs toward the dorms. By the time we got to the second floor, only a handful of the Society members were still sitting.

Oakland was already gone, and Mouse marched away toward her dorm, her shoes clacking on the hardwood floor.

The V's all went their own ways. We were defeated and paranoid, and no closer to a solution than we'd been before I'd shown them Jane.

Curtis walked slowly toward the dorm. I think it was the only time I'd ever seen him leave Carrie without a kiss or a hug. They'd been sitting in the room together, but I hadn't seen them holding hands.

Carrie watched him go and then turned for her dorm. She reached out a hand for Rosa, who went with her.

It was just the three of us left—me, Becky, and Mason.

Becky looked at me. She was nervous. "What now?"

I glanced at the window. It was early afternoon.

Reaching down, I unzipped a pocket on my cargo pants and pulled out one of the radios.

"Keep one with you in case something happens."

"What's going to happen?"

"No idea. But there's something on the other side of that wall that killed Lily. And something took Laura to detention."

Becky fiddled with the radio, twisting the dial from frequency to frequency. She didn't seem to be in much of a hurry to go anywhere.

I noticed that Becky and Mason hadn't said more than three words to each other. I had thought, perhaps foolishly, that we could trust each other a little more than that. I trusted both of them, or at least I thought I did. I wanted to.

Mason turned to leave. "I'm going back to bed," he said with a defeated sigh.

I looked back at Becky. She was smiling—the same tour-guide grin—only now with red swollen eyes.

"What if we just stick together for a while?"

She seemed almost embarrassed to ask the question, but I nodded and put on an optimistic smile.

"Sure. We're going to be okay, though."

Becky laughed, shaking her head and turning away. "I know *I'm* going to be okay," she joked. "I'm worried about you. Trouble seems to follow you."

There wasn't anywhere to go. There was no point in studying, and Havoc wasn't doing any cooking in the cafeteria. We sat in the common room and talked.

Becky was real. She had to be.

CHAPTER TWENTY-SIX

Becky leaned back in her overstuffed chair and giggled softly.

"My grandma was great," she said. "And she would have *hated* you."

I put up my hands in mock protest. "What's wrong with me?"

"I told you—I grew up on a ranch in the middle of nowhere. She didn't trust anyone from the city. You're all liars and criminals. She used to keep a rifle by the front door in case any of your kind came around."

"Oh yeah?" I laughed. "Well, in Pittsburgh we think people on ranches are hillbillies."

Becky stuck out her tongue.

"Hang on," she said, reaching for the back pocket of her jeans. "Someone's paging me."

"You brought your pager to a gang war?" I asked as she pulled the minicomputer from her pocket and opened it.

"Habit," she said with an embarrassed smile. "I'm always on call." She paused, reading whatever message had come through on her computer.

"Yours is networked?" I asked.

"It has to be so it can page me," she murmured. "A lot of . . ."

I watched as the color drained from her face. She glanced at me, terror in her eyes, and then back at the screen.

I jumped from my chair to read over her shoulder.

"They've given the security contract back to Isaiah," she said, her voice barely a whisper. "They're supposed to send you and Rosa to detention and lock down the school. Martial law."

Her eyes met mine.

"This is the school's answer?"

"He won't do it," Becky said, but her eyes betrayed her. She knew he would.

I stood up. "What's he going to do first? He'll have to get everyone together, right?"

She looked panicked. "Yeah, he'll get them together." She grabbed my arm. "But he knows that I've been with you all day. He's not going to waste any time."

"We have to get everyone out. Now. We have to escape right now."

Becky nodded, swallowing hard. She was trembling. "I'll—I'll go to the girls' dorm and warn Rosa. They don't know that I'm not in the Society anymore."

"What if they do?"

"Then I'll hurry." She took a step toward the door and then turned back. "What are you going to do?"

"I've got to get Curtis," I said, "and Oakland."

"You can't go in there. Even if they're not organized yet."

"I'll hurry, too."

We stared at each other for a moment. *We don't have time.*

"You have the radio," I said, and then turned and ran.

I was charging into a hornet's nest, and there was nothing I could do about it. Maxfield Academy had declared war on me and I was going to fight back.

Cracking open the door to the dorm, I peered inside. I couldn't see anyone, but people were definitely down there. There was the sound of a video game, the smell of microwave popcorn.

I stepped in, holding the doorknob so it wouldn't make any noise as it closed. I crept silently down the hall, keeping my feet close to the wall to avoid creaking. I don't know why that worked, but I'd been doing it for years to sneak out of my foster homes.

I moved quickly, getting to the junction that led to both Havoc and the Society. Noise came from both sides. For the first time since I'd gotten to the school, I wished I was wearing the school uniform. Everyone in the school had to know my black and yellow sweatshirt by now.

I paused, leaning into the wall, knowing that if I was spotted I could be hauled down to detention. Or just killed on the spot. No one would have been surprised.

But there was no sense in waiting. I couldn't tell what was going on around the corner of the hallway.

They must have been able to hear my heartbeat anyway.

Running the rest of the way, I reached Curtis's door. It was locked, and I knocked on it as quietly as I could. He was probably asleep.

I glanced back down the hall. No one was following me yet.

I knocked again, harder this time.

"What?" Curtis shouted from inside. A moment later he appeared at the door.

I held my finger to my lips.

"Isaiah's coming," I whispered. "I was with Becky and she got the message on—"

Curtis's eyes latched on to something down the hall, and I turned to see. One of Isaiah's thugs was watching. He disappeared as soon as our eyes met.

"Damn it," I said, turning back to Curtis. "The school put him back in charge. They're supposed to haul Rosa and me to detention. Becky called it martial law."

Curtis moved faster than I expected, grabbing his shoes and yanking them on. "You get the V's, I'll find Oakland."

"'Kay."

"And, Benson," he said. "They outnumber us. Get out of here, fast."

I opened my room, shouting to Mason to get off his bed, and then ran back to the hall. I knocked on every door. There was more noise down the hall now, and we were in a dead end. And the Society had all their security gear.

Some of the guys jumped to follow us, but not all of them. A couple didn't believe me, and no one seemed to think it was as urgent as I did. But they weren't marked for detention.

The radio squawked—it was loud, and I snatched it from my pocket to quiet it down.

"Benson," Becky said, her voice tin and staticky. "They've got her already."

"What?"

"Rosa's gone," she said, "and all the Society girls. They were gone before I got here."

"How could that happen?"

I turned and looked at the other V's, who were straining to hear Becky's words.

"I don't know," she said. "They must have gotten the message before I did."

My stomach dropped. Of course. They watched us on the cameras. They knew that Becky was with me—that she was lost to the Society. They'd done this to split us up. We were trapped.

"Get out," I shouted into the radio. "Go now."

Isaiah turned the corner, a dozen guys behind him. "She won't get far," he said. "The doors are all secured."

There were only seven V's here—five of us in the hall and two still in their rooms. Curtis was down with Havoc. Maybe he could find help there, but we were backed into a corner. Isaiah's hands were empty, but the rest of the guys were all armed. Three of them had the long metal rods that I'd seen Laura holding out in the forest, and others had knives and clubs.

"What is wrong with you guys?" I screamed. "Didn't you see what the rest of us saw?"

"Jane and Dylan are androids," Isaiah said simply. "So what? How is the school that much worse of a place? So the school lied to us—since when have they told us the truth? Are the androids killing us? No. They're just normal students."

Mason stepped forward. "What about Dylan?"

Isaiah's expression was smug and confident. "Dylan killed another android, not a human. Not one of us. The school isn't trying to kill anyone. You're the problems."

I stepped in front of the other guys. "Then get out of our way and we won't be a problem anymore."

"I can't do that," he said. "Now listen. Benson needs to go to detention. Anyone who tries to prevent that will also be taken to detention. Choose now."

Something slid across the floor, past my feet and toward the Society.

A paintball grenade.

Isaiah looked up at me, smirking. "Seriously?"

I turned away just in time, before the hiss of compressed air.

The Society erupted in chaos as the stench of pepper and alcohol filled the narrow hall. Paintballs were flying over my head and people were screaming—Hector and Joel had jumped out of their rooms and were firing paint at the Society's unprotected faces.

"Run," I shouted, and the seven of us charged past our scattering attackers, covering our noses and mouths.

Hector hurled another of my pepper spray grenades down the Society's corridor as we passed. Curtis joined us, followed by a handful of Havoc guys. Oakland was with him.

"Where is everyone else?" I shouted.

"Not coming."

We hit the door, only to find it locked, and our chips wouldn't open it.

"Get back," Curtis ordered, and then kicked. It held firm.

He kicked again, his foot hitting right next to the door-knob. There was a splintering sound.

"Come on, Hector," he said. "One, two, three—"

They both kicked, and the door flung wide open with a sharp crack.

There were thirteen of us—eight V's and five from Havoc—and we charged down the stairs. We were completely outnumbered and outgunned. The doors were locked and we didn't have any supplies to hike out, if we could even get over the wall.

I called Becky on the radio while we ran. "Where are you?"

There was no answer.

"Becky," I shouted. "Where are you?"

"Basement," Curtis said, breathing heavily. "If they're trying to save Rosa, they'll be in the basement."

We hit the first-floor foyer. A few students—Havoc girls—stood against the wall, watching, and Oakland barked at them to follow us. The polished marble was slick, and I slid as I rounded the corner, running for the stairwell to the basement.

"There are three different ways down," Curtis said. "We won't get cornered."

I knew that was optimistic. They'd have the high ground, and whether they were armed with paintball guns or pepper spray or just clubs, it would be a nightmare getting out.

We skidded around another corner, ready to jump down the stairs, only to find the girls standing at the top.

Becky was seething, her eyes red but dry. "She's gone. We were too late."

"What?"

Carrie ran forward and grabbed Curtis in a hug.

"What can we do?" I asked. We'd failed.

"Nothing," Becky said. "There's no button like on an elevator. You just put her in, and the school takes her. The room is empty."

Everyone stood, stunned and silent. Only the distant sound of the pursuing Society guys shook us back to life.

"Where are Isaiah's girls?" Oakland asked.

"Still down there," Gabby answered. There were a few Havoc girls here, but Mouse wasn't one of them. She must not have come.

"We need to go," Curtis said. "Now."

"Where are we going?" Anna asked, obviously frightened.

"Over the wall," he said. "And if you don't want to, go now. We don't have time to debate."

Curtis began running, and we followed. The doors were locked—we knew that—so now we just needed to find the easiest one to break. Curtis seemed to have the same idea I had. He ran for the back of the school, to the door that had been broken earlier that morning.

Isaiah was there ahead of us, his group of thugs spread to each side. They were all splattered with paint on their chests and face, and one had blood dripping from his swollen eye.

There was nothing smug about Isaiah now, who had a massive welt of his own on the side of his neck. His face was red and splotchy, his eyes still watering from the pepper spray.

"Let us out," I said. "What does it hurt you?"

"What does it hurt me?" he yelled. He was shouting at the group, fiery and animated. "What were things like before Benson showed up? We had parties and dances and went to class. These robots didn't change that. It was Benson!"

I felt a hand slip into mine. Becky.

"We can go back to that," Isaiah bellowed, "or you can die. Those are your only choices. Because make no mistake: If you cross that wall, you're dead. And it has nothing to do with me."

Oakland stepped forward, and I noticed for the first time that he was holding a long knife—at least twelve inches. It looked like a machete but had to have come from the kitchen.

Isaiah's eyes were growing increasingly wild. "It's all about cost and benefit with you people, isn't it?" he shouted. "You know that some of you will die, but it's worth it because some are going to live. That's a stupid, selfish idea. You all plan to be the ones who live. It's easy to write off the others, because you tell yourself that it won't be you."

"You could come with us," Curtis said, trying to stay calm.

"Or I could stay right here and live!"

I glanced behind us. The Society girls were back there, and they were armed, too.

"Or," Isaiah screeched, "maybe cost and benefit is the way to go." From the back of his pants he whipped out a pistol.

A .38, semiautomatic.

"How many of you do I need to shoot to stop you from leaving? It'll be fewer than will die out there."

The hall was dead silent. Finally Curtis spoke. "Where did you get the gun, Isaiah?"

Isaiah swung the pistol around and pointed it at Curtis. "How many V's have died, Curtis? It seems to happen every week." He aimed now at Oakland. "How many in Havoc?"

Oakland snarled. "You don't scare me."

"That's the problem!" Isaiah screamed. "You're staring down the barrel of a gun and you're not scared! That's why you idiots get killed. The Society doesn't get sent to detention. And we don't die in the forest."

Curtis took a step forward. "Give me the gun, Isaiah."

Isaiah stared back. Sweat was dripping down his face.

"No." He pulled the trigger.

The shot echoed in slow motion, sounding like a thunderclap in the marble hallway. Curtis fell to one knee, clutching his hip, and then slid all the way down to the floor.

Carrie screamed, leaping forward, and then dozens of voices exploded.

Isaiah simply stood there, his arm still outstretched, staring at the growing puddle of blood forming around Curtis. He didn't move as the thugs behind him slowly moved away. And he didn't move as Oakland stepped forward and took the pistol from his hand.

CHAPTER TWENTY-SEVEN

We ventured outside slowly and somberly, nearly silent as we crossed the lawn—more than fifty of us now. The sky was growing dark, and puffs of frozen breath rose above us as we moved.

A deer stood on the edge of the woods.

We left Isaiah tied to a radiator, but the dozen or so staunch Society members who stayed with him were probably already untying him.

Not everyone who was with us was armed, either. It was more about time than trust. We only had so many tools from maintenance and groundskeeping. I was carrying my paintball gun and a three-pronged rake. Becky held a pair of pruning shears.

Curtis was nearly unconscious, his arms around two other guys as he hobbled along on his good leg. The bullet passed through his upper thigh—it looked like a clean hole—but he'd lost a lot of blood. Carrie followed right behind. We wanted to take Curtis on the back of a four-wheeler, but none of them would start. One of the Society's former guards said that they only ever started for certain people—people Isaiah designated.

Despite his condition, Curtis had the pistol. The wound had proven one thing all too plainly to everyone who tried to help him. He was human. They'd seen inches of bloodied muscle and the white of his femur. He was the only one out of all of us who could prove he wasn't a robot.

I worried he wouldn't make it. We had hardly any medical supplies and no expertise to apply them. He was bandaged and given pain meds, and that was it. We didn't even have any antibiotics. I'd heard that Anna had rubbed hand sanitizer onto the wound.

We stared into the forest around us, watching for signs of trouble. It could come from anywhere in that dark forest. It could even come from the middle of our group, if anyone else turned out to be a robot. Would they have a gun, like Isaiah?

Becky held a small battery-powered reading light, but it only lit up the ground directly in front of us.

"What are you going to do?" Becky asked. "You know, when we get away."

Her voice sounded timid and nervous. I actually missed the confidence of the tour guide.

"I don't know," I said. "College. Do you think our credits will transfer from here?" I grinned at her and she smiled back.

"I think I might write a book about this place," she said.

"I didn't know you were a writer."

"I'm not really. Just my journal. I brought it, you know. So we can tell people what happened here."

"Well, maybe we'll all go on *Oprah*," I said.

She laughed softly, and rolled her eyes. "That's always been my dream."

Oakland and Mouse were leading the group. I wasn't sure why they chose the direction they did, but I supposed it was mostly guesswork anyway. After a lot of arguing we'd decided not to go to the culvert or the front gate—both of those seemed too obvious for escape, and we needed all the luck we could get.

We weren't moving directly opposite of the place with campfires, but we certainly weren't close.

"You were outside the wall a lot more recently than I was," Mason said, moving up next to me. He was using the mattock as a walking stick. "How far is it between that and the fence?"

"I don't know. Maybe half a mile? It's just more forest in between."

"That's where I'd be if I were them," he said. "Wait for us to get over the wall and then come after us. We'll be trapped."

"There's still room to run," I said, trying to be optimistic.

Becky held the shears at her side, but she looked uncomfortable with them. Not like Mason who had the heavy pipe wrench tight in his grip and his paintball gun slung over his shoulder. He was eager for a fight.

We were deep into the woods now, passing the first paintball field I'd played on, back when Havoc had ambushed me. It felt weird to be following Oakland's lead.

I looked back at Curtis, who was still hobbling along. He was at the back of the group, but seemed to be keeping up fairly well.

Becky's hand gently gripped my arm.

"Look," she whispered.

I turned and gazed out into the forest where she was pointing. The deer was there, walking alongside us, about thirty yards away.

"It's been following us for a few minutes now," she said. "It's awfully tame."

I bent down and picked up a stone, and then threw it at the deer. It bounced off a tree only inches from the animal, but there was no reaction.

"What'd you do that for?" Mason asked.

I shook my head. "I don't think that deer is real."

Becky frowned and then picked up and threw a stone of her own. I lost sight of it in the dark, though it clattered loudly on something hard.

The deer didn't change its course at all.

Becky's eyes met mine. "I don't like that."

"We made it!" someone shouted up ahead.

They'd reached the wall, a wide black line cutting through the dim gray forest. As far as I could see, there weren't any security cameras nearby. Unless that's what the deer was. I'd seen plenty of animals in the woods.

Oakland called Mason up to the front, and they unloaded all of the extension cords from his pack. There were three big ones—fifty-foot heavy orange cords from the maintenance room—and half a dozen twelve-foot cords we'd taken from various lamps around the building.

Hector climbed up into a tall skinny pine, carrying one of the heavy cords over his shoulder. The tree looked sickly, its needles rust colored and dry. When he got about thirty feet up, he tied the cords off and then scrambled back to the ground.

"Okay," Oakland barked. "Let's get this first one down." He pointed to several of the older, stronger students, including me, and we all grabbed the cord dangling out of the first tree. I wasn't going to be much help—after breaking into the steel door early that morning, the pain in my injured arm was strong and sharp. Even so, I took my place on the cord.

"Let's rock it back and forth," he said. "When it starts to break, get out of the way."

On Oakland's count, we tugged, the tree swaying a little

bit toward us. We let it swing back the other way.

"Pull," he shouted, as the tree naturally swung back in our direction. We yanked harder this time, pulling it farther and building more momentum. Then we let it swing toward the forest, away from the wall.

As we repeated this, over and over, I couldn't help but think of that first day in the school when I'd tried the same thing, except stupidly doing it from up in the tree. Three members of the Society had been there that night. Two of them were now dead. Well, one was dead and one was turned off and plugged into the wall. The third, a kid I still didn't really know, was now standing behind me on the cord, pulling with us.

The tree was swaying wildly now, back and forth, back and forth. With each bend toward the wall we pulled harder, until finally it roared with a thunderous crack. We scattered and the old tree collapsed, smashing into the wall.

As the dust settled, we could see the trunk leaning over the wall, a decent, if wobbly, bridge for climbing up to the top of the twelve feet of brick. We'd knock down another tree next to it and lash the two together.

"Hey," Mason said, moving toward the fallen tree. "The wall's leaning."

Sure enough, we could see that the white lines of mortar were no longer straight, but curved and bowed around the impact of the pine.

I noticed another weird thing about the wall—a fat raccoon, perched up on it, fifty feet away. If that had been a real raccoon, it would have run the instant the wall shook.

Oakland's voice shook me back to our task. "Let's get the next one," he shouted.

I nodded, staring at the raccoon for another few seconds. I'd seen the raccoon before, too.

Becky was also looking at the animal. Her eyes met mine. Tingles of panic were forming in my stomach, but I forced myself to turn back to the trees. There was too much to do.

We repeated the process, rocking a second tree—this one slightly thicker and with more branches—until it popped and fell. Unfortunately, our excitement at knocking the wall down was short-lived. The trunk hit the brick, continuing to bend the wall back, but it didn't collapse.

"We could take down a third one," someone suggested.

I looked at my watch. We'd already been working on the trees for almost half an hour. It was completely dark now, the only light coming from the glow of the low cold clouds.

Oakland gazed back at the other possible trees, including a big one that would easily crush the wall—if our cords could actually get it down without snapping. It was healthier than the two we'd felled.

"No," he finally said. "Let's get 'em stable and start going over."

We rolled the second tree along the wall toward the first. We only had to move it about eight feet, but it was almost impossible, and I was no use at all with my bad arm. Pushing with my palms hurt far worse than pulling on the cords. It took at least ten minutes to roll it into position, and by the time we'd tied the two trunks together it seemed to have dropped another fifteen degrees.

Hector climbed to the top of the wall, carrying the third extension cord with him. He paused at the top and then turned back, worry on his face.

"There are animals over here," he said, confused and nervous.

Oakland asked what he meant, but I immediately climbed up the logs to see for myself. Hector and I stood shoulder to shoulder on the top of the wall. Below us were a dozen animals—more raccoons and deer, and a hodgepodge of others: foxes, marmots, jackrabbits, and a porcupine. They waited around the wall, silent and still.

Beyond them was more forest.

"What the hell is this?" Hector breathed.

I pulled my paintball gun off my shoulder and fired three quick shots into the rabbit's face, which knocked it back in an awkward jump. But it didn't run. In the low light I couldn't see if any damage had been done, but it was once again staring at us.

People behind us were screaming for answers, and

Hector told them what was happening while I shot at a deer. I aimed for the eyes, trying to break whatever cameras were in there, but the deer hardly moved at all.

"Do they look like they're going to attack?" Oakland asked, obviously annoyed.

"I don't know," I said over my shoulder. "What could a marmot do?"

I kept my eyes on the animals while I listened to the murmurs below. These robots looked for all the world like real animals except they were completely motionless.

"Okay," Oakland shouted to the group. "Let's get over this thing. Jump if you can—it'll be faster—but don't be an idiot and break your ankle. We ain't carrying you."

"What about the robots?" someone shouted.

"Hit 'em if they get close," he answered. "That's why we're armed."

Hector tied the cord to a thick branch of the fallen tree, and then took a deep breath and lowered himself down to the ground. I kept my gun trained on the robots, but none of them made any motion to attack. Not that my gun would have stopped them.

Oakland sent a few of the bigger guys over the wall next, and once ten were down, one of the Havoc kids tried swinging a shovel at a raccoon. It jumped out of the way amazingly fast but didn't fight back.

I stayed on top of the wall, watching the rest of the

Havocs go, then the Society. Finally the V's climbed up the tree bridge. Becky stood on top of the wall now, and I climbed back down to help Carrie and Anna get Curtis up the logs. His fingers were curled tight, digging into my shoulder, and each breath sounded like an agonizing wheeze, as he tried to restrain himself from screaming in pain.

When he reached the top, he paused to catch his breath.

The students below were in a nervous cluster, staring outward at the endless sea of pines that continued before us. The animals had backed away, but were still in a loose semicircle around us.

We tied the cord around Curtis's chest, under his arms. It wasn't a good fix, and Carrie looked mortified as Anna, Becky, and I lowered him down. We couldn't help but do it jerkily—Curtis was heavy—and he cried out when he finally hit the ground.

Carrie jumped down next, and then Anna and Becky.

On top of the wall, I turned for one final look back. I couldn't see the school through the trees, and I wondered whether I'd ever see it in person again. Hopefully, I'd see it on the front page of the newspaper, with headlines about torture and imprisonment and I'd see Ms. Vaughn in an orange prison jumpsuit, being tried on dozens of counts of murder.

Below me, Oakland was already leading the group

forward and into the forest. Guys with long-handled weapons—rakes and shovels and pruning hooks—walked ahead of the others, trying to shoo the robot animals away. Carrie was helping Curtis stay upright, and Becky was standing at the base of the wall, waiting for me.

I jumped. The ground was harder than I expected, and my shins stung on impact, but I was also filled with a sudden sense of elation. I didn't know what lay ahead of us, but we had crossed the first obstacle.

This forest had sparser trees but thicker underbrush. We had to go slower now, fighting our way through the thick, dry bushes and grass. Becky and I were walking at the back now with Mason, Curtis hobbling up ahead of us. I felt isolated and vulnerable.

"This is bad," she whispered. We had to look down to keep our footing, unable to properly keep a watchful eye on the forest.

Someone screamed, and everyone started talking at once. I couldn't see what was going on, but they all started to run forward. Becky, Mason, and I jogged after them, slowed only by Curtis in front of us, who was staggering as quickly as he could.

"What happened?" I asked, trying to look ahead.

"Maybe they just got spooked," Mason said.

"I have the gun," Curtis wheezed.

I nodded, not taking my eyes off the people up front.

"We might need it."

Oakland's voice wasn't far, and I could hear him order-ing the students to stay together and to keep moving.

"We'll be okay," I said, almost automatically. I didn't know whether the assurance was more for them or for me.

People shouted up ahead. I tensed but quickly realized they were joyful cries. As we got closer we could see the fence, the chain link reflecting in the moonlight. We were there, and maybe the worst part was over. The animals were there, too, but everyone was ignoring them.

Hector and Joel were already up front, hacksaw and shovel in hand, attempting to get through the sturdy chain link. Becky ran forward, dropping to her knees at the fence line. She put the mouth of the pruning shears onto a wire and then strained to close it, trying to snap the thin steel. It wasn't cutting, so I joined her, my arms next to hers on the handles, trying to force the blades closed.

I grunted and Becky let out a labored cry, and the shears snapped the wire.

There were cheers behind us, and we moved to the next one.

My arms burned, and sweat dripped down my back, despite the freezing temperatures. Becky's forehead was wet with tiny droplets, and her skin was pulled tight as she clenched her jaw. We clipped another. And then another. By the time we'd snapped through ten of the wires, we were surrounded, everyone applauding each little success. Finally, Hector, who had given up with the hacksaw, told us to get out of the way and he began unweaving the steel links. In a few minutes there was a hole in the fence big enough to climb through.

He held it open proudly and gestured for Becky to go through. She grinned, her face beaming, and for the first time in almost a year and a half, Becky walked outside the fence. I followed her, and it was as though I were stepping out of a dark closet. Even though we remained in the same endless forest, it felt easier to breathe, like a heavy weight had been taken off my chest.

People were streaming through the hole now—Gabby, Hector, a few unarmed Society kids, Oakland, Mouse. All were moving with confidence and surprise; I don't think any of us expected we'd get this far.

"That's enough. Very good."

My heart fell into my stomach.

All the students were frozen. Ms. Vaughn had a Taser in her hand and another on her belt. Other than that, she was completely unarmed and alone.

She raised a finger and pointed. "I wouldn't go through there," she said simply and quietly. I looked back to see Mash standing at the hole.

"Why not?" he demanded and then tried to climb through. The moment his hand touched the chain link he froze and convulsed. We all stared in horror until one of the Society guys kicked Mash's feet out from under him and he fell, releasing his grip on the now-electrified fence.

"Turn it off," I shouted. "Let them through."

She shook her head. "I don't believe that's going to happen." Once again, she pointed at the fence. "You've broken the rules, quite severely, and you all know the punishments."

Firing erupted from somewhere behind the fence and I turned to see one of the Society girls firing her gun at the other students. Some shot back, but the same paint that was stinging their skin and threatening their eyes didn't phase her at all. She calmly lowered her gun and raised a butcher's knife.

"You see?" Ms. Vaughn said. "I'm not alone."

I spun, raising my gun at Ms. Vaughn.

Joel was in front of me, and his fist hit my jaw before I could react. I collapsed, lights dancing in my eyes, and watched as the few students on my side of the fence began fighting. The androids in the group were changing sides.

I grabbed Joel's leg and tried to trip him, but he managed to stay on his feet and smashed his gun down on my bad arm. I fell to the ground with a heavy thud and had to shake my head to try to see.

There were shouts and screams all around me, and the hissing sound of flying paint. I realized now that it was stupid to bring the guns. The paint couldn't hurt the robots—only the humans. And all the androids were armed with it.

I could see the fallen pruning shears a few yards away and wondered where Becky was, but there wasn't time to look. Joel grabbed me by the shoulder and lifted me off the ground—far stronger than any human could. But I twisted away, and his grip slipped, leaving him with a handful of shirt.

I reached for the pruning shears—my fingers could just touch the long handle—but I was too far. Joel flung me to the ground and then stepped on my braced wrist. I screamed in pain, and he kicked me in the ribs.

I couldn't move. My arm throbbed and burned, and I felt like my lungs had stopped working.

Joel was moving away from me, inching toward the unarmed Society kids. Becky was in the front, her arms outstretched in a vain attempt to protect those behind her. He swung his heavy arms at her, missing by inches.

Taking a desperate gulp of air, I pushed myself to my feet, my ribs flaring with pain.

Joel brought his fist down on Becky's shoulder, and she crumpled to the ground.

I grabbed the pruning shears. Recklessly, I lunged toward Joel, holding the shears in my right hand, just above the blade. I tackled him, plunging the sharp tool into his ribs.

He rolled underneath me, but I didn't let go. I yanked out the shears again—they were bloody, but I knew it was only from the skin; there was no blood in his mechanical body—and again rammed them in, this time just below the neck. He spun, trying to throw me. He brought his fists down against me, but I was too close for it to hurt much.

I felt someone behind me jump on Joel's fallen body and grab his thrashing legs. Another person—Becky—leapt on him, too, her arm around Joel's neck.

She screamed. "Kill it!"

With a surge of adrenaline, I thrust the shears back down into Joel's twisting body, again and again. On the last time the blade caught something, and I worked the handles back and forth cutting whatever cables or wires I'd snagged. Immediately, Joel stopped. His limbs and mouth frozen in place.

I lifted my head, surprised to see that no one else around us was still moving.

Mason stood disarmed, his hands on his bloodied head. On the other side of our group, Gabby was on the ground, moaning in pain, blood all over her shirt and arms. Mouse was down on the ground, Oakland's machete lodged in her chest. For an instant I wondered what that meant— I couldn't even tell who was on my side—but then I saw Oakland standing next to Ms. Vaughn, another knife at her throat.

"We're not going to be your guinea pigs anymore," Curtis yelled at the captive Ms. Vaughn. He was still standing on the other side of the electric fence. Many on that side were down on the ground now, crying in pain or cowering in fear, but I didn't think there were any other androids there.

Curtis's face was ashen. Carrie was trying to prop him up. "You can't test us anymore," he shouted. The pistol was in his hand, pointed at Ms. Vaughn. If Oakland didn't get her then Curtis would.

Ms. Vaughn stared back at him, her amused smile visible in the dim light.

"How very egocentric," she said, her voice cold and cruel. "We weren't testing you. We're testing *them*." She gestured at the bodies of Joel and Mouse.

The androids? Jane?

"We have to test the programs somewhere, in a controlled environment," she said scornfully. "This was never about you."

"The tests weren't for us," Carrie said, her voice almost a whimper.

"Well," Ms. Vaughn said, grinning at Carrie. "That's not precisely true."

And in an instant Curtis's pistol was in Carrie's hand. As he collapsed to the dirt—as Carrie let him fall—she fired three rounds into Oakland's chest.

Screams erupted again, and Carrie fell—maybe Curtis pulled her down, I couldn't tell.

I leapt from my place beside Joel, shears in my hand as I charged Ms. Vaughn. I knocked her backward and landed on top, the shears dangerously close to her throat.

"Call them off," I shouted, my face only inches from Ms. Vaughn's. I pressed the shears closer against her neck.

She laughed.

"Call them off!" I pushed the shears harder against her neck, and a thin line of blood appeared.

"You can't harm me," Ms. Vaughn said calmly. "I'm stored on the mainframe."

My eyes went wide.

Someone was shouting, "Run!"

"You've failed, Mr. Fisher," Ms. Vaughn said. "No one will get away. No one ever does."

Becky was next to me, pulling on my arm. "Come on!"

I glanced back at the others. Tapti had turned on them now, and another Havoc boy.

I saw Curtis's face. "Run!" Curtis yelled. "Go! Get help!"

Mason jumped toward Tapti, knocking her down. He snatched up someone's dropped wrench.

I jumped off Ms. Vaughn and darted toward Becky. We paused on the edge of the trees, looking back. She was taking huge panicked gulps of air. "Come on," I shouted to the others who were cowering against the fence, but they weren't moving.

"Go!" Curtis shouted again. "Go!" There was despair in his voice.

Carrie had stood up again, but the gun wasn't in her hands.

"Run!" It wasn't just Curtis now but Gabby, too, and Skiver, all pleading with us to go.

"We can't help them now," Becky gasped, grabbing me by the shirt, pulling me forward. Mason was only twenty feet behind us.

I took one last look and then turned to the forest, running beside Becky as fast as we could. It wouldn't be long before they sent someone after us.

Chapter Twenty-Eight

We ran for ten minutes at least, Becky a few steps ahead of me and Mason somewhere behind.

Fifty-four students had tried to escape, and only three had made it. And who knew whether we'd ever get out of the forest—there were miles and miles left to go before we could even start looking for help.

We couldn't go for the highway. They'd be watching the road. We had to go cross-country, pick a direction and hope we find help.

I thought of Curtis and Gabby, both viciously wounded. And others had been, too. If we weren't fast, they'd die.

They might die anyway.

What if the school got rid of everyone else? Killed them? I looked at Becky's small backpack and remembered the journal inside. It suddenly felt much more valuable.

We crested a low hill, and Becky slowed to a stop by a long-dead, fallen log. She was panting for breath. I noticed she'd been hit in the neck—there was a perfectly round cut where a firm paintball had broken the skin. The area around it was raised and bright red.

The clouds had broken around the moon, and there were fewer trees blocking the light up here. I could see a vague mass of forest—rolling hills stretching out toward the west. It felt strange to have a new vantage point after spending so long in one place.

"Look," Becky said, her outstretched arm pointing toward something in the distance that I couldn't see. "Is that smoke?"

I squinted. That was the general direction of the camp, but I couldn't see in this light.

Mason reached us.

And suddenly Becky collapsed, violently crashing onto the fallen log. She screamed in pain but it abruptly changed into a groan.

I took a step toward her. She must have tripped. She must have—

Mason was standing above her, and he turned to face me. He was holding the wrench.

He had hit her.

No. He couldn't be one of them. All the androids had given themselves away back with Ms. Vaughn. I stared at him, too stunned to speak. His eyes were dead.

I raised my hands, but it was too late to block him. He brought the club down onto my wrist brace and I crumpled to my knees. I tried to turn away, but he struck me in the ribs before I could.

He was still, looking down at me. He was going to kill us both. I glanced at Becky. She was struggling to move and softly gasping for air.

"Mason," I said, tasting blood in my mouth. "You're . . . like them?"

His lips didn't move, and it wasn't his voice. "Please return to the school."

He'd been taken over. Whatever I knew of Mason was gone, just like Jane. Someone else was controlling him now.

"Who are you?" I yelled. He'd raised the wrench again. "Come on, Mason. Don't do this. You have to be in there somewhere."

His body tensed, and then he swung.

But before it reached me I heard a pop and a buzz, and something shot toward Mason. He froze and then fell forward, as stiff and dead as if he'd been made of stone.

I looked at Becky. Her side was covered in blood, her face even paler than usual. She was holding a Taser.

She forced out the words. "I stole it off Ms. Vaughn."

I was too much in shock to answer. Becky was bleeding. I was wracked with pain. Mason was dead—short-circuited, maybe. *My own roommate . . .*

Becky had begun tugging at her sleeve, and I watched numbly. She had a cut on her head where Mason had hit her, and her upper arm was drenched in blood, which looked black in the darkness. I stared as she struggled to take off the jacket. It was cumbersome. She was only using one arm.

I shook my head to clear it, pushing myself off the ground and toward her. Gingerly, I helped guide the jacket sleeve off.

"I landed on the log," she said through gritted teeth, and nodded toward a mass of sharp, broken branches protruding from the trunk of the tree. One of them had pierced her bicep like a spear.

She leaned back, wincing at the pain, and I tried to clear the shredded strands of cloth from the wound. The cut wasn't wide, but it was deep. I could see the whiteness of her bone.

Yanking a wad of loose material from her jacket, I balled it up and then pushed it onto her arm. She pressed her lips tight together, trying to hide a groan.

"Hold that," I said. As she did, I pulled off my belt and cinched it around the makeshift bandage.

My hands were wet with her blood as I knelt beside her.

"We have to keep going," she said weakly.

"I know."

She leaned forward, trying to will herself to stand. She was tougher than I realized.

I stood shakily, reached for her good hand, and helped her to her feet.

Looking into her eyes, I smiled. Tears were forming but I blinked them away.

"What?" she said, cocking her head and grinning weakly.

"You're real," I said. "I saw the bone." Before she could respond, I wrapped my arms around her and pulled her against my chest. She hugged me back with her good arm, the other hanging limp at her side.

"We have to run," she said, not letting go.

"I know."

Looking beyond her, I watched the forest below us. Nothing was moving. That wouldn't last long. Once they knew that Mason had failed, there'd be someone else after us.

I put my hand on the back of her head, holding her against me, and I bent my face down into her brown hair. I couldn't help but cry.

"I wanted you to be real."

I felt her breathing, rapid and unsteady, as her arm tightened around me.

We had nothing. No supplies. We'd both taken off our packs to work on the fence. Becky was bleeding, and my ribs were as bad as they ever were.

But we were free. They were going to chase us, but right now we were free.

"We'll move downhill," I said, my eyes locked on the

smoky hills to the west. I was already picking out the trail in my mind.

Becky turned her head so she could see the forest floor but didn't let go of me.

"That's what they say," I said, remembering something I'd seen on TV. "Downhill until you find a stream, follow that to a river, follow that to people."

I felt her nod, and then she craned her neck to face me. She cracked a weak half smile. "Try to keep up."

I took a deep breath. "Let's run."

CHAPTER TWENTY-NINE

Snow had finally come.

Becky was beside me, shivering and pale. My arm was around her, holding her tight against me, trying to share body warmth as we huddled in the forest.

I'd tried everything I'd seen on TV to help us survive. When Becky couldn't walk any farther I'd found a hiding place in a cluster of junipers and laid down pine branches beneath us as insulation from the ground. I'd tried to cover us with leaves, but there weren't many to be found, so I made due with more pine. After a few hours of sitting there, freezing, I had to wonder if it was doing any good at all. I didn't dare make a fire.

She wasn't sleeping. Her breathing was heavy and uneven, and she winced frequently, balling her hands into tight, pained fists.

We'd made it past the wall, past the androids. We were out in the forest—we'd escaped. And she might die anyway.

As the light of dawn began to fill the sky, I inspected her

wound more closely. There was dried blood everywhere—and some that was still wet and oozing. Her skin was as white as the snowflakes.

"How is it?" she asked through gritted teeth.

"Oh, you're fine," I said, trying to joke. "I don't know what the big fuss is."

She smiled. If Becky had learned anything in the last year and a half, it was how to fake a smile.

"It hurts," she said, almost gasping the words.

"You'll be okay."

It was a lie. We both knew it. She'd lost too much blood, suffered too much trauma.

"Can you walk?" I asked. With light was sure to come more searches for us. So far we seemed to have avoided the guards, but I doubted that would last much longer.

"No choice," she said. Her eyes were closed, like she was trying to concentrate on something.

I sat up, trying not to bump her or dislodge our flimsy covering. "I'll be right back."

She nodded and bit her lip.

Trying to move silently, I climbed the hill slope. From the top, I couldn't see much more than endless forest, but I knew the mountains on the horizon—I'd seen them out the school's windows for weeks—and they gave me a good idea of where I was. We'd probably only traveled a few miles—maybe three or four—before stopping.

We'd never make it to the highway.

I turned my sights to the south. I couldn't see anything that way, either, but I knew something was there. The guards' camp, or whatever it was. It had to be close.

Scrambling back down the slope, I found Becky, eyes still shut. She looked dead. The only sign of life was her labored breathing.

"We need to go," I said.

She nodded, almost imperceptibly.

The going was difficult, but Becky kept moving, one foot in front of the other through the uneven terrain.

She didn't ask where I was leading her, and I didn't tell her. She wouldn't have agreed.

I held her hand while we walked, but even after half an hour of exercise it wasn't warming up. And now that the sky was even lighter, I could tell she wasn't pale but gray. I wondered if infection was setting in. Was it too soon for that?

And then I caught something, a scent in the air.

Becky noticed it, too, and her head turned quickly, suddenly alert. "What is that?"

"Wood smoke," I said.

"Is it the school?" she asked. She was looking at the sky, looking for smoke.

"I don't think so. We're close to the—whatever it is. The place you could see from the dorms."

There was fear in her eyes. "We can't turn ourselves in. Don't do this."

"I'm not. I'm just going to see if I can get some supplies—bandages or medicine or something. I'm guessing they'll all be out looking for us. No one will even be there."

Becky looked like she wanted to argue but was too exhausted. Instead, she just stood and stared into the woods.

"Okay," she said, her voice barely audible.

We hiked on for another mile, maybe. We were going slow and not in a straight line, so it was hard to judge the distance. Eventually, Becky couldn't go on. I helped her down into a sandy ravine and packed leaves and debris around her to keep her warm. It wouldn't do much good.

She took my hand. "Don't be gone long."

"I won't." I might have expected her to cry but was surprised to find tears forming in my eyes.

Before I left, I kissed her.

I almost ran through the woods now, still trying to be quiet, but knowing that taking my time could mean Becky dying alone.

The woods leveled out, the hills and valleys fading into a flat, sparse forest. There were no tracks—no footpaths or tire marks. No animals, either. I was all alone.

The scent of wood smoke was growing now, and I could see the haze between the trees. I had to be getting close.

And then the woods ended, and there was a town. Small farms and a few dozen buildings. Smoke was rising from four or five chimneys.

This wasn't a guard camp.

I ran to an empty garden that had been cleared for the winter, to the closest building. It looked like a barn.

I wanted to scream for help, to yell for the police, but my time in the school had made me paranoid. Maybe these people knew about the school. Maybe they ran the school.

Peering in the barn window, I didn't see anyone. But there were a few tarps. I could use those.

I carefully opened the door. It was warmer inside. There were animals there—half a dozen cows.

I ignored them and went for the tarps. They were large and sturdy and canvas—not soft, but they looked water-proof. There was a cabinet on the far wall, and I ran to it.

"Who are you?"

My heart dropped.

But it wasn't a guard's voice. It was a voice I recognized. A girl's voice.

I turned.

She was standing with the cows. She'd been milking them.

She didn't look the same, but I knew her. Her fair skin was darker and freckled—and she was taller. Older. But I knew her.

"Jane?"

She brushed a strand of red hair away from her face.

"We didn't think anyone survived," she said, her words slow and worried. "They're going to be looking for you."

I was frozen to the ground, unable to move, unable to speak.

Jane stepped out from behind the cows. Her clothes were old and worn. She stared back at me.

"I know you," she said, her words barely audible. Suddenly her eyes went wide. "I thought you died. I thought we both did."

END OF BOOK ONE

ACKNOWLEDGMENTS

This book would not have been written if my brother, Dan Wells, had not issued me an impossible challenge. It also wouldn't have been written if he hadn't invited me to his writing group ten years ago and, slowly and painfully, taught me to write. Whatever success I have in writing is due in large part to Dan, and I am in his debt.

I also owe a lot to my writer friends who have read, edited, and critiqued my manuscript. But more importantly, I'm grateful for their constant support and friendship. There are so many people to mention here that I probably shouldn't even try, but I particularly want to thank my amazing writing group: Annette Lyon, J. Scott Savage, Sarah Eden, Heather Moore, LuAnn Staheli, and Michele Holmes. Also, many thanks to my beta readers: Patty Wells, Ally Condie, Micah Bruner, Krista Jensen, Sheila Staley, Shauna Black, Stephanie Black, Bryan Hickman, Autumn Bruner, Christina Pettit, Joel Hiller, and Cameron Ruesch. (And, if I forgot you, it's only because I value your contribution far too much to trivialize it with a simple acknowledgment. Or whatever.)

Thanks to my wonderful agent, Sara Crowe, who worked tirelessly on this project and guided me through three major revisions.

And I can't thank my editor, Erica Sussman, and the awesome people at HarperTeen enough. This book is definitely a team effort, and I'm continually amazed by the miracles they produce.